THE PENGUIN CLASSICS

FOUNDER EDITOR (1944–64): E. V. RIEU

Editor: Betty Radice

TITUS PETRONIUS ARBITER is reputedly the author of the *Satyricon*. Historical and literary evidence confirms that he is the same Petronius whose character and strange death in A.D. 66 are so graphically described in Tacitus' *Annals*. As governor of Bithynia and as consul he showed vigour and ability, but his chief talent lay in the pursuit of pleasures, in which he displayed such exquisite refinement that he earned the unofficial title of the emperor Nero's 'arbiter of elegance' (*arbiter elegantiae*). Court rivalry and jealousy contrived to cast on Petronius the suspicion that he was conspiring against the emperor, and he was ordered to commit suicide. He gradually bled to death, opening his veins, binding and reopening them, passing his last hours in social amusement and the composition of a catalogue of Nero's debaucheries. Petronius is also the author of a small collection of lyric and elegiac poems.

LUCIUS ANNAEUS SENECA, statesman, philosopher, advocate and man of letters, was born at Cordoba in Spain around 4 B.C. Despite his relatively undistinguished background and ever-recurrent ill health, he rose rapidly to prominence at Rome, pursuing the double career in the courts and political life for which he had been trained. He began also quickly to acquire celebrity as an author of tragedies and of polished essays, moral, literary and scientific. On Nero's succession Seneca acted for some eight years as an unofficial chief minister, and upon retiring from public life he devoted his last three years to philosophy and writing, particularly the *Letters from a Stoic*. In A.D. 65, following the discovery of a plot against the emperor, which might have resulted in Seneca's elevation to the throne, he and many others were compelled by Nero to commit suicide. His fame as an essayist and dramatist lasted until two or three centuries ago when, unaccountably, he passed into literary oblivion.

J. P. SULLIVAN has held appointments in Classics or Arts and Letters at the Universities of Oxford, Cambridge, Texas, Buffalo and Hawaii.

PETRONIUS

THE SATYRICON

AND

SENECA

THE
APOCOLOCYNTOSIS

TRANSLATED

WITH INTRODUCTIONS AND NOTES BY

J. P. SULLIVAN

PENGUIN BOOKS

Penguin Books Ltd, Harmondsworth, Middlesex, England
Penguin Books, 625 Madison Avenue, New York, New York 10022, U.S.A.
Penguin Books Australia Ltd, Ringwood, Victoria, Australia
Penguin Books Canada Ltd, 2801 John Street, Markham, Ontario, Canada L3R 1B4
Penguin Books (N.Z.) Ltd, 182–190 Wairau Road, Auckland 10, New Zealand

—

This translation published 1965
Reprinted with revisions 1969
Reprinted 1971, 1972
Reprinted with revisions 1974
Reprinted 1976
Reprinted with *The Apocolocyntosis* 1977
Reprinted 1979, 1981

—

This translation of 'The Apocolocyntosis' first
published in the United States of America in *Arion*,
University of Texas, 1966

—

—

Made and printed in Great Britain
by Hazell Watson & Viney Ltd,
Aylesbury, Bucks
Set in Linotype Granjon

CONTENTS

THE APOCOLOCYNTOSIS
OR
THE DEIFICATION OF CLAUDIUS THE CLOD

INTRODUCTION

The Authorship and Date of the *Satyricon*

The *Satyricon* has been traditionally, and rightly, attributed to the courtier of Nero whose downfall and death in A.D. 66 are described by Tacitus (*Annals* 16. 17–20):

17. The space of a few days saw the fall, one after the other, of Annaeus Mela, Cerialis Anicius, Rufrius Crispinus, and C. Petronius ...

18. Gaius Petronius deserves some further attention. He was a man who spent his days sleeping and his nights working or enjoying himself. Industry is the usual foundation of success, but with him it was idleness. Unlike most people who throw away their money in dissipation, he was not regarded as an extravagant sensualist, but as one who made luxury a fine art. His conversation and his way of life were unconventional with a certain air of nonchalance, and they charmed people all the more by seeming so unstudied. Yet as proconsul in Bithynia and later as consul, he showed himself a vigorous and capable administrator. His subsequent return to his old habits, whether this was real or apparent, led to his admission to the small circle of Nero's intimates, where he became the Arbiter of Elegance. In the end Nero's jaded appetite regarded nothing as enjoyable or refined unless Petronius had given his sanction to it. Consequently the jealousy of Tigellinus was aroused against him: he saw in Petronius a rival, someone superior to himself in the whole art of pleasure. So he worked upon the Emperor's cruelty, his master-passion, to which all his other lusts were subordinate. Accusing Petronius of being an intimate of Scaevinus, he bribed a slave to give evidence against him. Petronius did not have a chance to reply and Tigellinus threw most of his household into prison.

19. The Emperor at that time happened to be on a visit to Campania. Petronius got as far as Cumae and was prevented from going any farther. He refused to prolong the suspense that hope or fear involved. Not that he was hasty in taking leave of life. On the contrary, he opened his veins and then, as the fancy took him, he bound them up or re-opened them. Meanwhile he talked with his friends, but not on serious topics or anything calculated to win admiration for his stoicism. He listened to their contributions – not discussions about

the immortality of the soul or the views of philosophers, but simply gay songs and light verse. He dealt out rewards to some of his slaves and floggings to others. He had a good dinner served and slept for a while, so that his death, although forced on him, should appear natural. Even in the codicils to his will, he refused to put down any of the usual death-bed flatteries for Nero or Tigellinus or any of the other courtiers. Instead he wrote out a full description of the Emperor's vicious activities, prefaced with the names of his male and female partners, and specifying the novel forms his lust had taken. This document he sent under seal to Nero. Then he broke his signet ring in case it should be used later to endanger others.

20. Nero's puzzlement as to how his nocturnal ingenuities were known was resolved by blaming Silia. This was a not insignificant person, a senator's wife, in fact, who had been a chosen partner in all the Emperor's vices and also a close friend of Petronius. She was exiled, out of personal spite, for her lack of discretion about what she had seen and experienced.

Plutarch, in his essay *On the Distinction between Flattery and Friendship* (60 d-e), adds an anecdote which may throw some light on Petronius' character and the methods by which he retained for a time his position with Nero.

These are minor faults. Next, however, comes that unscrupulous practice which has such a damaging effect on silly people. This consists in accusing them of tendencies and weaknesses the very opposite of their real failings ... This may take the form of sneering at reckless and extravagant spenders for their petty-minded and sordid ways – Titus Petronius did this with Nero.

Finally the elder Pliny (NH 37. 20) tells us that:

T. Petronius, a consular, when he was going to die through Nero's jealousy and envy, broke his fluorspar wine-dipper so that the Emperor's table would not inherit it. It had cost 300,000 sesterces.

It is probable that Pliny and Plutarch are right in giving his praenomen as Titus, and the name 'Arbiter' given him in the MSS was probably not his real cognomen. The most convincing attempt to identify our author precisely is that of K. F. C. Rose, who argued that he is T. Petronius Niger, who was consul around A.D. 63.[1]

However this may be, for centuries the dating of the *Satyricon*

1. *The Date and Author of the Satyricon* (Leiden, 1971), pp. 47 ff.

to Neronian times and the attribution of the work to Nero's courtier has been hotly disputed, and counter-suggestions range from the time of Augustus to after A.D. 200, but there was no consensus among the opponents of Neronian dating. There is now therefore more or less general agreement on both these points, but for the general reader, the main arguments for accepting this dating and attribution may be summarized as follows. The historical and economic references in the work point to the first century A.D.[1] The language and style belong to the same period: for example, the vulgarisms introduced into the speech of Trimalchio and his circle may be paralleled not only in the Senecan *Apocolocyntosis* (a work which surely belongs to the Neronian era)[2] but also in the wall-inscriptions preserved at Pompeii, all of which must belong to the period before A.D. 79. The literary criticism in the work is very like the criticism (particularly of rhetoric) that we find in other writings of the first century. And in particular the criticism prefacing the *Carmen de Bello Civili* (118 ff.) which seems directed at Lucan (*ob.* 30 April A.D. 65) without mentioning his name, can only be appropriate to the few years during which the *Pharsalia* was written and partially published. The literary sources of the work, the citations from other authors, arguably the literary intentions (which I shall discuss below), all fit this dating. The author of the work was obviously a highly literary and literate man; the court circle of Nero with an emperor of such literary ambitions would be naturally interested in criticism and literature. Consequently it is difficult to believe that the courtier Petronius became *elegantiae arbiter* simply because he knew which end of a spoon was which or how best to flavour wine, although it is perhaps significant that much of the satire directed against Trimalchio is satire of manners, not excluding table manners. The psycho-

1. Rose, op. cit., pp. 20 ff. Rose's penetrating and exhaustive study supersedes most previous work on the subject, but H. C. Schnur, 'The Economic Background of the *Satyricon*', *Latomus*, 18 (1959), 790 ff., and R. Browning, 'The Date of Petronius', *Classical Review*, 63 (1949), 12 ff., are still useful. A more detailed discussion, which takes account of Petronius' fictional purposes, is to be found in R. Duncan, *The Economy of the Roman Empire* (Cambridge, 1974), 238 ff.

2. Cf. G. Bagnani, *Arbiter of Elegance* (Toronto, 1954), pp. 80 ff., and see below pp. 211 ff.

logical similarity so frequently alleged between the man and the work, even if this is extended to the voyeurism which seems a characteristic of both, is perhaps too dubious to argue from,[1] but in addition to the broad considerations adduced above, one or two detailed arguments may be singled out from the mass of more dubious historical coincidences and references.

We know from the evidence of certain glass cups and inscriptions that Petraites (or Tetraites) was a famous gladiator of the time of Nero. A gladiator Petraites is mentioned twice by Trimalchio (52. 3 and 71. 6): he has Petraites' fights decorating cups in his possession, and he wants them depicted on his tomb. Similarly, two other Imperial entertainers, who can be dated fairly precisely, are both mentioned in the *Satyricon*: Menecrates, a lyre-playing protégé of Nero's, and Apelles, a *tragoedus* contemporary with Caligula. The mention of these two in the *Satyricon* fits precisely their actual chronological relationship.[2]

Such precise coincidences as these, as well as the broad similarities between features of the work and features of the language, the historical and economic background of the Roman world of the first century A.D., make the long-continued dispute about the dating of the work very puzzling, until one recalls the strange but not yet entirely quashed Baconian heresy in Shakespearian studies. Perhaps the identification of Tacitus' Petronius and our author seemed to some too good to be true.[3]

Now, however, we have more insight into the circumstances and motivation of the author of the *Satyricon*.

According to Tacitus (*Annals* 14. 16), in A.D. 59 Nero established a literary circle which went into session after dinner. It was made up of associates with some facility for verse, whose abilities

1. See J. P. Sullivan, *The Satyricon of Petronius: A Literary Study* (London and Bloomington, Indiana, 1968), pp. 238 ff.

2. The evidence for all this is laid out in H. T. Rowell, 'The Gladiator Petraites and the Date of the *Satyricon*', *Trans. Am. Philol. Assoc.* 89 (1958), 14 ff.

3. The most recent attempt to cast doubts on the identification may be found in *Petronii Arbitri Cena Trimalchionis*, Ed. M. S. Smith (Oxford 1975), 213 ff., who favours a somewhat earlier dating to the principate of Tiberius or Caligula. See also P. A. George, 'Petronius and Lucan *de Bello Civili*', *CQ*. 24 (1974), 119 ff.

had not yet attracted public attention. Here they would revise half-completed works or offer impromptu compositions for the Emperor's criticism and revision, since Nero was supposed to have a happy knack for such things, having been taught extempore composition by Seneca. One may assume that membership of this circle led to political advancement. M. Cocceius Nerva, the future emperor (A.D. 96–8) belonged to it. Born in A.D. 35, he was only two years older than Nero, who hailed him as the Tibullus of his age and had a high respect for his critical powers (Martial 8. 70; 8. 26). Later he played a vigorous role in the suppression of the Pisonian conspiracy and was praetor in A.D. 66. Aulus Vitellius, another future emperor (A.D. 68), also participated in Nero's literary activities; he presided at the *Neronia*, Nero's great literary and musical festival, and even after Nero's death arranged a recital from the *liber dominicus*, a collection of Neronian verse (Suetonius *Vitellius* 4; 11).

Ti. Silius Italicus, author of the *Punica*, was also close to Nero (Pliny *Letters* 37), becoming consul in A.D. 68; his contribution to the rampant literary activity at court was the *Ilias Latina*, now acknowledged to be his work. Fabricius Veiento, a satirist whose *Codicilli* attacked the senate and the priestly colleges, also rose to high honours and influence before his exile (Tacitus *Annals* 14. 3).

Others could be mentioned, although the most talented was obviously the poet Lucan, whose gifts according to the Voss *Life*, promoted him to a premature quaestorship before his fatal break with the emperor.

Into this circle, then, came T. Petronius Niger after his consulship in A.D. 63. He soon gained enormous influence over Nero, as his unofficial title of Arbiter of Elegance proves. His tastes, given Nero's enthusiasm for literature, must have been exercised in literary ways as well as in material refinements. His political power at court must have grown correspondingly; otherwise Tigellinus would not have grown jealous of him and encompassed his downfall. The *Satyricon*, so preoccupied with matters of taste, social and literary, and reflecting the growing hostility at court to the Annaean family, particularly to Seneca and Lucan, was the perfect vehicle for Petronius' talents. There was also the additional advantage that the chosen form did not constitute a challenge to Nero's own literary work, which was for neo-Alexandrian verse.

The Extent of the Work and the Plot

There are indications in our MSS which, if they are to be trusted, indicate that the extant portions and some fragments of the *Satyricon* may belong to Books XIV, XV, and XVI of the whole; this would mean that the work was originally perhaps twenty books long (six or ten times its present length), if it was ever finished – a great but not impossible length for a work of this sort. As we have it now, the text is interpolated, corrupt, and fragmentary. It is possible indeed that the market episode (c. 12 ff.) and the Quartilla episode (c. 16 ff.) are misplaced and belong to a slightly earlier part of the work (to Book XIV, if we could trust the interpolator of Fulgentius). But this has not yet been proved, and the abruptness of the transitions and the very odd sequence of meals in the earlier part of the work as we have it may be due simply to the loss of the connecting narrative. I have, therefore, left these episodes in the traditional place. I have followed the same practice with the occasional traces of a double tradition. It is tempting in the Quartilla episode to re-arrange and amalgamate, as Gaselee did, the two entrances of the catamite or catamites, and elsewhere in the text to remove the brief summaries of the action which are found in our MSS as part of the actual narrative. But a translation is not the place to do this: this is an editor's work. I have therefore translated the whole *textus receptus*, including the interpolations deleted by Müller, Fraenkel, and others, and excluding only certain obvious glosses.[1] After some consideration I have not interrupted the translation with summaries to bridge the gaps between the various fragments. On the whole the plot is fairly clear in the important essentials, and the intelligent reader can easily see for himself what must have been happening.

A brief recapitulation of the earlier lost episodes as they can be reconstructed from allusions in the work may be worth giving. The plot seems to consist of the adventures of the narrator

1. See my 'Interpolations in Petronius', *Proceedings of the Cambridge Philological Society* (1976).

Encolpius: sometimes he plays a direct part and is closely involved; at other times he is merely a witness of certain events
(Trimalchio's dinner-party is the best example of this). Such a
loose plot obviously and deliberately allows for frequent digressions, e.g., discussions of literature, short Milesian tales like 'The
Widow of Ephesus', poems of varying length, and so on. Nevertheless the plot gives some tenuous continuity to Encolpius'
adventures, and the basic plot is the wrath of Priapus against the
hero (*gravis ira Priapi*), a comic motif patently based on the
wrath of Poseidon against Odysseus in the *Odyssey*.[1] Encolpius
at some point has offended Priapus (it is unclear how), and
unfortunately, through various mishaps, he continues to offend
this god. Shortly before the surviving portion of the work begins
he and his two companions have witnessed and interrupted
some secret Priapean rites conducted by the priestess Quartilla,
perhaps near the long tunnel which links Naples and Puteoli,
and still later in the work he kills a goose sacred to the god.
Consequently the enmity of this powerful deity dogs him at intervals. Presumably for this reason he is still a poor exile, wandering from place to place, living by his wits. There are some
indications that he first fell foul of Priapus in Massilia (Mar-
seilles); he may have been exiled from that city (after a year's
entertainment at public expense) to avert a plague. If the doubt-
ful evidence can be trusted, he then took a hazardous journey by
sea to Italy. He may have been in Rome at some point. Possibly
it was here that he was providentially rescued from the gladiatorial arena. His activities, it is clear, frequently cause him to
run foul of the law and account for his constant travels and his
low connexions.

In Italy, Encolpius takes up with various companions, still
living by theft and free hospitality. He seems to be moving down
through Italy. At some point he is taken up by Lichas, a Taren-
tine ship owner, who is attracted by him. Encolpius, however,
seduces his wife Hedyle, commits some terrible outrage on
Lichas himself in the portico of Hercules at Baiae, the famous

---

1. This is not to suggest that the whole *Satyricon* was a close parody of
the *Odyssey*, but merely that the tenuous unifying theme and certain sub-
sidiary motifs were deliberately drawn from the *Odyssey*.

pleasure resort in south Italy, just above Puteoli, the *Graeca urbs* in which the surviving portion of the story opens, and also steals the robe and sacred rattle of the goddess Isis from Lichas' ship. In the same area, and no doubt about the same time, he falls in with the famous courtesan Tryphaena, who becomes his mistress. But becoming jealous of her fondness for the young and handsome Giton, whom he had at some point taken under his wing, he procures her public disgrace and runs off with Giton. Jealousy is a trait of Encolpius. Meeting a young man very like himself, Ascyltus, he tries to keep his relationship with Giton secret from him. The three of them are all involved in the murder of a certain Lycurgus, whose villa they then rob. The proceeds of this they sew up in a ragged tunic for safety, but during a temporary separation, perhaps while stealing an expensive cloak from some country people, they are separated and Encolpius loses the cloak with the stolen money inside. Ascyltus plainly suspects his companion's honesty. This sort of conflict, added to the jealousy over Giton (not the last occasion on which Encolpius suffers from it), will eventually cause the break-up of the trio.

It is not always easy to decide the order of the above events. As I have said, it is not impossible that some of the earlier episodes in the extant fragments are misplaced (e.g., the attempt to sell the stolen cloak). If the present ordering in the MSS is accepted, then we find the trio lodged in Puteoli and associating as men of culture with the teacher of rhetoric Agamemnon, who has a school there. Encolpius is in the middle of a discussion of the present system of rhetorical education with him, when the work as we have it abruptly opens.

The Literary Qualities of the *Satyricon*

The dubious reputation of the *Satyricon* from quite early times and its unfortunate association with literary *curiosa*, privately printed editions and copies bound in black morocco, have militated against much serious discussion of the work as literature. Many have recognized its value, but as one Frenchman said, '*on lit Pétrone, on ne cite pas*'. The German scholar Niebuhr

(1776–1831) summarized the accepted opinion when he remarked:

The disgusting indecencies of which the remains of Petronius are full ... give him so bad a name, that he who confesses an intimate acquaintance with the fiction, and expresses gratification in it, exposes himself to a severe judgement, and affords a good opportunity for the display of sanctimonious hypocrisy.

A modern reader is unlikely to have much patience with such strictures, being reared on gamier fare than anything Petronius provides. In the words of Judge Woolsey on Joyce's *Ulysses*, the few sections to which exception might be taken are 'emetic' rather than 'aphrodisiac', and these are ingredients inseparable from Petronius' literary purposes. The final word on this aspect of the *Satyricon* was said by D. H. Lawrence in a letter to Lady Ottoline Morrell (dated 1 February 1916):

He startled me at first, but I liked him. He is a gentleman when all is said and done ... Petronius is straight and above board. Whatever he does, he doesn't try to degrade and dirty the pure mind in him.

There have been many characterizations of the *Satyricon* and for most of them there is some evidence in the work. It has been seen as an early picaresque novel like *Gil Blas*, *Guzman d'Alfarache*, or even *Don Quixote*, the parody on knightly romances being matched by the parody on the *Odyssey* which runs through the *Satyricon*; it has been regarded simply as a connected collection of Milesian tales and comic sketches; it has been described as an elaborate satire on the basis of Epicurean morality against the violent and frustrating passions of greed, sex, and anger; or, even more frequently, it has been taken as the first realistic novel in European literature.[1] The disconnected nature of the fragments, the loss of so much of the work, and the diversity of what remains, all make it hard to classify, even though there is something critically inadequate about throwing up one's hands and agreeing to regard it as something of a *beau*

1. See B. E. Perry, *The Ancient Romances* (Berkeley and Los Angeles, 1967), pp. 96 ff.; E. Courtney, 'Parody and Literary Allusion in Menippean Satire', Philogus 106 (1962) 86 ff.; P. G. Walsh, *The Roman Novel* (Cambridge, 1970), pp. 4, 8 ff.

monstre, some unique portent like *Tristram Shandy*, *Finnegans Wake*, or Pound's *Cantos*, works that are at once a beginning and an end.

The best way to understand its nature is to consider it organically as a development of a literary tradition in the context of a certain milieu, and it will be found to be, I believe, an explicable literary phenomenon whose features cease to surprise us and so cease to baffle our evaluation. In this way one may explain all the features which have led to one-sided characterizations of the work, while dispensing with those equally one-sided comparisons to single works of earlier or later literature which often serve to hide its exact nature.

Formally, the work belongs to the tradition of Menippean satire, the mélange of prose and verse invented by Menippus of Gadara in the first half of the third century B.C. and developed in Rome by Varro and others. We know that it was an available form in Neronian times from the evidence of the extant *Apocolocyntosis* by Petronius' contemporary, the younger Seneca (see below, pp. 211–24), a crudely humorous squib directed against the dead Emperor Claudius. And a main characteristic of Menippean satire was the union of humour and philosophy (or whatever moral or aesthetic basis an author might substitute for this).[1]

We cannot, however, say off-hand that Petronius' motive in writing his work was predominantly satirical in our sense, for he differs vastly from Persius, the other Neronian satirist who has survived. But what we can say with fair assurance is that, granted the continuance of a Roman tradition of Menippean satire, the very form and loose structure of Menippean satire might be attractive to the sort of genius and temperament we find in Petronius. It would require merely the enlargement of its potentialities to become an ideal vehicle of Petronius' literary abilities. I said earlier that it was unlikely that Nero's Arbiter of Elegance was not a literary arbiter as well as an arbiter of more tangible refinements. If this was so, Menippean satire was a perfect form for literary criticism, both directly and through parody, particularly as the fashion of writing books of criticism was not yet so firmly established as with us and criticism was generally

1. See, e.g. P. Parsons, 'A Greek *Satyricon*?', *Bulletin of the Institute of Classical Studies* 18 (1971) 53 ff.

offered in satire form. It allowed also for the exercise of Petronius' admittedly meagre verse talents, with the additional advantage that their attribution to fictional *personae* would not constitute any very high claims for their merit. The final and rather extraneous attraction of the form would be its suitability for the continuous recitals which Nero's literary court circle undoubtedly indulged in.

Yet for all its formal seductions, Menippean satire was still a branch of Roman satire, whose characteristic content had gradually become – despite its earlier broadness – a commentary on life and morals. It is clear from the evidence of Persius, and there is no reason to think the case different with Menippean satire, that Roman satire had developed into what we think of as true satire. The one difference there might be between Menippean and regular satire is the strong tradition of humour and fantasy, which is clearly indicated in the titles of Varro's lost works. As a consequence, Petronius, who was a literary traditionalist, would be impelled – or attracted – by the exigencies of the form as he found it (for the degeneration of Menippean satire into a mere mélange of prose and verse, in Boethius for example, came later) to take a large account, somehow or other, of this element as well as the more basic element of satire proper. This is perhaps a misleading way to put it, and it is not the way the artist works. We are talking here about the tension between the artist and the claims of his chosen form, claims which are imposed on the artist in one sense, but are voluntarily accepted by him for the artistic process. Even if the choice of Menippean satire was initially for its peripheral advantages (namely, looseness of structure, tolerance of digressions, opportunities for versification), an unlikely hypothesis with so impressive an artist as Petronius, his genius would then respond to the more essential nature of the form, even though his own literary excellence might develop or even change that nature into something other.

All this may seem oversubtle, but it is important to exclude the idea of Petronius' inventing a new *genre* which corresponds closely to the modern sprawling novel as practised by its more realistic and digressive practitioners, and, naturally, failing in its execution. The similarity to the novel is there, but it has another explanation.

If my view is correct, several important aspects of the *Satyricon* now find, directly or indirectly, their explanation. The digressions, such as the *Carmen de Bello Civili*, although they fit so adventitiously into the loose Menippean form, may be left aside: their *raison d'être* is obvious enough. But the integral episodes of the work derive from satire and were determined by Petronius' choice of *genre*. At least three of them are paralleled in extant Roman satire, notably the '*Cena Trimalchionis*', which has obvious affinities with Horace's '*Cena Nasidieni*' (*Sat.* 2. 8), the episode at Croton, which intermittently satirizes legacy hunters, a theme common to Horace and Juvenal (cf. Hor. *Sat.* 2. 5 and Juv. *Sat.* 1. 37 ff, 55 ff), and, finally, the satiric description of women such as Circe, who prefer low-class lovers, a type prominent in Juvenal's sixth satire and to be found also in Herondas and elsewhere. No doubt other episodes, such as Encolpius' soliloquy over the dead body of Lichas, might also have had literary ancestors – a study of Varro's fragments and titles suggests further interesting possibilities. And if we leave satire proper, Encolpius' impotence has its parallel in Ovid's mock-serious lament over his own fiasco in *Amores* 3. 7, a subject as appropriate to satire as to elegy, if not more so. And of course we must not make the mistake of thinking that the Romans were unsophisticated about literary cross-fertilization – Horace's discussion of Lucilius and his predecessors in Atttic comedy is proof enough of this. The main themes of the work then seem predominantly satiric and the close relation of humour or wit with moral satire, in ancient as well as modern times, might seem to explain the nature of most of the *Satyricon*, particularly if we add that ancient satirists, like Jonathan Swift and some seventeenth-century writers such as Rochester and Dorset, often chose prurient and disgusting targets for their humorous or ironic shafts. But the truth is that Petronius, on a careful reading, does not strike us, for all his satiric themes, as a truly classical satirist. There is something oddly wrong in this classification, and the long debate over the nature of the work reinforces our doubts. For Petronius does not strike us as a serious moralist or even, like Juvenal, as an adopter of a conventional *morale* from which to launch into his more vital and artistic preoccupations. He is completely disengaged from the moral situations he depicts and the episode at Croton is given an atmosphere of fantasy and humour rather than moral concern.

The 'Cena Trimalchionis' offers the real clue to this difficulty. The theme is traditional, even if considerably deepened by experience and observation, but the standard adopted is clearly one of taste, as one might expect of its author, rather than any moral standard. But even this standard is constantly undercut by the deliberate satire on Encolpius, the mouthpiece of the satire. All his strictures on Trimalchio's vulgarity and pretentiousness lose their effect when Petronius makes his narrator expose himself time and again to the reader's contempt, however indulgent. As a partial consequence, although the sheer vitality of Petronius' creation must not be overlooked, Trimalchio more and more assumes the status of a great comic character rather than a mercilessly flayed object of satire. (Petronius' original *intentions* are naturally irrelevant – his initial aim may easily have been transcended.) Much the same may be said of Trimalchio's circle.

What has happened, I think, is this: Petronius' themes are at first dictated by the tradition of the *genre* he has chosen and his success or relative failure with them depends on their challenge to his imagination. Obviously the Trimalchio episode is more of a masterpiece than anything that happens elsewhere in Puteoli or at Croton. The challenge that he has been able to meet has been essentially a novelist's challenge, for we have seen that his artistic impulse is not really a satirist's impulse at all. His claim to be a satirist is no more than the fact that he has chosen traditional satiric topics where the air of disengagement is too obvious to be missed, and when he does approach satire from an implicit standard, it is a standard of taste which he constantly undercuts by irony. Encolpius is a failure both as a moral and an aesthetic repository, but at no point, except possibly in cc. 118 and 132 (both literary), does Petronius appear to offer his own views.

One important association of satire had obviously gone home to him, an association that was perhaps reinforced by a variety of circumstances, not all of them literary. Satire not only had a tradition of more or less conversational language (*sermoni propriora*, in Horace's phrase), but it also prided itself on its 'realism'. Of course Roman literature is always highly dependent on tradition and sometimes one might suspect that some of the 'realistic' topics which recur so often had become in fact stylized, if not fossilized – much as second-rate modern novels convert originally daring narrations of the sexual act into conventional and stylized descriptions. Still, the Roman satirists continued to decry stale mythological themes and proclaim that their form of art alone depicted reality ... *quidquid agunt homines, hominem pagina nostra sapit, quodque facit populus*, etc.

Naturally when one looks at the subjects of satire, one sees that this claim to represent reality is actually, in Mary McCarthy's phrase, 'a denigration of the real'. The satirist, like many so-called 'realistic' novelists, is presenting a partial view of reality and claiming that only the seamier, the more vulgar, side of life is truly real, the rest is the humbug of the canting moralist. Hence the predominance of sexual themes in the satirists, Petronius included: sex is the one subject at least for satire which outlives legacy-hunting, the ill-treatment of the Irish, and contemporary manifestations of bad taste.

In certain ages and milieu this view of life is more seductive than in others. Certain periods of high literary culture and material refinement seem affected by a *nostalgie de la boue*, which may make itself felt both in life and in literature. Nero, we are told by Suetonius (*Nero*, 26), used to wander at night in disguise into low taverns and get involved in disreputable escapades in Rome, and Petronius' interest in lower-class life, sordid sex, and crime seems almost the literary counterpart of this. A comparison might be made with the 1890s in Europe where a high degree of literary sophistication went hand in hand with an interest in the more disreputable areas of life – Dorian Gray and Des Esseintes have the same peculiar contrasts of refinement and sordidness in their characters as Encolpius or Eumolpus.

Were this all, Petronius would find himself in the company of those satirists, and novelists, whose purblind view of reality makes them either inadequate commentators on life or highly partial visionaries saved from inadequacy only by their intensity and literary gifts. But Petronius, for all his acceptance of satiric themes and the satirist's view of life, is saved by his own irony and artistic ambivalence towards satire. He can accept the satiric themes, but he does not accept the moral premiss, whether because of his Epicureanism or his own view of existence. The sordid becomes humorous; the sexual never becomes salacious or disgusting; the objects of his 'satire' become literary creations. If there is any commentary on existence, it is ultimately a novelist's commentary, almost a poet's, not the cruder and over-simplified commentary of the satirist. In Petronius we see the novelist taking over the satirist's task, while working with the satirist's themes – and it is not the so-called 'realistic' novelist who does what the satirist does even though he omits the more obvious moralizing, but rather the creative novelist who enlarges on life and reshapes it to his own artistic ends.

The proof is there in Trimalchio, although evidence may be found scattered throughout the work. The basic object of satire, the vulgar, uneducated but pretentious freedman, had no doubt a thousand counterparts in life, and Horace provided Petronius with an adequate model of satiric treatment in the somewhat similar character of Nasidienus. But the novelist's impulse in Petronius was greater than the satirist's and to build up the elaborate character of Trimalchio, Petronius drew on what he knew of life, including a considerable number of real persons. Trimalchio's fondness for the insipid rebus game (c. 56) he shares with the Emperor Augustus (cf. Suetonius, *Augustus* 75); his eccentricity about the importance of the digestive tract he shares with the Emperor Claudius (cf. Suetonius, *Claudius* 32); his morbid game of playing dead he has in common with at least two other Romans, Pacuvius and Turannius, both mentioned by Seneca (*Epistulae Morales* 12. 8 and *De brevitate Vitae* 20. 3); and of course an important model was the millionaire Calvisius Sabinus, described by Seneca (*Epistulae Morales* 27. 5–8). Similarly, his astrological disquisition in c. 39 is not simply a piece of free invention, but a careful and witty compilation of current popular beliefs, just as the language and sentiments of Trimalchio's humbler friends seem convincing and plausible evidence of a careful study of their putative milieu. (It is worth comparing those passages in D. H. Lawrence's *Lady Chatterley's Lover*, where the housekeeper, Mrs Bolton, discusses affairs in the village with Clifford Chatterley.) All this amalgamation of direct observation and literary hearsay (for we cannot deny realism to a novelist because his source is reportage or what he takes to be reportage) is of course subordinated to the imaginative grasp which we feel at work in the presentation of that true novelistic creation, Trimalchio.

On the Translation

The translation of such a highly original and artistic work as the *Satyricon*, written in a mixture of prose and verse, offers special problems. The amount of imitation and parody of other authors is considerable; the style moves from serious and elaborate discussion of literature to the humorous vernacular conversations of Trimalchio and his circle. And these are set within the basic narrative framework which is the generally terse, swift-moving Latinity of Encolpius. The complex problem of the prose style thus takes us to the very heart of the work.

Before discussing this major obstacle for the translator, it might be well to turn at once to the question of Petronius' verse insertions.

The verse of the *Satyricon* is of course dramatic *vers d'occasion* and, as such, subject to the exigencies of his plot. As a result, one cannot expect too much – nor does one get it. Petronius, on the evidence of the verse insertions and certain fragments, is not a great poet, despite the claims occasionally made for him. The few poems of merit sometimes included in the Fragments (e.g., XXXVIII and LIV in this translation) are probably not by Petronius. Some of the discredit must go to his reactionary critical principles in poetry. Petronius set himself against the mainstream of Latin verse, which was moving towards the wit of Martial and the pointed rhetoric of Juvenal, and is already well established in Latin literature by Nero's time in the works of Lucan. Whatever criticisms may be made of this, a mere traditionalism based on Vergil and Horace would be powerless to deflect or revolutionize contemporary poetic diction. Petronius' metrical virtuosity is however clear – he employs a variety of metres: choliambics, elegiacs, dactylic hexameters, hendecasyllables, etc. This too has to be taken into account by the translator, if only to the extent of trying to reproduce this *variety* of verse forms. Patently it is impossible to offer readable versions which reproduce these metres in English and so, like most translators, I have chosen whatever type of verse seemed suitable for the subject. It is, of course, an easy matter to ensure that the verse is bad where the Latin verse was intended to be bad. For the most part, I have attempted to be readable and therefore I have felt free to use modern methods of verse translation, notably *vers libre*, modern rhythm and diction, and pastiche. In various ways, like so many translators, I am indebted to Ezra Pound, and most notably to his *Homage to Sextus Propertius*, although this translation is in no way intended to be a 'creative translation' like that work. Pound's own epic, like Lucan's, is unfinished; and I have adopted the *Cantos* as my model for translating the long poem on the Civil War (c. 119 ff.). The original was meant to be a rehandling of the *Pharsalia* of Lucan, a sort of epic parody. There is no contemporary verse translation of Lucan to play host to the parasite, as the first three books of Lucan played host to Petronius' poem, and as in any case the whole rationale of the exercise is too remote to us, I have concentrated on making this strange fragment of an epic comprehensible to the modern reader by retaining the subject matter and making the style the style of the *Cantos*.

This opportunistic method of translation, however, will not serve for the prose sections. It would be gratifying if the translator, like Matthew Arnold with Homer, could simply point to a limited number of qualities in the original which he had tried to bring out in the translation. But this is difficult to do except sketchily: in the main, Petronius is deliberately and deceptively simple over large stretches of his work; there is, furthermore, a pervasive irony which leaves the reader often in some doubt as to the author's intentions at certain points (how serious, for example, is the opening discussion of contemporary rhetoric?); above all, there is the constant auctorial sophistication which makes itself felt through the pretentious or unsuccessful sophistication which the narrator Encolpius tries to adopt. In few works do we have such a separation of the author and his narrative vehicle.

These qualities are difficult to reproduce and indeed their interplay and local appearance in the work are sometimes hard to pin down exactly. I have tried in the preceding section to lay out my critical estimate of the work as a whole, but sometimes the particular intentions of a given section are problematic and it would be a dangerous optimism to force too blatant or crude an interpretation simply for the sake of brightness in translation. In Petronius above all the tone is of supreme importance, more important even than the range and flexibility of his style and subject matter, for it is through the tone that the objectivity and irony of the author make themselves apparent.

THE SATYRICON

1. ... Our professors of rhetoric are hag-ridden in the same way, surely, when they shout 'I got these wounds fighting for your freedom ! This eye I lost for you. Give me a hand to lead me to my children. I am hamstrung, my legs can't support me.' We could put up with even this stuff if it were a royal road to eloquence. But the only result of these pompous subjects and this empty thunder of platitudes, is that when young speakers first enter public life they think they have been landed on another planet. I'm sure the reason such young nitwits are produced in our schools is because they have no contact with anything of any use in everyday life. All they get is pirates standing on the beach, dangling manacles, tyrants writing orders for sons to cut off their fathers' heads, oracles advising the sacrifice of three or more virgins during a plague – a mass of sickly sentiments: every word, every move just so much poppycock.[1]

2. People fed on this kind of thing have as much chance of learning sense as dishwashers have of smelling clean. If you'll pardon my saying so, you professors of rhetoric are mainly responsible. You have ruined good speaking. Your smooth and empty sound effects provided a few sniggers, and as a result you took the guts out of real oratory, and that was the end of it. Young men were not tied down to rhetorical exercises when Sophocles and Euripides managed to write the way people should speak.[2] Academic pedants had not addled their wits when Pindar and the nine lyric poets grew nervous of the Homeric style.[3] And apart from the poets I can cite, I certainly cannot see Plato or Demosthenes going in for this sort of training.[4] The elevated, what one might call the *pure* style, is not full of purple patches and bombast : it is lifted up by its intrinsic beauty. It is not so long since that long-winded spouting of yours travelled from Asia to Athens and its foul pestilential breath infected every youthful ambition.[5] Once standards drop, eloquence loses vigour and voice. Who since then has attained the stature of Thucydides or the reputation of Hyperides?[6] Why, not even poetry has shown a spark of life. All forms of literature have

been faced with the same diet and lost their chance of a ripe old age. Even the great art of painting has met the same fate since the unscrupulous Egyptians produced their 'Handbook for Painters'.[7]

3. Agamemnon, after his own sweat in the class room, did not allow me to hold forth in the colonnade for longer than himself.

'Young man,' he said, 'your opinions show extraordinary good taste and you have that extremely rare quality – a love for intellectual merit. So I shall not baffle you with any expertise. It is not surprising that teachers make immoral concessions with these exercises – they *have* to humour the madmen. If the speeches they make do not win the approval of their young pupils, as Cicero says, "they will be the only ones in their schools".[8] When spongers[9] are trying to get a dinner out of their rich friends, their main object is to find out what they would most like to hear. The only way they will get what they are after is by winning over their audience. It is the same with a tutor of rhetoric. Like a fisherman he has to bait his hook with what he knows the little fishes will rise for; otherwise he's left on the rocks without a hope of their biting.

4. 'What's the answer? It's the parents you should blame. They won't allow their children to be properly controlled. In the first place they sacrifice everything, even their hopes, to their ambition. Then in their overeagerness they direct these immature intellects into public life. They will tell you that there is no mightier power than oratory and they dress up their boys as orators while they are still drawing their first breath. If only parents would not rush them through their studies! Then young men who are prepared to work would cultivate their minds with solid reading, mould their characters with sensible advice, and prune their style with a ruthless pen.[10] They would wait and listen before they tried themselves and they would realize that an adolescent taste is quite worthless. Then the noble art of oratory would have its true weight and dignity. Boys today are frivolous in school; young men are laughing stocks in public life; and, the greatest shame of all, even when they are old they refuse to give up the mistakes they learnt in the classroom.

'But just to show you how I am not above a bit of low-level

improvisation in the manner of Lucilius,[11] I'll throw you off a few lines expressing my feelings:

5. Ambition to fulfil the austere demands of Art,
   The mind moving to major themes,
   Demands discipline, the tight belt,
   The heart like a mirror.
   Disdain the high seats of the mighty,
   The begrudged invitations to drunken dinners,
   The addictions, the low pleasures,
   The mental spark guttering out with the wine.
   Refuse theatre invitations,
   Refuse to sell your applause
   To the actor's empty mouthings.

   Near smiling battlements of martial Athens,
   In Lacedaemonian colony,
   By the home of the Sirens even,
   No matter:
   Verse for your early education,
   Deep joyful drafts from Homeric springs
   Then full of the Socratic circle,
   Let your reins ride loose,
   Rattle the great sword of Demosthenes.
   Now our Roman squadrons swirl round you like a flood,
   Lighter from an injection of Greek music,
   Changing their savour.
   Then leave the forum behind
   And let your reading advance
   Till the power of Fortune makes itself heard in History,
   Clearly and distinctly
                     in running cadences.
   War's brutal sounds should feast your ears;
   Shudder at the mighty orotundities
   Of Cicero,
             who never lost a cause.
   This is the right armoury of genius –
   "Drink deep or taste not the Pierian spring."
   And now you may write.'[12]

6. As I was listening carefully to him, I did not notice Ascyltus slipping away ... and while I paced about very impressed by this flood of ideas, a huge crowd of students entered the colonnade. Apparently they had been listening to an extempore

declamation by whoever it was who took over Agamemnon's lecture. While the young men were laughing at the points he made and picking to pieces the arrangement of the whole speech, I took the opportunity to slip away and started off hastily after Ascyltus. But I was not paying much attention to the way I went, and I had no idea where our lodging was.[13] Whichever direction I took, I came back to the same spot. Finally, worn out with running and dripping with sweat, I went up to an old woman selling fresh vegetables.

7. 'Excuse me, mother,' I began, 'I don't suppose you know where I'm staying, do you?'

She was amused by my naïve politeness.

'Of course I do,' she said. She got to her feet and set off in front of me. I thought she was uncanny, < and followed her >. And then, as we reached an out of the way place, the kind old lady threw back a patchwork curtain and said to me:

'This is where you must be staying.'

I was just telling her I did not recognize the place, when I caught sight of some naked old prostitutes and some customers furtively prowling up and down in the middle of them.[14] Slowly, in fact too late, I realized I had been taken to a brothel. Cursing the old woman's tricks I covered my face and began hurrying right through the whore-house to the other side. At the very door who should bump into me but Ascyltus. Like me he was worn out and practically dead. It looked as though he had been brought there by the same little old woman. Greeting him with a smile, I asked what he was doing in this dreadful place.

8. He wiped away the sweat with his hands and said:

'If only you knew what has been happening to me!'

'What happened?' I said.

'I wandered through the whole town,' he began faintly, 'and I couldn't find where I'd left our lodgings. Then a respectable-looking gentleman came up and very kindly offered to show me the way. He went down various pitch-dark turnings and brought me to this place. Then he offered me money and began making improper suggestions. The woman had already got her money for the cubicle and he had his hand on me. If I'd not been stronger that he was, I should have been in a bad way.'

In fact, everyone around seemed to have been drinking aphrodisiac . . .[15]

*

Our combined forces made short work of the nuisance.

*

9. As though through a fog I caught sight of Giton standing at the side of the street. I rushed to the spot . . .

*

I asked my little friend if he'd prepared anything for supper. At this the boy sat down on the bed and wiped away a stream of tears with his thumb. I was deeply shocked at the dear boy's state and urged him to tell me what had happened. Slowly and reluctantly – in fact I had to plead and threaten alternately – he told me:

'It was your dear friend, the fellow you go round with, anyway. Just a few minutes ago he ran into my room and began wanting to rape me. When I shouted for help, he took out his big knife and said: "If you're playing Lucretia, I'm your Tarquin." '[16]

When I heard this, I shook my fist in front of Ascyltus's face: 'What have you to say, you filthy little pansy! Your very breath stinks from your dirty ways!'

Ascyltus pretended to be horrified. Then he made an even braver show with his own fists and shouted far more loudly than I had: 'Shut up, you dirty pug! Even the arena was glad to be rid of you. Shut up, you stab-in-the-dark! Even when you were at your best, you never managed to lay a decent woman. I was very close to you in the park, wasn't I? Just the way the boy is now in the hotel.'

'Didn't you slip away,' I said, 'when we were talking to the professor?'

10. 'Well, you fool, what did you expect me to do, when I was dying of hunger? I should have been listening to his rubbishy platitudes, I suppose! They're not worth a row of broken bottles – he'd be interpreting his dreams next! *You* are a hell of a sight worse than I am – I didn't praise his poetry to cadge a dinner.'

... So our mortifying quarrel collapsed in roars of laughter, and we turned peaceably to other things ...

*

But his treachery stuck in my mind, so I said: 'Look, Ascyltus, I see it is impossible for us to get along together. I suggest we divide our belongings and try to make a living by ourselves. You're a literary sort of man and so am I. I don't want to interfere with your earnings, so I'll offer some other line. Otherwise every day hundreds of different things will set us at each other's throat, and get us talked about all over town.'

Ascyltus had no objection. He merely said: 'Look, at the moment we've accepted an invitation to dinner as men of letters – don't let us waste the evening. Tomorrow, if this is the way you want it, I'll find myself lodgings and someone else to live with.'

'It's just wasting time,' I pointed out, 'why put off our pleasures?' My desires were responsible for the suddenness of this split. For some time now I had been wanting to be rid of my troublesome chaperon and be back on my old footing with dear little Giton.

*

11. I looked everywhere in the town before going back to our little room. At last I enjoyed his kisses without looking for excuses. I held the boy in my arms as though I'd never let him go. I had what I wanted and anyone would have envied me my luck. But we were still in the middle of this when Ascyltus came quietly to the door, forcibly shattered the bolts, and found me playing around with Giton. He filled the little room with laughter and applause. He rolled me out of the cloak I was lying in and said:

'What *were* you up to, my pious old friend? What's this? Are you just sharing the same tent?'

And he did not limit himself to insults, but taking the strap from his bag he began to lay into me in earnest, punctuating it with insolent remarks like – 'So that's your idea of fair shares, is it?'

*

12. It was getting dark when we came into the square.[17] We

noticed a lot of things on sale, none of them of any great worth – in fact, the sort of things whose dubious origin is best concealed in the dim light of evening. As we ourselves had brought along the cloak we had stolen we decided to take advantage of this excellent opportunity by unfolding just the edge of it in a corner. Our hope was that the high-quality cloth would attract some chance buyer. It was not long before a countryman, who looked familiar to me, approached with a young woman companion and started examining the garment very closely. Ascyltus in turn shot a keen glance at the tunic dangling over the shoulders of the fellow. Suddenly he almost fainted and couldn't open his mouth. Even I lost some of my composure when I looked at the man. He appeared to be the very person who had found our tunic in the wilds. Clearly it was the same man. Ascyltus however was afraid to trust his eyes in case he did something rash. So he began by moving closer like a potential customer, then he pulled the edge of it from his shoulders and ran his fingers carefully over it.

13. What a marvellous stroke of luck! The countryman's prying hands so far hadn't even tried the stitches. He was selling it like something a tramp had picked up and wanted to be rid of. As soon as Ascyltus realized our hoard was intact and the man selling it was a person of no account, he took me a little way out of the crowd and said :

'Do you know, dearie, the loot I was so cross about has returned to us. That's our tunic and it looks as if it's still stuffed with the money – it hasn't been touched. Now what are we going to do? How are we going to claim our property?'

I was delighted not only because I saw the loot but because I was now fortunately free of that loathsome suspicion. I opposed anything underhand : legal methods were clearly our best line of attack. If he would not hand the property over to its rightful owner, then it would come to a court-order.

14. Ascyltus on the other hand was afraid of the law. 'Who knows us in this place?' he said. 'And who is going to believe us if we press our claim? I'm all for buying it now we have spotted it, even though it is our own. I would rather lay out a small sum to recover valuable property than go to court, where the outcome is very uncertain.

What use are laws where money is king,
Where poverty's helpless and can't fix a thing?
Even Cynics[18] who sneer are rarely averse
To selling their scruples to fill up their purse.
There's no justice at law – it's the bidding that counts
And the job of the judge is to fix the amounts.'

However, apart from a solitary coin which we had intended to spend on lupines, we had no ready money. So in case the loot should slip from our fingers in the meantime, we decided to knock down the price of the cloak and take a small loss for the sake of the greater gain. As soon as we unwrapped our merchandise, the woman standing by the countryman with her head covered carefully examined the marks on it, grabbed the edge with both hands and screamed at the top of her voice: 'Help, thieves!' As for us, we became panicky in case we looked at a loss, so we began hanging on to the torn and shabby tunic, and shouting just as indignantly that they had *our* property. But the two sides were in a very different position, and the dealers who had come milling round at the noise ridiculed our spite.[19] For they saw one side demanding back an extremely valuable cloak, while the other side was after a tattered old thing, which it would be a waste to use good patches on. In the end Ascyltus managed to quieten their laughter and get himself heard:

15. 'Everyone obviously likes his own things best. Let them give us back our tunic and take back their cloak.' Although the countryman and the woman were in favour of this exchange, the night police however had been summoned (it was almost night now)[20] and they insisted that both articles should be deposited with them, so that a magistrate could look into the matter the next day. It was not merely the articles themselves that were at stake, but there was the quite different question that both parties were suspected of theft. It was agreed that persons to take charge of them should be appointed, and one of the dealers, a bald-headed man with a very knobbly forehead, who sometimes handled court cases too, had pounced on the cloak and was swearing that the exhibit would appear next day. Of course it was obvious what he was after: once the cloak was left with him it could be sat on by these thieves, and we would be too afraid of legal proceedings to come to court. This was obviously what

we wanted too, and by a piece of luck both sides got what they were after. The countryman, infuriated by our claim that this patched old thing was an exhibit, threw the tunic into Ascyltus' face. So much for our particular charge – the cloak was the only thing in dispute and we were told to hand it over into custody . . .

The prize was ours again, we thought, and we went hastily back to our lodgings. Once behind locked doors we began ridiculing the sharp wits of our accusers and the dealers equally – it was very smart of them to give us our money back.

> Anything on which I'm set
> Should be hard to get;
> A ready-made victory
> Is always a bore to me.

*

16. But we had only just filled ourselves up with the supper Giton had kindly prepared, when there came a knock, savage enough to make the door rattle. We turned pale and asked who it was. 'Open and you'll find out!' came the answer. As we were speaking, the bolt gave way of its own accord and fell to the floor : the door was suddenly thrown open to admit the caller. It was a woman, in fact, with her head covered.

'Did you think you could make a fool out of me?' she said. 'I am Quartilla's personal maid and it was her religious service you burst into at the entrance to the grotto. And now she is on her way to the inn and she wants to talk to you. Don't get upset. She won't blame you or punish you for your mistake. She is really wondering what in heaven brought such charming young men to her part of the world.'

17. We had not yet said a word nor had we agreed one way or the other, when the lady herself entered with one young girl in attendance. She sat on my bed and cried for a long time. Not even this drew comment from us : in complete amazement we waited for this tearful show of grief to end. When the calculated storm of tears subsided, she uncovered her haughty head and wrung her hands till the joints cracked.

'What monstrous conduct is this?' she said. 'Where did you pick up such unimaginably criminal ways? Heaven knows, I'm deeply sorry for you. You see, it's absolutely forbidden – no one has ever seen it without being punished. Especially as our part of the world is so full of watchful powers that it's easier to run across a god than a man. And don't think I have come here for vengeance. I am more worried about your youth than my own injuries. Through sheer ignorance – I still believe this – you have committed an unforgivable sin. That very night I was full of unrest: I shivered with such a deadly chill I was afraid it was an attack of fever. And so I looked for a cure in my dreams and I was instructed to get hold of you and alleviate the onset of the attack by a subtle method which was revealed to me. But it is not the remedy I am so greatly concerned about; there is a deeper pain raging in my heart, which has brought me almost to death's door – I am afraid that in your youthful recklessness you will be driven to make public what you saw in the shrine of Priapus [21] and let out to all and sundry the workings of the divine mind. So I throw myself at your feet and I solemnly beg you not to make our nocturnal rites into a laughing-stock, and not to spread abroad the secrets of centuries – secrets which hardly a thousand people have ever shared.'

18. After this moving plea, she again burst into tears; shaking with great sobs she pressed her face and bosom to my bed. I was torn between sympathy and fear. I told her not to be upset and not to worry on either score. No one would spread abroad her holy mysteries; and if the god had revealed to her some further cure for her fever, then we were ready to further the will of heaven, no matter what it cost us.

This promise made her more cheerful; she covered me with kisses, her tears turned to laughter, and she slowly smoothed the hair falling over my ears.

'I'll make a truce with you,' she said. 'I withdraw my charges. Though if you had not been amenable about this medicine I'm after, there was a mob waiting for tomorrow to avenge my injuries and vindicate my honour.

> Trample on cravens; Pride makes its own laws:
> My passion is to go as I please.
> Even philosophers fight when offended,
> And the victor is merciful, when the fight's ended.'

*

Then she clapped her hands and suddenly burst into such a peal of laughter that she frightened us. The maid who had arrived before her did the same and so did the little girl who had come in with her.

19. The whole place rang with their theatrical laughter, while we were still wondering why this sudden change of mood and looking now at each other, now at the women.[22]

*

'So I have given orders that not a living soul is to be allowed into this inn today, so I can get from you the remedy for my fever without any interruption.'

As Quartilla said this, Ascyltus looked stupefied for a moment. I personally went colder than winter in Gaul, and I couldn't get a word out. But our numbers banished any fears I felt of worse to come. After all, they were three weak women, if they wanted to try anything; if nothing else, we, on the other hand, were the stronger sex, and we were certainly less hampered by clothes. In fact, I had already decided how we were to be matched, so that if it came to a fight, I would face Quartilla myself, Ascyltus the maid, and Giton the girl.

*

Then all our courage absolutely vanished. Our surprise was complete. Our eyes began to close at the prospect of certain death.

*

20. 'Please, lady,' I said, 'if you have anything worse in store for us, get it over quickly. Surely we have not committed such a great crime that we deserve to be tortured before we die.'

*

The maid called Psyche carefully spread a blanket on the hard floor.

*

. . . tried to excite me, but the thing was cold with the chill of a thousand deaths.

*

Ascyltus had pulled his cloak over his head; obviously he had been warned it was dangerous to pry into other people's secrets.

*

The maid produced two thongs from her pocket and tied our hands and feet with them.

*

Our amusing conversation was just tailing off, when Ascyltus asked: 'Hey, don't I deserve a drink?' Summoned by my laughter, the maid clapped her hands and said: 'I did put it down near you, young man. But have you drunk all that medicine by yourself?' 'Really?' said Quartilla. 'Has Encolpius drunk all the aphrodisiac there was?'

*

Her sides shook with her charming laughter.

*

In the end even Giton joined in the joke, particularly when the little girl threw her arms round his neck and kissed him an incredible number of times without any struggle.

*

21. We were in such a dreadful way we wanted to shout for help, but there was no one to come to our aid. Besides, whenever I showed signs of calling for assistance from outside, Psyche stuck a hairpin into my cheeks. Meanwhile the girl was stifling Ascyltus with a cosmetic brush which she had soaked in aphrodisiac.

Finally, up came a pansy, dressed in myrtle-green shaggy felt, which was tucked up under his belt. He pulled the cheeks of our bottoms apart, then he slobbered vile, greasy kisses on us, until Quartilla, carrying a whale-bone rod, with her skirts up round her, put an end to our sufferings.

*

Both of us swore a solemn oath that our dreadful secret would die with us.

*

A crowd of gymnasium attendants came in, who rubbed us with the proper oil and made us feel better. Somehow or other we threw off our weariness, put on dinner clothes again and were taken into the next room. There were three couches ready and every other refinement of gracious living magnificently laid out. We took our places as we were told, and beginning with some wonderful hors d'oeuvre we were then practically swimming in Falernian wine. After helping ourselves to a long series of dishes, we were beginning to fall asleep, when Quartilla said, 'Do you actually intend to go to sleep when you know the whole night has to be a vigil in honour of our guardian Priapus?'

*

22. Ascyltus, overcome by all he had gone through, was dropping off to sleep, so the maid he had rudely rejected took some soot and rubbed it all down his face and, without his feeling it in his drunken stupor, she painted his sides and shoulders with wine lees. I was also worn out, and I had already dropped into the lightest possible doze. In fact, the whole household, indoors and out, had done the same. Some were lying here and there round the feet of the guests, others were propped up against the walls, a number stayed in the doorway with their heads together. The lamps were running out of oil too, and were casting only a dim dying light, when two Syrians on the prowl entered the dining room. They began quarrelling greedily among the silver and smashed a decanter they'd taken. Over went one of the tables, silver and all, and a cup which was knocked off from quite a height cracked the maid's skull as she drooped over the couch. The blow made her scream and she gave the thieves away, as well as waking up some of the drunken guests. The Syrians, realizing they were trapped, dropped side by side next to a couch – you'd have thought it was pre-arranged – and began snoring as though they had been asleep for hours.

By now the butler likewise was awake and poured oil into the guttering lamps. The slaves, after rubbing their eyes a bit, had returned to their duties, and a girl with cymbals entered and the clash of brass woke everyone up.

23. The party began again and Quartilla called us back to drinking, the girl with the cymbals adding to the conviviality.

*

In comes a male prostitute, a low creature and just what you would expect in that house. Cracking his fingers with a groan, he blurted out some verses of this sort:

> 'Pansy boys, come out to play,
> You've been cropped the Delian way:
> Young or old, there's room for you
> And room for roaming fingers too!
> Hips and bottoms, waggle away,
> Pansy boys, come out to play.'

Once his lines were finished, he slobbered a filthy kiss on me. Then he even came on the couch and tried with all his strength to pull my clothes off. He kept working away fruitlessly between my legs. Trickles of acacia-pomade ran down his sweaty forehead and there was so much powder in the wrinkles on his cheeks that he looked like a peeling wall in a thunderstorm.

24. I couldn't keep my tears back any longer, I was in the depths of misery.

'Please, lady,' I said, 'surely you ordered me a night-cap.'[23] She clapped her hands daintily and said: 'Oh, you clever man. You're bubbling over with native wit. Well now, hadn't you discovered that a pansy could be a night-cap?'

Then in case my comrade-in-arms should get off too lightly, I said: 'Be fair. Is Ascyltus the only one at the table to have a holiday?'

'Really,' said Quartilla, 'let Ascyltus have a night-cap too.'

Thereupon the pansy swapped horses and after making the changeover to my companion, pestered him with his buttocks and kisses.

Giton was standing there while all this went on and splitting his sides laughing. And Quartilla, catching sight of him, asked with great interest whose was the boy. I replied that he was my boy-friend.

'Then why hasn't he given me a kiss?' said Quartilla. And calling him to her, she pressed her lips to his. Then she slipped her hand into his clothes and felt his immature little tool. 'To-morrow this will serve nicely as hors d'oeuvre to tempt my appetite,' she said. 'For the present, I don't want any ordinary stuffing after such a nice cod-piece.'

25. As she said this, Psyche came and laughingly whispered something in her ear:

'Yes, yes,' said Quartilla, 'thanks for reminding me. It's such an excellent opportunity, why shouldn't our little Pannychis lose her virginity?'

The girl was brought forward immediately – quite a pretty thing who appeared no more than seven years old. Everyone applauded and called for a wedding. I was quite taken aback by this and insisted that Giton, who was a very nice boy, was not up to this loose behaviour, nor was the girl old enough to take on the heavy duties of womanhood.

'Really?' said Quartilla. 'Is she any younger than I was when I had my first man? Juno's curse on me, if I can even remember being a virgin. When I was a child I played dirty games with boys of the same age, then as the years went by, I turned to bigger boys till I reached maturity. I even think this is the origin of the proverb – if you carry the calf, you can carry the bull.'

So in case my little friend should suffer worse treatment out of my sight, I got up to help with the ceremony.[24]

26. Psyche had already put a veil round the girl's head and old Night-cap was leading the way with a torch. The tipsy women, still clapping, had formed a long line and had fixed up a bridal chamber with draperies in the appropriate sacrilegious way. Then Quartilla, highly excited by all this playful obscenity, rose to her feet herself, seized Giton, and dragged him into the chamber.

It was obvious the boy had not struggled and even the girl had not been dismayed or scared by the mention of marriage. And so, when they were shut in and lying down, we sat round the chamber doorway, and Quartilla was one of the first to put an inquisitive eye to a crack she had naughtily opened, and spy on their childish play with prurient eagerness. Her insistent hand pulled me down also to have a similar look, and since our faces were pressed together as we watched, whenever she could spare a moment, she would move her lips close to mine in passing and bruise me with sly kisses.[25]

*

We threw ourselves on our beds and spent the rest of the night without fear.

DINNER WITH TRIMALCHIO

BOOK XV

26. The next day but one finally arrived. But we were so knocked about that we wanted to run rather than rest. We were mournfully discussing how to avoid the approaching storm, when one of Agamemnon's slaves broke in on our frantic debate.

'Here,' said he, 'don't you know who's your host today? It's Trimalchio – he's terribly elegant. . . . He has a clock in the dining-room and a trumpeter all dressed up to tell him how much longer he's got to live.'

This made us forget all our troubles. We dressed carefully and told Giton, who was very kindly acting as our servant, to attend us at the baths.

27. We did not take our clothes off but began wandering around, or rather exchanging jokes while circulating among the little groups. Suddenly we saw a bald old man in a reddish shirt, playing ball with some long-haired boys. It was not so much the boys that made us watch, although they alone were worth the trouble, but the old gentleman himself. He was taking his exercise in slippers and throwing a green ball around. But he didn't pick it up if it touched the ground; instead there was a slave holding a bagful, and he supplied them to the players. We noticed other novelties. Two eunuchs stood around at different points: one of them carried a silver chamber pot, the other counted the balls, not those flying from hand to hand according to the rules, but those that fell to the ground. We were still admiring these elegant arrangements when Menelaus hurried up to us.

'This is the man you'll be dining with,' he said. 'In fact, you are now watching the beginning of the dinner.'

No sooner had Menelaus spoken than Trimalchio snapped his fingers. At the signal the eunuch brought up the chamber pot for him, while he went on playing. With the weight off his bladder, he demanded water for his hands, splashed a few drops on his fingers and wiped them on a boy's head.

28. It would take too long to pick out isolated incidents. Any-

way, we entered the baths where we began sweating at once and we went immediately into the cold water. Trimalchio had been smothered in perfume and was already being rubbed down, not with linen towels, but with bath-robes of the finest wool. As this was going on, three masseurs sat drinking Falernian in front of him. Through quarrelling they spilled most of it and Trimalchio said they were drinking his health.[1] Wrapped in thick scarlet felt he was put into a litter. Four couriers with lots of medals went in front, as well as a go-cart in which his favourite boy was riding – a wizened, bleary-eyed youngster, uglier than his master. As he was carried off, a musician with a tiny set of pipes took his place by Trimalchio's head and whispered a tune in his ear the whole way.

We followed on, choking with amazement by now, and arrived at the door with Agamemnon at our side. On the doorpost a notice was fastened which read:

ANY SLAVE LEAVING THE HOUSE WITHOUT HIS MASTER'S PERMISSION WILL RECEIVE ONE HUNDRED LASHES

Just at the entrance stood the hall-porter, dressed in a green uniform with a belt of cherry red. He was shelling peas into a silver basin. Over the doorway hung – of all things – a golden cage from which a spotted magpie greeted visitors.

29. As I was gaping at all this, I almost fell over backwards and broke a leg. There on the left as one entered, not far from the porter's cubbyhole, was a huge dog with a chain round its neck. It was painted on the wall[2] and over it, in big capitals, was written:

BEWARE OF THE DOG

My colleagues laughed at me, but when I got my breath back I went on to examine the whole wall. There was a mural[3] of a slave market, price tags and all. Then Trimalchio himself, holding a wand of Mercury and being led into Rome by Minerva. After this a picture of how he learned accounting and, finally, how he became a steward. The painstaking artist had drawn it all in great detail with descriptions underneath. Just where the colonnade ended Mercury hauled him up by the chin and rushed him to a high platform. Fortune with her flowing cornucopia

46

and the three Fates spinning their golden threads were there in attendance.

I also noticed in the colonnade a company of runners practising with their trainer. In one corner was a large cabinet, which served as a shrine for some silver statues of the household deities with a marble figure of Venus and an impressive gold casket in which, they told me, the master's first beard was preserved.[4]

I began asking the porter what were the pictures they had in the middle.

'The Iliad, the Odyssey, and the gladiatorial show given by Laenas,' he told me.

30. Time did not allow us to look at many things there . . . by now we had reached the dining-room, at the entrance to which sat a treasurer going over the accounts. There was one feature I particularly admired: on the door-posts were fixed rods and axes[5] tapering off at their lowest point into something like the bronze beak of a ship. On it was the inscription:

PRESENTED TO C. POMPEIUS TRIMALCHIO
PRIEST OF THE AUGUSTAN COLLEGE[6]
BY HIS STEWARD CINNAMUS

Beneath this same inscription a fixture with twin lamps dangled from the ceiling and two notices, one on each door-post. One of them, if my memory is correct, had written on it:

30 AND 31 DECEMBER
OUR GAIUS
IS OUT TO DINNER[7]

The other displayed representations of the moon's phases and the seven heavenly bodies. Lucky and unlucky days were marked with different coloured studs.[8]

Having had enough of these interesting things, we attempted to go in, but one of the slaves shouted: 'Right foot first!' Naturally we hesitated a moment in case one of us should cross the threshold the wrong way. But just as we were all stepping forward, a slave with his back bare flung himself at our feet and began pleading with us to get him off a flogging. He was in trouble for nothing very serious, he told us – the steward's clothes, hardly worth ten sesterces, had been stolen from him at the baths. Back went our feet, and we appealed to the steward, who was counting out gold pieces in the office, to let the man off.

He lifted his head haughtily: 'It is not so much the actual loss that annoys me,' he said, 'it's the wretch's carelessness. They were my dinner clothes he lost. A client had presented them to me on my birthday – genuine Tyrian purple, of course; however they had been laundered once. So what does it matter? He's all yours.'

31. We were very much obliged to him for this favour; and when we did enter the dining-room, that same slave whose cause we had pleaded ran up to us and, to our utter confusion, covered us with kisses and thanked us for our kindness.

'And what's more,' he said, 'you'll know right away who it is you have been so kind to. "The master's wine is the waiter's gift." '

Finally we took our places.[9] Boys from Alexandria poured iced water over our hands. Others followed them and attended to our feet, removing any hangnails with great skill. But they were not quiet even during this troublesome operation: they sang away at their work. I wanted to find out if the whole staff were singers, so I asked for a drink. In a flash a boy was there, singing in a shrill voice while he attended to me – and anyone else who was asked to bring something did the same. It was more like a musical comedy than a respectable dinner party.

Some extremely elegant hors d'oeuvre were served at this point – by now everyone had taken his place with the exception of Trimalchio, for whom, strangely enough, the place at the top was reserved. The dishes for the first course included an ass of Corinthian bronze with two panniers, white olives on one side and black on the other. Over the ass were two pieces of plate, with Trimalchio's name and the weight of the silver inscribed on the rims. There were some small iron frames shaped like bridges supporting dormice sprinkled with honey and poppy seed. There were steaming hot sausages too, on a silver gridiron with damsons and pomegranate seeds underneath.[10]

32. We were in the middle of these elegant dishes when Trimalchio himself was carried in to the sound of music and set down on a pile of tightly stuffed cushions. The sight of him drew an astonished laugh from the guests.[11] His cropped head

stuck out from a scarlet coat; his neck was well muffled up and he had put round it a napkin with a broad purple stripe and tassels dangling here and there. On the little finger of his left hand he wore a heavy gilt ring and a smaller one on the last joint of the next finger. This I thought was solid gold, but actually it was studded with little iron stars. And to show off even more of his jewellery, he had his right arm bare and set off by a gold armlet and an ivory circlet fastened with a gleaming metal plate.

33. After picking his teeth with a silver toothpick, he began: 'My friends, I wasn't keen to come into the dining room yet. But if I stayed away any more, I would have kept you back, so I've deprived myself of all my little pleasures for you. However, you'll allow me to finish my game.'

A boy was at his heels with a board of terebinth wood with glass squares, and I noticed the very last word in luxury – instead of white and black pieces he had gold and silver coins.[12] While he was swearing away like a trooper over his game and we were still on the hors d'oeuvre, a tray was brought in with a basket on it. There sat a wooden hen, its wings spread round it the way hens are when they are broody. Two slaves hurried up and as the orchestra played a tune they began searching through the straw and dug out peahens' eggs, which they distributed to the guests.

Trimalchio turned to look at this little scene and said: 'My friends, I gave orders for that bird to sit on some peahens' eggs. I hope to goodness they are not starting to hatch. However, let's try them and see if they are still soft.'

We took up our spoons (weighing at least half a pound each) and cracked the eggs, which were made of rich pastry. To tell the truth, I nearly threw away my share, as the chicken seemed already formed. But I heard a guest who was an old hand say: 'There should be something good here.' So I searched the shell with my fingers and found the plumpest little figpecker, all covered with yolk and seasoned with pepper.

34. At this point Trimalchio became tired of his game and demanded that all the previous dishes be brought to him. He gave permission in a loud voice for any of us to have another glass of mead if we wanted it. Suddenly there was a crash from

the orchestra and a troop of waiters – still singing – snatched away the hors d'oeuvre. However in the confusion one of the side-dishes happened to fall and a slave picked it up from the floor. Trimalchio noticed this, had the boy's ears boxed and told him to throw it down again. A cleaner came in with a broom and began to sweep up the silver plate along with the rest of the rubbish. Two long-haired Ethiopians followed him, carrying small skin bottles like those they use for scattering sand in the circus, and they poured wine over our hands – no one ever offered us water.

Our host was complimented on these elegant arrangements. 'You've got to fight fair,' he replied. 'That is why I gave orders for each guest to have his own table. At the same time these smelly slaves won't crowd so.'

Carefully sealed wine bottles were immediately brought, their necks labelled :

FALERNIAN

CONSUL OPIMIUS

ONE HUNDRED YEARS OLD[13]

While we were examining the labels, Trimalchio clapped his hands and said with a sigh :

'Wine has a longer life than us poor folks. So let's wet our whistles. Wine is life. I'm giving you real Opimian. I didn't put out such good stuff yesterday, though the company was much better class.'

Naturally we drank and missed no opportunity of admiring his elegant hospitality. In the middle of this a slave brought in a silver skeleton, put together in such a way that its joints and backbone could be pulled out and twisted in all directions.[14] After he had flung it about on the table once or twice, its flexible joints falling into various postures, Trimalchio recited :

> 'Man's life alas ! is but a span,
> So let us live it while we can,
> We'll be like this when dead.'

35. After our applause the next course was brought in. Actually it was not as grand as we expected, but it was so novel that everyone stared. It was a deep circular tray with the twelve signs

of the Zodiac arranged round the edge. Over each of them the chef had placed some appropriate dainty suggested by the subject.[15] Over Aries the Ram, butter beans; over Taurus the Bull, a beef-steak; over the Heavenly Twins, testicles and kidneys; over Cancer the Crab, a garland; over Leo the Lion, an African fig; over Virgo the Virgin, a young sow's udder; over Libra the Scales, a balance with a tart in one pan and a cake in the other; over Scorpio, a lobster; over Sagittarius the Archer, a bull's eye; over Capricorn, a horned fish; over Aquarius the Water-carrier, a goose; over Pisces the Fishes, two mullets. In the centre was a piece of grassy turf bearing a honeycomb. A young Egyptian slave carried bread around in a silver oven ... and in a sickening voice he mangled a song from the show *The Asafoetida Man*.

36. As we started rather reluctantly on this inferior fare, Trimalchio said:

'Let's eat, if you don't mind. This is the sauce of all order.' As he spoke, four dancers hurtled forward in time to the music and removed the upper part of the great dish, revealing underneath plump fowls, sows' udders, and a hare with wings fixed to his middle to look like Pegasus.[16] We also noticed four little figures of Marsyas,[17] which let a peppery fish-sauce go running over some fish which seemed to be swimming in a little channel. We all joined in the servants' applause and amid some laughter we helped ourselves to these quite exquisite things.

Trimalchio was every bit as delighted as we were with this piece of ingenuity: 'Carve 'er!' he cried. Up came the man with the carving knife and with his hands moving in time to the orchestra, he sliced up the victuals like a charioteer battling to the sound of organ music. And still Trimalchio went on saying insistently: 'Carve 'er! Carve 'er!'

I suspected this repetition was connected with some joke, and I went so far as to ask the man on my left what it meant. He had watched this sort of game quite often and said:

'You see the fellow doing the carving – he's called Carver. So whenever he says "Carver!", he's calling out his name and his orders.'

37. I couldn't face any more food. Instead I turned to this man to find out as much as I could. I began pestering him for gossip

and information – who was the woman running round the place?

'Trimalchio's wife,' he told me, 'Fortunata is her name and she counts her money by the sackful. And before, before, what was she? You'll pardon me saying so, but you wouldn't of touched a bit of bread from her hand. Nowadays – and who knows how or why – she's in heaven, and she's absolutely everything to Trimalchio. In fact, if she tells him at high noon it's dark, he'll believe her. He doesn't know himself how much he's got, he's so loaded – but this bitch looks after everything, even places you wouldn't think of. She's dead sober and full of ideas, but she's got a rough tongue and she's a real magpie when she gets her feet up. If she likes you, she likes you – if she doesn't like you, she doesn't like you.

'The old boy himself now, he's got estates it'd take a kite to fly over – he's worth millions of millions.[18] There's more silver plate lying in his porter's cubbyhole than any other man owns altogether. As for his servants – boy, oh boy! I honestly don't think there's one in ten knows his own master. In fact he could knock any of these smart boys in the dirt.

38. 'And don't you think he buys anything, either. Everything is home-grown: wool, lemons, pepper. If you ask for hen's milk, you'll get it. In fact, there was a time when the wool he got wasn't good enough for him, so he brought some rams from Tarentum and put them in with his sheep. To get home-grown Attic honey, he ordered some bees from Athens – the Greek strain improved his own bees a bit at the same time.

'And here's something more – this last few days he wrote off for mushroom spores from India. Why, he hasn't a single mule that wasn't sired by a wild ass. You see all these cushions – everyone of them has either purple or scarlet stuffing. There's happiness for you!

'But mind you, don't look down on the other freedmen here. They're dripping with the stuff. You see that man on the very bottom couch. At present he's got eight hundred thousand of his own. He started out with nothing. It's not long since he was humping wood on his own back. They say – I don't know myself, I've just heard it – they say he stole a hobgoblin's cap and found its treasure. I don't begrudge anyone what God has given him. Besides, he can still feel his master's slap and wants to give himself a good time. For instance, the other day he put up a notice which said:

GAIUS POMPEIUS DIOGENES
IS MOVING TO HIS OWN HOUSE AND
WILL LET THE ROOM OVER
HIS SHOP FROM I JULY

'Now that fellow in the freedman's place – look how well off he was once! I'm not blaming him – he had a million in his hands, but he slipped badly. I don't think he can call his hair his own. Yet I'd swear it wasn't his fault: there's not a better man alive. Some dirty freedmen pocketed everything he had. One thing you can be sure of – you have partners and your pot never boils and once things take a turn for the worse, friends get out from underneath. What a respectable business he had and look at him now! He was an undertaker. He used to eat like a king – boars roasted in their skins, elaborate pastry, game birds, complete with chefs and confectioners. More wine was spilt under the table than another man keeps in his cellar. He wasn't a man, he was an absolute dream. When things were looking black, he didn't want his creditors to think he was bankrupt, so he put up notice of an auction like this:

GAIUS JULIUS PROCULUS
AUCTION OF SURPLUS STOCK'

Trimalchio interrupted these pleasant reminiscences. The dish had already been removed and the convivial guests had begun to concentrate on the drink and general conversation. Leaning on his elbow, Trimalchio said:

39. 'Now you're supposed to be enjoying the wine. Fishes have to swim. I ask you, do you think I'm just content with that course you saw in the bottom of the dish? "Is this like the Ulysses you know?"[19] Well then, we've got to display some culture at our dinner. My patron – God rest his bones! – wanted me to hold up my head in any company. There's nothing new to me, as that there dish proves.[20] Look now, these here heavens, as there are twelve gods living in 'em, changes into that many shapes. First it becomes the Ram. So whoever is born under that sign has a

lot of herds, a lot of wool, a hard head as well, a brassy front, and a sharp horn. Most scholars are born under this sign, and most muttonheads as well.'

We applauded the wit of our astrologer and he went on:

'Then the whole heavens turns into the little old Bull. So bull-headed folk are born then, and cow-herds and those who find their own feed. Under the Heavenly Twins on the other hand – pairs-in-hand, yokes of oxen, people with big ballocks, and people who have it both ways. I was born under the Crab, so I have a lot of legs to stand on and a lot of property on land and sea, because the Crab takes both in his stride. And that's why I put nothing over him earlier, so as not to upset my horoscope. Under Leo are born greedy and domineering people. Under the Virgin, effeminates, runaways, and candidates for the chain-gang. Under the Scales butchers, perfume-sellers, and anyone who weighs things up. Under Scorpio poisoners and murderers. Under Sagittarius are born squint-eyed people who look at the vegetables and take the bacon. Under Capricorn, people in trouble who sprout horns through their worries. Under the Water-Carrier, bar-tenders and jugheads. Under the Fishes, fish-fryers and people who spout in public.

'So the starry sky turns round like a mill-stone, always bringing some trouble, and men being born or dying.

'Now as for what you see in the middle, the piece of grass and on the grass the honeycomb, I don't do anything without a reason – it's Mother Earth in the middle, round like an egg, with all good things inside her like a honeycomb.'

40. 'Oh clever!' we all cried, raising our hands to the ceiling and swearing that Hipparchus and Aratus[21] couldn't compete with *him*.

Then the servants came up and laid across the couches embroidered coverlets showing nets, hunters carrying broad spears, and all the paraphernalia of hunting. We were still wondering which way to look when a tremendous clamour arose outside the dining-room, and would you believe it? – Spartan hounds began dashing everywhere, even round the table. Behind them came a great dish and on it lay a wild boar of the largest possible size, and, what is more, wearing a freedman's cap on its head. From its tusks dangled two baskets woven from palm leaves, one full of fresh Syrian dates, the other of dried Theban dates. Little piglets made of cake were all round as though at its dugs, suggesting it was a brood sow now being served. These were actually gifts to take home. Surprisingly the man who took his place to cut up the boar was not our old friend Carver[22] but a huge bearded fellow, wearing leggings and a damask hunting coat. He pulled out a hunting knife and made a great stab at the boar's side and as he struck, out flew a flock of thrushes. But there were fowlers all ready with their limed reeds, who caught them as soon as they began flying round the room.

Trimalchio gave orders for each guest to have his own bird, then added: 'And have a look at the delicious acorns our pig in the wood has been eating.'

Young slaves promptly went to the baskets and gave the guests their share of the two kinds of date.

41. As this was going on, I kept quiet, turning over a lot of ideas as to why the boar had come in with a freedman's cap on it. After working through all sorts of wild fancies, I ventured to put to my experienced neighbour the question I was racking my brains with. He of course replied:

'Even the man waiting on you could explain this obvious point – it's not puzzling at all, it's quite simple. The boar here was pressed into service for the last course yesterday, but the guests let it go. So today it returns to the feast as a freedman.'

I damned my own stupidity and asked no more questions in case I looked like someone who had never dined in decent company.

As we were talking, a handsome youth with a garland of vine-leaves and ivy round his head, pretending to be Bacchus the Reveller, then Bacchus the Deliverer and Bacchus the Inspirer, carried grapes round in a basket, all the time giving us a recital of his master's lyrics in a high-pitched voice. At the sound, Trimalchio called out, 'Dionysus, now be Bacchus the Liberat . . .'

The lad pulled the freedman's cap off the boar and stuck it on his head. Then Trimalchio commented:

'Now you won't deny my claim to be a liberal fellow.'[23] We applauded his joke and kissed the boy hard as he went round.

After this course Trimalchio got up and went to the toilet. Free of his domineering presence, we began to strike up a general conversation. Dama started off by calling for bigger glasses.

'The day's nothin',' he said. 'It's night 'fore y'can turn around. So the best thing's get out of bed and go straight to dinner. Lovely cold weather we've had too. M'bath hardly thawed me out. Still, a hot drink's as good as an overcoat. I've been throwin' it back neat, and I'm pretty tight – the wine's gone to m'head.'

This started Seleucus off.

42. 'Me now,' he said, 'I don't have a bath every day. It's like gettin' rubbed with fuller's earth, havin' a bath. The water bites into you, and as the days go by, your heart turns to water. But when I've knocked back a hot glass of wine and honey, kiss-my-arse I say to the cold weather. Mind you, I couldn't have a bath – I was at a funeral today. Poor old Chrysanthus has just given up the ghost – nice man he was! It was only the other day he stopped me in the street. I still seem to hear his voice. Dear, dear! We're just so many walking bags of wind. We're worse than flies – at least flies have got some strength in them, but we're no more than empty bubbles.

'And what would he have been like if he hadn't been on a diet? For five days he didn't take a drop of water or a crumb of bread into his mouth. But he's gone to join the majority. The doctors finished him – well, hard luck, more like. After all, a doctor is just to put your mind at rest. Still, he got a good send-off – he had a bier and all beautifully draped. His mourners – several of his slaves were left their freedom – did him proud, even though his widow was a bit mean with her tears. Suppose now he hadn't been so good to her! But women as a sex are real vultures. It's no good doing them a favour, you might as well throw it down a well. An old passion is just an ulcer.'

43. He was being a bore and Phileros said loudly:

'Let's think of the living. He's got what he deserved. He lived an honest life and he died an honest death. What has he got to complain about? He started out in life with just a penny and he was ready to pick up less than that from a muck-heap, if he had to use his teeth. He went up in the world. He got bigger and bigger till he got where you see, like a honeycomb. I honestly think he left a solid hundred thousand and he had the lot in hard cash. But I'll be honest about it – seeing I'm a bit of a cynic – he had a foul mouth and too much lip. He wasn't a man, he was just murder.

'Now his brother was a fine man, a real friend to his friends, always ready with a helping hand or a decent meal.

'Chrysanthus had bad luck at first, but the first vintage set him on his feet. He fixed his own price when he sold the wine. And what properly kept his head above water was a legacy he came in for, when he pocketed more than was left to him. And the blockhead, when he had a quarrel with his brother, cut him out of his will in favour of some sod we've never heard of. You're leaving a lot behind when you leave your own flesh and blood. But he took advice from his slaves and they really fixed him. It's never right to believe all you're told, especially for a business man. But it's true he enjoyed himself while he lived. You got it, you keep it. He was certainly Fortune's favourite – lead turned to gold in his hand. Mind you, it's easy when everything runs smoothly.

'And how old do you think he was? Seventy or more! But he was hard as nails and carried his age well. His hair was black as a raven's wing. I knew the man for ages and ages and he was still an old lecher. I honestly don't think he left the dog alone. What's more, he liked little boys – he could turn his hand to anything. Well, I don't blame him – after all, he couldn't take anything else with him.'

44. This was Phileros, then Ganymedes said:

'You're all talking about things that don't concern heaven or earth. Meanwhile, no one gives a damn the way we're hit by the corn situation. Honest to God, I couldn't get hold of a mouthful of bread today. And look how there's still no rain. It's been absolute starvation for a whole year now. To hell with the food officers! They're in with the bakers – "You be nice to me and I'll be nice to you." So the little man suffers, while those grinders of the poor never stop celebrating. Oh, if only we still had the sort of men I found here when I first arrived from Asia. Like lions they were. That was the life! Come one, come all!

If white flour was inferior to the very finest,[24] they'd thrash those bogeymen till they thought God Almighty was after them.

'I remember Safinius – he used to live by the old arch then; I was a boy at the time. He wasn't a man, he was all pepper. He used to scorch the ground wherever he went. But he was dead straight – don't let him down and he wouldn't let you down. You'd be ready to play *morra*[25] with him in the dark. But on the city council, how he used to wade into some of them – no beating about the bush, straight from the shoulder! And when he was in court, his voice got louder and louder like a trumpet. He never sweated or spat – I think there was a touch of the old acid[26] about him. And very affable he was when you met him, calling everyone by name just like one of us. Naturally at the time corn was dirt cheap. You could buy a penny loaf that two of you couldn't get through. Today – I've seen bigger bull's-eyes.

'Ah me! It's getting worse every day. This place is going down like a calf's tail. But why do we have a third-rate food officer who wouldn't lose a penny to save our lives? He sits at home laughing and rakes in more money a day than anyone else's whole fortune. I happen to know he's just made a thousand in gold. But if we had any balls at all, he wouldn't be feeling so pleased with himself. People today are lions at home and foxes outside.

'Take me, I've already sold the rags off my back for food and if this shortage continues, I'll be selling my bit of a house. What's going to happen to this place if neither god nor man will help us? As I hope to go home tonight, I'm sure all this is heaven's doing.

'Nobody believes in heaven, see, nobody fasts, nobody gives a damn for the Almighty. No, people only bow their heads to count their money. In the old days high-class ladies used to climb up the hill barefoot, their hair loose and their hearts pure, [27] and ask God for rain. And he'd send it down in bucket-fuls right away – it was then or never – and everyone went home like drowned rats. Since we've given up religion the gods nowadays keep their feet well wrapped up. The fields just lie . . .'

45. 'Please, please,' broke in Echion the rag merchant, 'be a

bit more cheerful. "First it's one thing, then another," as the yokel said when he lost his spotted pig. What we haven't got today, we'll have tomorrow. That's the way life goes. Believe me, you couldn't name a better country, if it had the people. As things are, I admit, it's having a hard time, but it isn't the only place. We mustn't be soft. The sky don't get no nearer wherever you are. If you were somewhere else, you'd be talking about the pigs walking round ready roasted back here.

'And another thing, we'll be having a holiday with a three-day show that's the best ever – and not just a hack troupe of gladiators but freedmen for the most part. My old friend Titus has a big heart and a hot head. Maybe this, maybe that, but something at all events. I'm a close friend of his and he does nothing by halves. He'll give us cold steel, no quarter and the slaughterhouse right in the middle where all the stands can see it. And he's got the wherewithal – he was left thirty million when his poor father died. Even if he spent four hundred thousand, his pocket won't feel it and he'll go down in history. He's got some big brutes already, and a woman who fights in a chariot and Glyco's steward, who was caught having fun with his mistress. You'll see quite a quarrel in the crowd between jealous husbands and romantic lovers. But that half-pint Glyco threw his steward to the lions, which is just giving himself away. How is it the servant's fault when he's forced into it? It's that old pisspot who really deserves to be tossed by a bull. But if you can't beat the ass you beat the saddle. But how did Glyco imagine that poisonous daughter of Hermogenes would ever turn out well? The old man could cut the claws off a flying kite, and a snake don't hatch old rope. Glyco – well, Glyco's got his. He's branded for as long as he lives and only the grave will get rid of it. But everyone pays for their mistakes.

'But I can almost smell the dinner Mammaea is going to give us – two denarii apiece for me and the family. If he really does it, he'll make off with all Norbanus's votes, I tell you he'll win at a canter. After all, what good has Norbanus done us? He put on some half-pint gladiators, so done in already that they'd have dropped if you blew at them. I've seen animal-killers[28] fight better. As for the horsemen killed, he got them off a lamp – they ran round like cocks in a backyard. One was just a cart-horse, the other couldn't stand up, and the reserve was just one corpse instead of another – he was practically hamstrung. One boy did have a bit of spirit – he was in Thracian armour,[29] and even he didn't show any initiative. In fact, they were all flogged afterwards, there were so many shouts of "Give 'em what for !" from the crowd. Pure yellow, that's all.

'"Well, I've put on a show for you," he says. "And I'm clapping you," says I. "Reckon it up – I'm giving more than I got. So we're quits."

46. 'Hey, Agamemnon ! I suppose you're saying "What is that bore going on and on about?" It's because a good talker like you don't talk. You're a cut above us, and so you laugh at what us poor people say. We all know you're off your head with all that reading. But never mind ! Some day I'll get you to come down to my place in the country and have a look at our little cottage. We'll find something to eat – a chicken, some eggs. It'll be nice, even though the unreliable weather this year has made off with everything. Anyway, we'll find enough to fill our bellies.

'And my kid is growing up to be a pupil of yours. He can divide by four already. If God spares him, you'll have him ready to do anything for you. In his spare time, he won't take his head out of his exercise book. He's clever and there's good stuff in him, even if he is crazy about birds. Only yesterday I killed his three goldfinches and told him a weasel ate them. But he's found some other silly hobbies, and he's having a fine time painting. Still, he's already well ahead with his Greek, and he's starting to take to his Latin, though his tutor is too pleased with himself and unreliable – he just comes and goes.[30] He knows his stuff but doesn't want to work. There is another one as well, not so clever but he is conscientious – he teaches the boy more than he knows himself. In fact, he makes a habit of coming around on holidays, and whatever you give him, he's happy.

'Anyway, I've just bought the boy some law books, as I want him to pick up some legal training for home use. There's a living in that sort of thing. He's done enough dabbling in poetry and such like. If he objects, I've decided he'll learn a trade – barber, auctioneer, or at least a barrister – something he can't lose till he dies. Well, yesterday I gave it to him straight:

"Believe me, my lad, any studying you do will be for your own good. You see Phileros the solicitor – if he hadn't studied, he'd be starving today. It's not so long since he was humping round loads on his back. Now he can even look Norbanus in the face. An education is an investment, and a proper profession never goes dead on you." '

47. This was the sort of conversation flying round when Trimalchio came in, dabbed his forehead and washed his hands in perfume. There was a short pause, then he said:

'Excuse me, dear people, my inside has not been answering the call for several days now. The doctors are puzzled. But some pomegranate rind and resin in vinegar has done me good. But I hope now it will be back on its good behaviour. Otherwise my stomach rumbles like a bull. So if any of you wants to go out, there's no need for him to be embarrassed. None of us was born solid. I think there's nothing so tormenting as holding yourself in. This is the one thing even God Almighty can't object to. Yes, laugh, Fortunata, but you generally keep me up all night with this sort of thing.

'Anyway, I don't object to people doing what suits them even in the middle of dinner – and the doctors forbid you to hold yourself in. Even if it's a longer business, everything is there just outside – water, bowls, and all the other little comforts. Believe me, if the wind goes to your brain it starts flooding your whole body too. I've known a lot of people die from this because they wouldn't be honest with themselves.'

We thanked him for being so generous and considerate and promptly proceeded to bury our amusement in our glasses. Up to this point we'd not realized we were only in mid-stream, as you might say.

The orchestra played, the tables were cleared, and then three white pigs were brought into the dining-room, all decked out in muzzles and bells. The first, the master of ceremonies announced, was two years old, the second three, and the third six. I was under the impression that some acrobats were on their way in and the pigs were going to do some tricks, the way they do in street shows. But Trimalchio dispelled this impression by asking:

'Which of these would you like for the next course? Any

clodhopper can do you a barnyard cock or a stew and trifles like that, but my cooks are used to boiling whole calves.'

He immediately sent for the chef and without waiting for us to choose he told him to kill the oldest pig.

He then said to the man in a loud voice:

'Which division are you from?'

When he replied he was from number forty, Trimalchio asked:

'Were you bought or were you born here?'

'Neither,' said the chef, 'I was left to you in Pansa's will.'

'Well, then,' said Trimalchio, 'see you serve it up carefully – otherwise I'll have you thrown into the messenger's division.'

So the chef, duly reminded of his master's magnificence, went back to his kitchen, the next course leading the way.

48. Trimalchio looked round at us with a gentle smile: 'If you don't like the wine, I'll have it changed. It is up to you to do it justice. I don't buy it, thank heaven. In fact, whatever wine really tickles your palate this evening, it comes from an estate of mine which as yet I haven't seen. It's said to join my estates at Tarracina and Tarentum.[31] What I'd like to do now is add Sicily to my little bit of land, so that when I want to go to Africa, I could sail there without leaving my own property.

'But tell me, Agamemnon, what was your debate about today? Even though I don't go in for the law, still I've picked up enough education for home consumption. And don't you think I turn my nose up at studying, because I have two libraries, one Greek, one Latin. So tell us, just as a favour, what was the topic of your debate?'

Agamemnon was just beginning, 'A poor man and a rich man were enemies . . .' when Trimalchio said: 'What's a poor man?' 'Oh, witty!' said Agamemnon, and then told us about some fictitious case or other. Like lightning Trimalchio said: 'If this happened, it's not a fictitious case – if it didn't happen, then it's nothing at all.'

We greeted this witticism and several more like it with the greatest enthusiasm.

'Tell me, my dear Agamemnon,' continued Trimalchio, 'do you remember the twelve labours of Hercules and the story of Ulysses – how the Cyclops tore out his thumb with a pair of pincers.[32] I used to read about them in Homer, when I was a boy. In fact, I actually saw the Sibyl at Cumae[33] with my own eyes dangling in a bottle, and when the children asked her in Greek: "What do you want, Sybil?" she used to answer: "I want to die." '

49. He was still droning on when a server carrying the massive pig was put on the table. We started to express our amazement at this speed and swear that not even an ordinary rooster could be cooked so quickly, the more so as the pig appeared far larger than we remembered. Trimalchio looked closer and closer at it, and then shouted:

'What's this? Isn't this pig gutted? I'm damn certain it isn't. Call the chef in here, go on, call him!'

The downcast chef stood by the table and said he'd forgotten it.

'What, you forgot!' shouted Trimalchio. 'You'd think he'd only left out the pepper and cumin. Strip him!'

In a second the chef was stripped and standing miserably between two men with whips. But everyone began pleading for him:

'It does tend to happen,' they said, 'do let him off, please. If he does it any more, none of us will stand up for him again.'

Personally, given my tough and ruthless temperament, I couldn't contain myself. I leaned over and whispered in Agamemnon's ear:

'How could anyone forget to clean a pig? I damn well wouldn't let him off if he forgot to clean a fish.'

But not Trimalchio. His face relaxed into a smile.

'Well,' he said, 'since you have such a bad memory, gut it in front of us.'

The chef recovered his shirt, took up a knife and with a nervous hand cut open the pig's belly left and right. Suddenly, as the slits widened with the pressure, out poured sausages and bloodpuddings.

50. The staff applauded this piece of ingenuity and gave a concerted cheer – 'Hurray for Gaius!' The chef of course was rewarded with a drink and a silver crown, and was also given a drinking cup on a tray of Corinthian bronze. Seeing Agamemnon staring hard at this cup, Trimalchio remarked:

'I'm the only person in the world with genuine Corinthian.'

I was expecting him with his usual conceit to claim that all his plate came from Corinth. But he was not as bad as I thought.

'Perhaps you're wondering,' he went on, 'how I'm the only one with genuine Corinthian dishes. The simple reason is that the manufacturer I buy from is named Corinth – but what can be Corinthian, if you don't have a Corinth to get it from?

'You mustn't take me for a fool: I know very well where Corinthian metalwork first came from. When Troy was captured that crafty snake Hannibal piled all the bronze, silver, and gold statues into one heap and set them on fire, and they were all melted to a bronze alloy. The metalworkers took this solid mass and made plates, dishes, and statuettes out of it. That is how Corinthian plate was born, not really one thing or another, but everything in one.[34] You won't mind my saying so, but I prefer glass – that's got no taste at all. If only it didn't break, I'd prefer it to gold, but it's poor stuff the way it is.

51. 'Mind you, there was a craftsman once who made a glass bowl that didn't break. So he got an audience with the emperor,[35] taking his present with him. Then he made as though to hand it to him and dropped it on the floor. The emperor couldn't have been more shaken. The man picked the bowl off the ground – it had been dinted like a bronze dish – took a hammer from his pocket and easily got the bowl as good as new. After this performance he thought he'd be taken for God Almighty, especially when the emperor said to him:

' "Is there anyone else who knows this process for making glass?"

'But now see what happens. When the man said no, the emperor had his head cut off, the reason being that if it was made public, gold would have been as cheap as muck.

52. 'Now I'm very keen on silver. I have some three-gallon bumpers ... showing how Cassandra killed her sons,[36] and the boys are lying there dead – very lifelike. I have a bowl my patron left – with Daedalus shutting Niobe in the Trojan Horse. What's more, I have the fights of Hermeros and Petraites on some cups – all good and heavy. No, I wouldn't sell my know-how at any price.'

While he was talking, a young slave dropped a cup. Trimalchio looked in his direction.

'Get out and hang yourself,' he said, 'you're utterly useless.' Immediately the boy's lip trembled and he begged Trimalchio's pardon.

'What are you asking me for?' snapped his master, 'as though I was the trouble! I'm just asking you not to let yourself be such a useless fool.'

In the end however, as a favour to us, he let him off and the boy ran round the table to celebrate . . .

Trimalchio shouted 'Out with the water – in with the wine!' . . .

We all showed our appreciation of his amusing wit – especially Agamemnon, who knew how to angle for further invitations. But our admiration went to Trimalchio's head. He drank with even greater cheerfulness and was very nearly drunk by now.

'Doesn't anyone want my dear Fortunata to dance?' he said. 'Honestly, no one dances the *Cordax*[37] better.'

Then he stuck his hands up over his forehead and gave us a personal imitation of the actor Syrus, while all the staff sang in chorus:

'Madeia, Perimadeia.'

In fact, he would have taken the floor, if Fortunata had not whispered in his ear. She must have told him, I suppose, that such low fooling did not suit his dignity. But you never saw anyone so changeable – one minute he would be frightened of Fortunata and the next minute he would be back in character again.

53. What really interrupted his coarse insistence on dancing was his accountant, who sounded as though he was reading out a copy of the Gazette:

'26 July: Births on the estate at Cumae: male 30, female 40. Wheat threshed and stored: 500,000 pecks. Oxen broken in: 500.

'On the same date: the slave Mithradates crucified for insulting the holy spirit that watches over our dear Gaius.

'On the same date: Deposits to the strong-room (no further investment possible): 10,000,000 sesterces.

'On the same date: a fire broke out on the estate at Pompeii beginning at the house of Nasta the bailiff.'

'What!' said Trimalchio. 'When was an estate bought for me at Pompeii?'

'Last year,' said the accountant, 'so it hasn't yet come on the books.'

Trimalchio flared up:

'If any land is bought for me and I don't hear of it within six months, I refuse to have it entered on the books.'

The official edicts were read out and the wills of certain game-keepers. In specific codicils they said they were leaving Trimalchio nothing. Then the names of some bailiffs; the divorce of a freedwoman, the wife of a watchman, on the grounds of adultery with a bath-attendant; the demotion of a hall-porter to a job at Baiae; the prosecution of a steward; and the result of an action between some bedroom attendants.

Finally the acrobats arrived. One was a silly idiot who stood there holding a ladder and made his boy climb up the rungs, give us a song and dance at the top, then jump through blazing hoops, and hold up a large wine-jar with his teeth.

Only Trimalchio was impressed by all this: art wasn't appreciated, he considered, but if there were two things in the world he really liked to watch, they were acrobats and horn-players. All the other shows were not worth a damn.

'As a matter of fact,' he said, 'once I even bought some comic-actors, but I preferred them putting on Atellan farces,[38] and I told my conductor to keep his songs Latin.'

54. Just as he was saying this, the boy tumbled down on Trimalchio's couch.[39] Everyone screamed, the guests as well as the servants – not because they were worried over such an awful person (they would happily have watched his neck being broken) but because it would have been a poor ending to the party if they had to offer their condolences for a comparative stranger. Trimalchio himself groaned heavily and leaned over his arm as though it were hurt. Doctors raced to the scene, but practically the first one there was Fortunata, hair flying and cup in hand, telling the world what a poor unfortunate thing she was. As for the boy who had fallen, he was already crawling round our feet, begging for mercy. I had an uneasy feeling that his pleadings might be

the prelude to some funny surprise ending, as I still remembered the chef who had forgotten to gut his pig. So I began looking round the dining-room for some machine to appear out of the wall, especially after a servant was beaten for using white instead of purple wool to bandage his master's bruised arm.

Nor were my suspicions far out, because instead of punishment, there came an official announcement from Trimalchio that the boy was free, so that no one could say that such a great figure had been injured by a slave.

55. We all applauded his action and started a desultory conversation about how uncertain life was.

'Well,' says Trimalchio, 'an occasion like this mustn't pass without a suitable record.' He immediately called for his notebook, and without much mental exertion he came out with:

> 'What comes next you never know,
> Lady Luck runs the show,
> So pass the Falernian, lad.'

This epigram brought the conversation round to poetry and for quite a time the first place among poets was given to Mopsus of Thrace[40] until Trimalchio said:

'Tell me, professor, how would you compare Cicero and Publilius? I think Cicero was the better orator, but Publilius the better man. Now could there be anything finer than this:

> 'Down luxury's maw, Mars' walls must wilt.
> Your palate pens peacocks in plumage of gilt:
> These Babylon birds are plumped under lock
> With the guinea hen and the capon cock.
> That long-legged paragon, winged castanet,
> Summer's lingering lease and winter's regret –
> Even the stork, poor wandering guest,
> Is put in your pot and makes that his nest.
> Why are Indian pearls so dear in your sight?
> So your sluttish wife, draped in the diver's delight,
> May open her legs on her lover's divan?
> What use are green emeralds, the glass ruin of man,
> Or carbuncles from Carthage with fire in their flint?
> Unless to let goodness gleam out in their glint.
> Is it right for a bride to be clad in a cloud
> Or wearing a whisp show off bare to the crowd?

56. 'Well now, whose profession do we think is most difficult after literature? I think doctors and bankers. A doctor has to know what people have in their insides and what causes a fever – even though I do hate them terribly the way they put me on a diet of duck. A banker has to spot the brass under the silver. Well, among dumb animals the hardest worked are cattle and sheep. It's thanks to cattle we have bread to eat, and it's thanks to sheep and their wool that we're well dressed. It's a low trick the way we eat mutton and wear woollens. Bees, now, I think are heavenly creatures – they spew honey, though people suppose they get it from heaven. But at the same time they sting, because where there's sweet you'll find bitter there too.'

He was still putting the philosophers out of work when tickets were brought round in a cup and the boy whose job it was read out the prizes.[41] '*Rich man's prison* – a silver jug. *Pillow* – a piece of neck came up. *Old man's wit and a sour stick* – dry salt biscuits came up and an apple on a stick. *Lick and spit* got a whip and a knife. *Flies and a fly-trap* was raisins and Attic honey. *Dinner-clothes and city-suit* got a slice of meat and a notebook. *Head and foot* produced a hare and a slipper. *Lights and letters* got a lamprey and some peas.' We laughed for ages. There were hundreds of things like this but they've slipped my mind now.

57. Ascyltus, with his usual lack of restraint, found everything extremely funny, lifting up his hands and laughing till the tears came. Eventually one of Trimalchio's freedman friends flared up at him – the one sitting above me, in fact.

'You with the sheep's eyes,' he said, 'what's so funny? Isn't our host elegant enough for you? You're better off, I suppose, and used to a bigger dinner. Holy guardian here preserve me! If I was sitting by him, I'd make him bleat! A fine pippin he is to be laughing at other people! Some fly-by-night from god knows where – not worth his own piss. In fact, if I pissed round him, he wouldn't know where to turn.

'By god, it takes a lot to make me boil, but if you're too soft, worms like this only come to the top. Look at him laughing! What's he got to laugh at? Did his father pay cash for him? You're a Roman knight, are you? Well, my father was a king.

"Why are you only a freedman?" ' did you say? Because I
went into service voluntarily. I wanted to be a Roman citizen, not
a subject with taxes to pay.[42] And today, I hope no one can
laugh at the way I live. I'm a man among men, and I walk with
my head up. I don't owe anybody a penny – there's never been
a court-order out for me. No one's said *"Pay up!"* to me in the
street.

'I've bought a bit of land and some tiny pieces of plate. I've
twenty bellies to feed, as well as a dog. I bought my old woman's
freedom so nobody could wipe his dirty hands on *her* hair.
Four thousand I paid for myself. I was elected to the Augustan
College and it cost me nothing. I hope when I die I won't have
to blush in my coffin.

'But you now, you're such a busybody you don't look behind
you. You see a louse on somebody else, but not the fleas on
your own back. You're the only one who finds us funny. Look at
the professor now – he's an older man than you and we get
along with him. But you're still wet from your mother's milk
and not up to your ABC yet. Just a crackpot – you're like a
piece of wash-leather in soak, softer but no better! You're
grander than us – well, have two dinners and two suppers! I'd
rather have my good name than any amount of money. When
all's said and done, who's ever asked me for money twice? For
forty years I slaved but nobody ever knew if I was a slave or a
free man. I came to this colony when I was a lad with long hair
– the town-hall hadn't been built then. But I worked hard to
please my master – there was a real gentleman, with more in his
little finger-nail than there is in your whole body. And I had
people in the house who tried to trip me up one way or another,
but still – thanks be to his guardian spirit! – I kept my head
above water. That's real success: being born free is as easy as
all get-out. Now what are you gawping at, like a goat in a
vetch-field?'

58. At this remark, Giton, who was waiting on me, could not
suppress his laughter and let out a filthy guffaw, which did not
pass unnoticed by Ascyltus' opponent. He turned his abuse on
the boy.

'So!' he said, 'you're amused too, are you, you curly-headed
onion? A merry Saturnalia to you! Is it December, I'd like to

know?[43] When did *you* pay your liberation tax?[44] Look, he doesn't know what to do, the gallow's bird, the crow's meat.

'God's curse on you, and your master too, for not keeping you under control! As sure as I get my bellyful, it's only because of Trimalchio that I don't take it out of you here and now. He's a freedman like myself. We're doing all right, but those good-for-nothings, well – . It's easy to see, like master, like man. I can hardly hold myself back, and I'm not naturally hot-headed – but once I start, I don't give a penny for my own mother.

'All right! I'll see you when we get outside, you rat, you excrescence. I'll knock your master in the dirt before I'm an inch taller or shorter. And I won't let you off either, by heaven, even if you scream down God Almighty. Your cheap curls and your no-good master won't be much use to you then – I'll see to that. I'll get my teeth into you, all right. Either I'm much mistaken about myself or you won't be laughing at us behind your golden beard. Athena's curse on you and the man who first made you such a forward brat.

'I didn't learn no geometry or criticism and such silly rubbish, but I can read the letters on a notice board and I can do my percentages in metal, weights, and money. In fact, if you like, we'll have a bet. Come on, here's my cash. Now you'll see how your father wasted his money, even though you do know how to make a speech.

'Try this:

> Something we all have.
> Long I come, broad I come. What am I?

'I'll give you it: something we all have that runs and doesn't move from its place: something we all have that grows and gets smaller.[45]

'You're running round in circles, you've had enough, like the mouse in the pisspot. So either keep quiet or keep out of the way of your betters, they don't even know you're alive – unless you think I care about your box-wood rings that you swiped from your girl friend! Lord make me lucky! Let's go into town and borrow some money. You'll soon see they trust this iron one.

'Pah! a drownded fox makes a nice sight, I must say. As

I hope to make my pile and die so famous that people swear by my dead body, I'll hound you to death. And he's a nice thing too – the one who taught you all these tricks – a muttonhead, not a master. We learned different. Our teacher used to say: "Are your things in order? Go straight home. No looking around. And be polite to your elders." Nowadays it's all an absolute muck-heap. They turn out nobody worth a penny. I'm like you see me and I thank God for the way I was learnt.'

59. Ascyltus began to answer this abuse but Trimalchio, highly amused by his friend's fluency, said:

'No slanging matches! Let's all have a nice time. And you, Hermeros, leave the young fellow alone. His blood's a bit hot – you should know better. In things like this, the one who gives in always comes off best. Besides, when you were just a chicken, you shouted cock-a-doodle too, and you had no more brains yourself. So let's start enjoying ourselves again, that'll be much better. Let's watch the recitations from Homer.'

In came the troupe immediately and banged their shields with their spears. Trimalchio sat up on his cushion and while the reciters spouted their Greek lines at one another in their usual impudent way, he read aloud in Latin in a sing-song voice. After a while, he got silence and asked:

'Do you know which scene they were acting? Diomede and Ganymede were the two brothers. Their sister was Helen. Agamemnon carried her off and offered a hind to Diana in her place. So now Homer is describing how the Trojans and Tarentines fought each other. Agamemnon, of course, won and married off his daughter Iphigenia to Achilles. This drove Ajax insane, and in a moment or two he'll explain how it ended.'[46]

As Trimalchio said this, the reciters gave a loud shout, the servants made a lane, and a calf was brought in on a two-hundred-dred pound plate: it was boiled whole and wearing a helmet. Following it came Ajax, slashing at the calf with a drawn sword like a madman. Up and down went his arm – then he collected the pieces on the point of his sword and shared them among the surprised guests.

60. But we were not given long to admire these elegant turns, for all of a sudden, the coffered ceiling began rumbling and the whole dining-room shook. I leapt to my feet in panic, as I

was afraid some acrobat was coming down through the roof. The other guests also looked up to see what strange visitation this announced. Would you believe it – the panels opened and suddenly an enormous hoop was let down, with gold crowns and alabaster jars of toilet cream hanging from it. While we were being told to accept these as presents, I looked at the table . . . Already there was a tray of cakes in position, the centre of which was occupied by a Priapus made of pastry, holding the usual things in his very adequate lap – all kinds of apples and grapes.

Greedily enough, we stretched out our hands to this display, and in a flash a fresh series of jokes restored the general gaiety. Every single cake and every single apple needed only the slightest touch for a cloud of saffron to start pouring out and the irritating vapour to come right at us.

Naturally we thought the dish must have some religious significance to be smothered in such an odour of sanctity, so we raised ourselves to a sitting position and cried:

'God save Augustus, the Father of his People!'

All the same, even after this show of respect, some of the guests were snatching the apples – especially me, because I didn't think I was pushing a generous enough share into Giton's pocket.

While all this was going on, three boys in brief white tunics came in. Two of them set down the household deities[47] in all their finery on the table; the other, carrying round a bowl of wine, kept shouting: 'God save all here!' . . .

Our host said that one of the gods was called Cobbler, the second Luck, and the third Lucre. There was also a very faithful likeness of Trimalchio himself and as all the others were pressing their lips to it, we felt too embarrassed not to do the same.

61. After we had all wished each other health and happiness, Trimalchio looked at Niceros and said:

'You used to be better company at a party. You're keeping very quiet nowadays: you don't say a word – I don't know why. Do me a favour to please me. Tell us about that adventure you had.'

Niceros was delighted by his friend's affable request and said:

'May I never make another penny if I'm not jumping for joy to see you in such form. Well, just for fun – though I'm worried about those professors there in case they laugh at me. That's up to them. I'll tell it all the same. Anyway, what do I care who laughs at me. It's better to be laughed at than laughed down.'

Thus he spake and began this story :

'When I was still in service, we were living down a narrow street – Gavilla owns the house now – and there as heaven would have it, I fell in love with the wife of Terentius the innkeeper.

'You all used to know Melissa from Tarentum, an absolute peach to look at. Honest to god, it wasn't her figure or just sex that made me care for her, it was more because she had such a nice nature. If I asked her for anything, it was never refused. She made a penny, I got half of it. I gave her what I had to look after and she never let me down.

'One day her husband died out on the estate. So I did my best to get her by hook or by crook. After all, you know, a friend in need is a friend indeed.

62. 'Luckily the master had gone off to Capua to fix up some odds and ends. I seized my chance and I talked a guest of ours into walking with me as far as the fifth milestone. He was a soldier as it happened, and as brave as hell. About cock-crow we shag off, and the moon was shining like one o'clock. We get to where the tombs are and my chap starts making for the grave-stones, while I, singing away, sits down and starts counting them. Then just as I looked in my mate's direction, he stripped off and laid all his clothes by the side of the road. My heart was in my mouth, I stood there like a corpse. Anyway, he pissed a ring round his clothes and suddenly turned into a wolf. Don't think I'm joking, I wouldn't tell a lie about this for a fortune. However, as I began to say, after he turned into a wolf, he started howling and rushed off into the woods.

'At first I didn't know where I was, then I went up to collect his clothes – but they'd turned to stone. If ever a man was dead with fright, it was me. But I pulled out my sword, and I fairly slaughtered the early morning[48] shadows till I arrived at my girl's house.

'I was just like a ghost when I got in, I practically gasped my last, the sweat was pouring down my crotch, my eyes were blank and staring – I could hardly get over it. It came as a surprise to my poor Melissa to find I'd walked over so late.

' "If you'd come a bit earlier," she said, "at least you could've helped us. A wolf got into the grounds and went for all the livestock – it was like a shambles. But he didn't have the last laugh, even though he got away. One of the slaves put a spear right through his neck."

'I couldn't close my eyes again after I heard this. But when it was broad daylight I rushed off home like the innkeeper after the robbery. And when I came to the spot where his clothes had turned to stone, I found nothing but bloodstains. However, when I got home, my soldier friend was lying in bed like a great ox with the doctor seeing to his neck. I realized he was a werewolf and afterwards I couldn't have taken a bite of bread in his company, not if you killed me for it. If other people think differently about this, that's up to them. But me – if I'm telling a lie may all your guardian spirits strike me down!'

63. Everyone was thrilled.

'I wouldn't disbelieve a word,' said Trimalchio. 'Honestly, the way my hair stood on end – because I know Niceros doesn't go in for jokes. He's really reliable and never exaggerates.

'Now I'll tell you a horrible story myself. A real donkey on the roof! When I was still in long hair (you see, I led a very soft life from my boyhood) the master's pet slave died. He was a pearl, honest to God, a beautiful boy, and one of the best. Well, his poor mother was crying over him and the rest of us were deep in depression, when the witches suddenly started howling – you'd think it was a dog after a hare.

'At that time we had a Cappadocian chap, tall and a very brave old thing, quite the strong man – he could lift an angry ox. This fellow rushed outside with a drawn sword, first wrapping his left hand up very carefully, and he stabbed one of the women right through the middle, just about here – may no harm come to where I'm touching! We heard a groan but – naturally I'm not lying – we didn't see the things themselves. Our big fellow, however, once he was back inside, threw himself on his bed. His whole body was black and blue, as though he'd been whipped.

'We closed the door and went back to what we had to do, but as the mother puts her arms round her son's body, she touches it and finds it's only a handful of straw. It had no heart, no inside, no anything. Of course the witches had already stolen the boy and put a straw baby in its place.

'I put it to you, you can't get away from it – there are such things as women with special powers and midnight hags that can turn everything upside down. But that great tall fellow of ours never got his colour back after what happened. In fact, not many days later, he went crazy and died.'

64. Equally thrilled and convinced, we kissed the table and asked the midnight hags to stay at home till we got back from dinner.

By this time, to tell the truth, there seemed to be more lights burning and the whole dining-room seemed different,[49] when Trimalchio said:

'What about you, Plocamus, haven't you a story to entertain us with. You used to have a fine voice for giving recitations with a nice swing and putting songs over – ah me, the good old days are gone.'

'Well,' said Plocamus, 'my galloping days finished after I got gout. Besides when I was really young I nearly got consumption through singing. How about my dancing? How about my recitations? How about my barber's shop act? When was there anybody so good apart from Apelles[50] himself?'

Putting his hand to his mouth he let out some sort of obscene whistle which he afterwards insisted was Greek.

Trimalchio, after giving us his own imitation of a fanfare of trumpets, looked round for his little pet, whom he called Croesus. The boy however, a bleary-eyed creature with absolutely filthy teeth, was busy wrapping a green cloth round a disgustingly fat black puppy. He put half a loaf on the couch and was cramming it down the animal's throat while it kept vomiting it back. This sight reminded Trimalchio to send out for Scylax, 'protector of the house and the household'.

A hound of enormous size was immediately led in on a chain. A kick from the hall-porter reminded him to lie down and he stretched himself out in front of the table. Trimalchio threw him a piece of white bread, remarking:

'Nobody in the house is more devoted to me.'

The boy, however, annoyed by such a lavish tribute to Scylax, put his own little pup on the floor and encouraged her to hurry up and start a fight. Scylax, naturally following his canine instincts, filled the dining-room with a most unpleasant barking and almost tore Croesus' Pearl to pieces. Nor was the trouble limited to the dog-fight. A lampstand was upset on the table as well and not only smashed all the glass but spilled hot oil over some of the guests.

Not wanting to seem disturbed by the damage, Trimalchio gave the boy a kiss and told him to climb on his back. The lad mounted him without hesitation, and slapping his shoulder-blades with the flat of his hand, shouted amid roars of laughter:

'Big mouth, big mouth, how many fingers have I got up?'

After a while Trimalchio calmed down and gave instructions for a huge bowl of drink to be mixed and served to all the servants, who were sitting by our feet. He added the condition:

'If anyone won't take it, pour it over his head. Day's the time for business, now's the time for fun.'

65. This display of generosity was followed by some savouries, the very recollection of which really and truly makes me sick. Instead of thrushes, a fat capon was brought round for each of us, as well as goose-eggs in pastry hoods. Trimalchio surpassed himself to make us eat them; he described them as boneless chickens. In the middle of all this, a lictor knocked at the double doors and a drunken guest entered wearing white, followed by a large crowd of people. I was terrified by this lordly apparition and thought it was the chief magistrate arriving. So I tried to rise and get my bare feet on the floor. Agamemnon laughed at this panic and said:

'Get hold of yourself, you silly fool. This is Habinnas – Augustan College and monumental mason.'

Relieved by this information I resumed my position and watched Habinnas' entry with huge admiration. Being already drunk, he had his hands on his wife's shoulders; loaded with several garlands, oil pouring down his forehead and into his eyes, he settled himself into the place of honour[51] and immediately demanded some wine and hot water. Trimalchio, delighted by these high spirits, demanded a larger cup for himself and asked how he had enjoyed it all.

'The only thing we missed,' replied Habinnas, 'was yourself – the apple of my eye was here. Still, it was damn good. Scissa was giving a ninth-day dinner[52] in honour of a poor slave of hers she'd freed on his death-bed. And I think she'll have a pretty penny to pay in liberation tax because they reckon he was worth fifty thousand. Still, it was pleasant enough, even if we did have to pour half our drinks over his wretched bones.'

66. 'Well,' said Trimalchio, 'what did you have for dinner?'

'I'll tell you if I can – I've such a good memory that I often forget my own name. For the first course we had a pig crowned with sausages and served with blood-puddings and very nicely done giblets, and of course beetroot and pure wholemeal bread – which I prefer to white myself: it's very strengthening and I don't regret it when I do my business. The next course was cold tart and a concoction of first-class Spanish wine poured over hot honey. I didn't eat anything at all of the actual tart, but I dived right into the honey. Scattered round were chickpeas, lupines, a choice of nuts and an apple apiece – though I took two. And look, I've got them tied up in a napkin, because if I don't take something in the way of a present to my youngster, I'll have a row on my hands.

'Oh yes, my good lady reminds me. We had a hunk of bear-meat set before us, which Scintilla was foolish enough to try, and she practically spewed up her guts; but I ate more than a pound of it, as it tasted like real wild-boar. And I say if bears can eat us poor people, it's all the more reason why us poor people should eat bears.

'To finish up with, we had some cheese basted with new wine, snails all round, chitterlings, plates of liver, eggs in pastry hoods, turnips, mustard, and some filthy concoction – good riddance to that.[53] There were pickled cumin seeds too, passed round in a bowl and some people were that bad-mannered they took three handfuls. You see, we sent the ham away.

67. But tell me something, Gaius, now I ask – why isn't Fortunata at the table?'

'You know her,' replied Trimalchio, 'unless she's put the silver away and shared out the left-overs among the slaves, she won't put a drop of water to her mouth.'

'All the same,' retorted Habinnas, 'unless she sits down, I'm shagging off.'

And he was starting to get up, when at a given signal all the

servants shouted 'Fortunata' four or five times. So in she came
with her skirt tucked up under a yellow sash to show her cerise
petticoat underneath, as well as her twisted anklets and gold-
embroidered slippers. Wiping her hands on a handkerchief
which she carried round her neck, she took her place on the
couch where Habinnas' wife was reclining. She kissed her. 'Is it
really you?' she said, clapping her hands together.

It soon got to the point where Fortunata took the bracelets
from her great fat arms and showed them to the admiring Scintilla. In the end she even undid her anklets and her gold hair net,
which she said was pure gold. Trimalchio noticed this and had
it all brought to him and commented:

'A woman's chains, you see. This is the way us poor fools[54]
get robbed. She must have six and a half pounds on her. Still,
I've got a bracelet myself, made up from one-tenth per cent to
Mercury[55] – and it weighs not an ounce less than ten pounds.'

Finally, for fear he looked like a liar, he even had some scales
brought in and had them passed round to test the weight.

Scintilla was no better. From round her neck she took a little
gold locket, which she called her 'lucky box'. From it she extracted two earrings and in her turn gave them to Fortunata to
look at.

'A present from my good husband,' she said, 'and no one has
a finer set.'

'Hey!' said Habinnas, 'you cleaned me out to buy you a glass
bean. Honestly, if I had a daughter, I'd cut her little ears off. If
there weren't any women, everything would be dirt cheap. As it
is, we've got to drink cold water and piss it out hot.'

Meanwhile, the women giggled tipsily between themselves and
kissed each other drunkenly, one crying up her merits as a
housewife, the other crying about her husband's demerits and
boy friends. While they had their heads together like this,
Habinnas rose stealthily and taking Fortunata's feet, flung them
up over the couch.

'Oh, oh!' she shrieked, as her underskirt wandered up over
her knees. So she settled herself in Scintilla's lap and hid her
disgusting[56] red face in her handkerchief.

68. Then came an interval, after which Trimalchio called for
dessert. Slaves removed all the tables and brought in others.

They scattered sawdust tinted with saffron and vermilion, and something I had never seen before – powdered mica. Trimalchio said at once:

'I could make you just settle for this. There's dessert for you! The tables've deserted.[57] However, if you people have anything nice, bring it on!'

Meanwhile a slave from Alexandria, who was taking round the hot water, started imitating a nightingale, only for Trimalchio to shout: 'Change your tune!'

More entertainment! A slave sitting by Habinnas' feet, prompted, I suppose, by his master, suddenly burst out in a sing-song voice:

'Meanwhile Aeneas was in mid-ocean with his fleet.'[58]

No more cutting sound ever pierced my eardrums. Apart from his barbarous meandering up and down the scale, he mixed in Atellan verses,[59] so that Vergil actually grated on me for the first time in my life. When he did finally stop through exhaustion, Habinnas said:

'He's never had any real training. I just had him taught by sending him along to peddlers on the street corner. He's no one to equal him if he wants to imitate mule-drivers or hawkers. He's desperately clever, really. He's a cobbler, a cook, a confectioner – a man that can turn his hand to anything. But he's got two faults; if he didn't have them he'd be one in a million – he's circumcised and he snores. I don't mind him being cross-eyed – so is Venus. That's why he's never quiet and his eyes are hardly ever still. I bought him for twelve hundred sesterces.'

69. Scintilla interrupted him: 'Of course, you're not telling them all the tricks the wretch gets up to. He's a pimp – but I'll make sure he gets branded for it.'

Trimalchio laughed: 'I know a Cappadocian[60] when I see one. He's not slow in looking after himself and, by heaven, I admire him for it. You can't take it with you.

'Now, Scintilla, don't be jealous. Believe me, we know all about you women too. As sure as I stand here, I used to knock up the mistress so much that even the old boy suspected; so he sent me off to look after his farms. But I'd better save my breath to cool my porridge.'

As though he'd been complimented the wretched slave took out an earthenware lamp from his pocket and for more than half an hour gave imitations of trumpet-players, while Habinnas hummed an accompaniment, pressing down his lower lip with his hand. Finally coming right into the middle, he did a flute-player with some broken reeds, then he dressed up in a greatcoat and whip and did the Life of the Muleteer, till Habinnas called him over, kissed him, and gave him a drink:

'Better and better, Massa!' he said, 'I'll give you a pair of boots.'

There would have been no end to all these trials if an extra course had not arrived – pastry thrushes stuffed with raisins and nuts. After them came quinces with thorns stuck in them to look like sea-urchins. All this would have been all right, but there was a far more horrible dish that made us prefer even dying of hunger. When it was put on the table, looking to us like a fat goose surrounded by fish and all sorts of game, Trimalchio said:

'Whatever you see here, friends, is made from one kind of stuff.'

I, of course, being very cautious by nature, spotted immediately what it was and glancing at Agamemnon, I said:

'I'll be surprised if it isn't all made of wax, or at any rate mud. I've seen that sort of imitation food produced at the Saturnalia in Rome.'

70. I hadn't quite finished what I was saying when Trimalchio said:

'As sure as I hope to expand – my investments of course, not my waist-line – my chef made it all from pork. There couldn't be a more valuable man to have. Say the word and he'll produce a fish out of a sow's belly, a pigeon out of the lard, a turtle dove out of the ham, and fowl out of the knuckle. So he's been given a nice name I thought of myself – he's called Daedalus.[61] And seeing he's a clever lad, I brought him some carvers of Styrian steel as a present from Rome.'

He immediately had them brought in and gazed at them with admiration. He even allowed us to test the point on our cheeks.

All of a sudden in came two slaves, apparently having had a quarrel at the well; at any rate they still had water jugs on their shoulders. But while Trimalchio was giving his decision about their respective cases, neither of them paid any attention to his verdict: instead they broke each other's jugs with their sticks. Staggered by their drunken insolence, we couldn't take our eyes away from the fight till we noticed oysters and scallops sliding out of the jugs, which a boy collected and carried round on a dish. The ingenious chef was equal to these elegant refinements – he brought in snails on a silver gridiron, singing all the time in a high grating voice.

I blush to say what happened next. Boys with their hair down their backs came round with perfumed cream in a silver bowl and rubbed it on our feet as we lay there,[62] but first they wrapped our legs and ankles in wreaths of flowers. Some of the same stuff was dropped into the decanter and the lamp.

Fortunata was now wanting to dance,[63] and Scintilla was doing more clapping than talking, when Trimalchio said:

'Philargyrus – even though you are such a terrible fan of the Greens[64] – you have my permission to join us. And tell your dear Menophila to sit down as well.'

Need I say more? We were almost thrown out of our places, so completely did the household fill the dining-room. I even noticed that the chef was actually given a place above me, and he was reeking of pickles and sauce. And he wasn't satisfied with just having a place, but he had to start straight off on an imitation of the tragedian Ephesus,[65] and then challenge his master to bet against the Greens winning at the next races.

71. Trimalchio became expansive after this argument.

'My dear people,' he said, 'slaves are human beings too. They drink the same milk as anybody else, even though luck's been agin 'em. Still, if nothing happens to me, they'll have their taste of freedom soon. In fact, I'm setting them all free in my will. I'm giving Philargyrus a farm, what's more, and the woman he lives with. As for Cario, I'm leaving him a block of flats, his five per cent manumission tax, and a bed with all the trimmings. I'm making Fortunata my heir, and I want all my friends to look after her.

'The reason I'm telling everyone all this is so my household will love me now as much as if I was dead.'

Everyone began thanking his lordship for his kindness, when he became very serious and had a copy of his will brought in.

Amid the sobs of his household he read out the whole thing from beginning to end.

Then looking at Habinnas, he said:

'What have you to say, my dear old friend? Are you building my monument the way I told you? I particularly want you to keep a place at the foot of my statue and put a picture of my pup there, as well as paintings of wreaths, scent-bottles, and all the contests of Petraites, and thanks to you I'll be able to live on after I'm dead. And another thing! See that it's a hundred feet facing the road and two hundred back into the field. I want all the various sorts of fruit round my ashes and lots and lots of vines. After all, it's a big mistake to have nice houses just for when you're alive and not worry about the one we have to live in for much longer. And that's why I want this written up before anything else:

THIS MONUMENT DOES NOT GO TO THE HEIR

'But I'll make sure in my will that I don't get done down once I'm dead. I'll put one of my freedmen in charge of my tomb to look after it and not let people run up and shit on my monument. I'd like you to put some ships there[66] too, sailing under full canvas, and me sitting on a high platform in my robes of office, wearing five gold rings[67] and pouring out a bagful of money for the people. You know I gave them all a dinner and two denarii apiece. Let's have in a banqueting hall as well, if you think it's a good idea, and show the whole town having a good time. Put up a statue of Fortunata on my right, holding a dove, and have her leading her little dog tied to her belt – and this dear little chap as well, and great big wine jars sealed up so the wine won't spill. And perhaps you could carve me a broken wine jar and a boy crying over it. A clock in the middle, so that anybody who looks at the time, like it or not, has got to read my name. As for the inscription now, take a good look and see if this seems suitable enough:

HERE SLEEPS
GAIUS POMPEIUS TRIMALCHIO
MAECENATIANUS[68]
ELECTED TO THE AUGUSTAN COLLEGE IN HIS ABSENCE
HE COULD HAVE BEEN ON EVERY BOARD IN ROME

BUT HE REFUSED
GOD-FEARING BRAVE AND TRUE
A SELF-MADE MAN
HE LEFT AN ESTATE OF 30,000,000
AND HE NEVER HEARD A PHILOSOPHER
FAREWELL
AND YOU FARE WELL, TRIMALCHIO.'

72. As he finished Trimalchio burst into tears. Fortunata was in tears, Habinnas was in tears, in the end the whole household filled the dining-room with their wailing, like people at a funeral. In fact, I'd even begun crying myself, when Trimalchio said:

'Well, since we know we've got to die, why don't we live a little. I want to see you enjoying yourselves. Let's jump into a bath – you won't be sorry, damn me! It's as hot as a furnace.'

'Hear! Hear!' said Habinnas. 'Turning one day into two – nothing I like better.' He got up in his bare feet and followed Trimalchio on his cheerful way.

I looked at Ascyltus. 'What do you think?' I said. 'Now me, if I see a bath, I'll die on the spot.'

'Let's say yes,' he suggested, 'and while they're going for their bath, we can slip out in the crowd.'

This seemed a good idea, so Giton led us through the portico till we reached the door, where the hound chained there greeted us with such a noise that Ascyltus actually fell into the fish-pond. Not only that, as I was drunk too, when I tried to help the struggling Ascyltus I was dragged into the same watery trap. However, the hall-porter saved us and by his intervention pacified the dog and dragged us trembling to dry land. Giton had already bought off the beast in a most ingenious way. He had scattered whatever he had got from us at dinner in front of the barking hound, and distracted by the food, it had choked down its fury.

Nevertheless, when, shivering and wet, we asked the hall-porter to let us out through the front door, he said: 'You're wrong if you think you can leave through the door you came in. No guest has ever been let out through the same door. They come in one way and go out another.'

73. What could we do after this piece of bad luck, shut up in

this modern labyrinth and now beginning to regret that bath. We asked him to please show us the way to the bath-hall, and, throwing off our clothes, which Giton began drying at the door, we went in.[69] There stood Trimalchio, and not even there could we get away from his filthy ostentation. He told us there was nothing better than a private bath, and that he once had a bakery on that very spot. Then he sat down as though tired, and being tempted by the acoustics of the bath, with his drunken mouth gaping at the ceiling, he began murdering some songs by Menecrates[70] – or so we were told by those who understood his words.

The rest of the guests ran round the edge hand in hand, giggling away with a tremendous noise. Some were trying to pick up rings from the floor with their hands tied behind their backs, or were kneeling and trying to bend backwards and touch the tips of their toes. We left them to their games and got down into the tub which was being prepared for Trimalchio.

Well, after shaking off our drunken stupor, we were taken to another dining-room where Fortunata had laid out an elegant spread.... In fact, I noticed some bronze fishermen on the lamps as well as tables of solid silver, with gold inlaid pottery spread around and wine pouring from a leather wine flask before our very eyes.

'Today, my friends,' said Trimalchio, 'my personal servant had his first shave: he's a careful man – and that's a compliment – who watches the pennies. So let's whet our throttles and not stop eating till daylight.'

74. Just as he was speaking, a cock crowed. Upset by this, Trimalchio ordered some wine to be poured out under the table and even had the lamps sprinkled with it undiluted. He actually changed his ring to his right hand.[71]

'That trumpeter,' he said, 'didn't give the signal without good reason. There should be a fire next or else somebody will be dying in the neighbourhood – God spare us! So whoever gets me that bringer of bad news, there's a tip for him.'

Before the words were out of his mouth, the cock was brought in and Trimalchio ordered it to be put in the pan and cooked. It was cut up by that very skilful chef and it was thrown into the pot. While Daedalus drew off the scalding liquid, Fortunata ground pepper in a box-wood grinder.

After this dish Trimalchio looked at the servants and said:
'Why haven't you had dinner yet? Off you go and let some others come on duty.'

Up came another squad and as the first set called out: 'Good night, Gaius!' the new arrivals shouted: 'Good evening, Gaius!'

This led to the first incident that damped the general high spirits. Not a bad-looking boy entered with the newcomers and Trimalchio jumped at him and began kissing him at some length. Fortunata, asserting her just and legal rights, began hurling insults at Trimalchio, calling him a low scum and a disgrace, who couldn't control his beastly desires. 'You dirty dog!' she finally added.

Trimalchio took offence at this abuse and flung his glass into Fortunata's face. She screamed as though she'd lost an eye and put her trembling hands across her face. Scintilla was terrified too and hugged the quaking woman to her breast. An obliging slave pressed a little jug of cold water to her cheek, while Fortunata rested her head on it and began weeping. Trimalchio just said:

'Well, well, forgotten her chorus days, has she? She doesn't remember, but she was bought and sold,[72] and I took her away from it all and made her as good as the next. Yet she puffs herself up like a frog and doesn't even spit for luck. Just a great hunk, not a woman. But those as are born over a shop don't dream of a house. May I never have a day's good luck again, if I don't teach that Cassandra in clogs[73] some manners!

'There was I, not worth twopence, and I could have had ten million. And you know I'm not lying about it. Agatho, who ran a perfume shop for the lady next door,[74] he took me on one side and said: "You don't want to let your family die out, you know!" But me, trying to do the right thing and not wanting to look changeable, I cut my own throat.

'All right! I'll make you want to dig me up with your bare nails. Just so you'll know on the spot what you've done for yourself – Habinnas! I don't want you to put her statue on my tomb, so at least when I'm dead I won't have any more squabbles. And another thing! just to show I can get my own back – when I'm dead I don't want her to kiss me.'

75. After this thunderbolt, Habinnas began asking him to calm

down: 'None of us are without faults,' he said, 'we're not gods, we're human!' Scintilla said the same, calling him Gaius, and she began asking him, in the name of his guardian spirit, to give in.

Trimalchio held back his tears no longer. 'I ask you, Habinnas,' he said, 'as you hope to enjoy your bit of savings – if I did anything wrong, spit in my face. I kissed this very careful little fellow, not for his pretty face, but because he's careful with money – he says his ten times table, he reads a book at sight, he's got himself some Thracian kit out of his daily allowance, and he's bought himself an easy chair and two cups out of his own pocket. Doesn't he deserve to be the apple of my eye? But Fortunata won't have it.

'Is that the way you feel, high heels? I'll give you a piece of advice: don't let your good luck turn your head, you kite, and don't make me show my teeth, my little darling – otherwise you'll feel my temper. You know me: once I've decided on something, it's fixed with a twelve-inch nail.

'But to come back to earth – I want you to enjoy yourselves, my dear people. After all, I was once like you are, but being the right sort, I got where I am. It's the old headpiece that makes a man, the rest is all rubbish. "Buy right – sell right!" – that's me! Different people will give you a different line. I'm just on top of the world, I'm that lucky.

'But you, you snoring thing, are you still moaning? I'll give you something to moan about in a minute.

'However, as I'd started to say, it was my shrewd way with money that got me to my present position. I came from Asia as big as this candlestick. In fact, every day I used to measure myself against it, and to get some whiskers round my beak quicker, I used to oil my lips from the lamp. Still, for fourteen years I was the old boy's fancy. And there's nothing wrong if the boss wants it. But I did all right by the old girl too. You know what I mean – I don't say anything because I'm not the boasting sort.

76. 'Well, as heaven will have it, I became boss in the house, and the old boy, you see, couldn't think of anything but me. That's about it – he made me co-heir with the Emperor[75] and I got a senator's fortune.[76] But nobody gets enough, never. I wanted to go into business. Not to make a long story of it, I built

five ships, I loaded them with wine – it was absolute gold at the time – and I sent them to Rome. You'd have thought I ordered it – every single ship was wrecked. That's fact, not fable! In one single day Neptune swallowed up thirty million. Do you think I gave up? This loss honestly wasn't more than a flea-bite to me – it was as if nothing had happened. I built more boats, bigger and better and luckier, so nobody could say I wasn't a man of courage. You know, the greater the ship, the greater the confidence. I loaded them again – with wine, bacon, beans, perfumes and slaves. At this point Fortunata did the decent thing, because she sold off all her gold trinkets, all her clothes, and put ten thousand in gold pieces in my hand. This was the yeast my fortune needed to rise. What heaven wants, soon happens. In one voyage I carved out a round ten million. I immediately bought back all my old master's estates. I built a house, I invested in slaves, and I bought up the horse trade.[77] Whatever I touched grew like a honeycomb. Once I had more than the whole country, then down tools! I retired from business and began advancing loans through freedmen.

'Actually I was tired of trading on my own account, but it was an astrologer who convinced me. He happened to come to our colony, a sort of Greek, Serapa by name, and he could have told heaven itself what to do. He even told me things I'd forgotten. He went through everything for me from A to Z. He knew me inside out – the only thing he didn't tell me was what I ate for dinner the day before. You'd have thought he'd never left my side.

77. 'Wasn't there that thing, Habinnas? – I think you were there: "You got your lady wife out of those *certain circumstances*. You are not lucky in your friends. Nobody thanks you enough for your trouble. You have large estates. You are nursing a viper in your bosom."

'And he said – though I shouldn't tell you – I have thirty years, four months, two days to live. What's more, I shall soon receive a legacy. My horoscope tells me this. If I'm allowed to join my estates to Apulia,[78] I'll have lived enough.

'Meantime, under the protection of Mercury, I built this house. As you know, it was still a shack,[79] now it's a shrine. It has four dining-rooms,[80] twenty bedrooms, two marble colonnades, a row of box-rooms up above, a bedroom where I sleep myself, a nest for this viper, and a really good lodge for the porter. The guest apartment takes a hundred guests. In fact, when Scaurus[81] came here, he didn't want to stay anywhere else, even though he's got his father's guest house down by the sea. And there are a lot of other things I'll show you in a second.

'Believe me: have a penny, and you're worth a penny. You got something, you'll be thought something. Like your old friend – first a frog, now a king.

'Meantime, Stichus, bring out the shroud and the things I want to be buried in. Bring some cosmetic cream too, and a sample from that jar of wine I want my bones washed in.'

78. Stichus did not delay over it, but brought his white shroud and his formal dress into the dining-room ... Trimalchio told us to examine them and see if they were made of good wool. Then he said with a smile:

'Now you, Stichus, see no mice or moths get at those – otherwise I'll burn you alive. I want to be buried in style, so the whole town will pray for my rest.'

He opened a bottle of nard on the spot, rubbed some on all of us and said:

'I hope this'll be as nice when I'm dead as when I'm alive.' The wine he had poured into a big decanter and he said:

'I want you to think you've been invited to my wake.'

The thing was becoming absolutely sickening, when Trimalchio, showing the effects of his disgusting drunkenness, had a fresh entertainment brought into the dining-room, some cornet players. Propped up on a lot of cushions, he stretched out along the edge of the couch and said: 'Pretend I'm dead and say something nice.'

The cornet players struck up a dead march. One man in particular, the slave of his undertaker (who was the most respectable person present) blew so loudly that he roused the neighbourhood. As a result, the fire brigade, thinking Trimalchio's house was on fire, suddenly broke down the front door and began kicking up their own sort of din with their water and axes.

Seizing this perfect chance, we gave Agamemnon the slip and escaped as rapidly as if there really were a fire.

79. There was no torch available to show us the way, and as it was halfway through the night, the silence gave us little hope of meeting anyone with a light. Add to this too much wine and our ignorance of the place, which would have been a problem even in daylight. So after we had dragged our bleeding feet over all the sharp stones and jutting pieces of broken crockery for nearly a full hour, we were rescued by Giton's ingenuity. Afraid of losing his way even in daytime, he had shrewdly marked all the pillars and posts with chalk, and the bright marks, gleaming through even the thickest darkness, showed us the way. Yet we had to sweat just as much once we arrived at the inn. The old woman, after soaking herself so long with her guests, wouldn't have felt it if you'd put a fire under her, and we should probably have had to spend the night on the doorstep, if a courier had not turned up and jumped down from his carriage.[1] He naturally refused to knock any longer but broke the inn-door down and finally let us in that way.

> Ye gods and goddesses! O what a night!
> The bed, so soft! Our souls had lost
> Their way – we lay so warm and tight –
> Goodbye, care. I've said my last good night.

I congratulated myself too soon. For once the wine had made me relax my drunken hands, Ascyltus, being utterly unscrupulous, took the boy away from me in the night and transferred him to his bed. And rolled up coolly with someone else's boyfriend (was Giton unconscious or was he pretending?) he fell asleep wrapped in an embrace he had no right to, lost to all sense of justice.

When I awoke and ran my hands over the empty joyless bed – if you can trust what a lover says, I wondered whether to run my sword through both of them and continue their sleep into death. Following a safer policy, I roused Giton with my fists, but looking at Ascyltus with a savage expression I said:

'You have wrecked all mutual confidence and friendship with your criminal ways, so pack up right away and find somewhere else to practise your filthy habits.'

He made no opposition but once we had shared the loot equally, he said:

'Right, now let's split the boy too.'

80. I thought this was a parting joke. But he drew his sword with a murderous hand, saying:

'You are not going to enjoy this prize you are sitting on alone. I must have my share even if I cut it off with this sword to avenge myself.'

I did the same and wrapping my cloak round my arm, dropped into a fighting crouch. In the middle of this heartbreaking lunacy the poor boy held on to our knees in tears and begged us not to let the inn see another pair of Theban brothers[2] or to sully the sanctity of our beautiful friendship with each other's blood.

'If there must be bloodshed at any price,' he cried, 'look, I offer you my throat, get your hands on it, press your points home. I'm the one to die, because I broke up a sworn friendship.'

We put up our steel after this plea. Ascyltus was the first to speak:

'I'll put an end to this quarrel. Let the boy himself go with the one he wishes, so that he at least may have the liberty of choosing his lover.'

Imagining our long intimacy had come to mean as much as ties of blood, I had no fears. On the contrary, I jumped headlong at the offer and gave the decision to the judge. There was no hesitation, not the slightest appearance of it. The last syllable was scarcely out of my mouth when he got up and chose Ascyltus as his lover. Thunderstruck by this verdict, just as I was, I fell on the bed. I would have laid violent hands on myself like an executioner, if I hadn't begrudged my rival that victory. Ascyltus left proudly with his prize and abandoned his comrade-in-arms, his dearest friend a little while ago, his companion even in misfortune; he abandoned him in all his misery in a place full of strangers.

Friendship's a word and friends know its value –
The counters slide merrily all through the game –

Your friends broadly smiling, while fortune was by you:
Their backs even broader when trouble came.

*

(The mime has begun
And the father is there,
And here is the son
And the millionaire.
Then closes the page,
When played is their part,
On the laughter upstage
And the masks of their art –
Then their true faces appear.)[3]

81. I soon dried my tears, but being afraid that in addition to all my other troubles, Menelaus the assistant tutor might find me alone in my lodgings, I collected my bags and sadly rented a quiet place along the seafront. I holed up there for three days, constantly aware of my loneliness and humiliation; I would beat my breast, already sore with sobbing, and again and again I'd cry out loud through all the groans that racked me:

'Why couldn't that earthquake have swallowed me up? Or the sea, such a menace even to innocent people? Did I escape the law, did I outwit the arena, did I kill my host, only to end up, despite my claims to be a daring criminal, just lying here, a beggar and an exile, abandoned in a lodging-house in a Greek town? And who brought this loneliness upon me? An adolescent wallowing in every possible filth, who even on his own admission had been rightly run out of town, who had known freedom and respectability only in contexts of vice, and who had been hired as a girl even by someone who knew he was a man. As for the other one! Putting on women's clothes the day he became a man, talked into effeminacy by his mother, doing only woman's work in the slave pen, and after he couldn't meet his debts and had to change his sexual ground, he abandoned the claims of an old friendship and – in the name of decency! – sold out everything like a whore on the strength of a one-night stand. Now the loving pair lie clutching each other every night and perhaps when they are worn out by their love-play, they laugh at my loneliness. But they won't get away with it. As sure as I'm a man and not a slave, I'll wipe out the insult with their guilty blood.'

82. With these words I fastened my sword to my side and not to let bodily weakness endanger my mission, I restored my strength with a heavy meal. Then I rushed out into the street and went round all the arcades like a madman. But while I was thinking of nothing but blood and destruction, my face like thunder and my heart full of rage (I was dropping my hand continually to my dedicated hilt), a soldier noticed me, a deserter or a thug.

'Hey there, friend,' he said, 'what's your regiment and who's your company commander?'

I lied boldly about my regiment and my company until he said:

'Well, tell me something. Do the soldiers in your army walk about in white slippers?'

As my face and my very trembling betrayed the lie, he told me to give up my weapons and keep out of trouble. I'd been robbed and worse, my revenge had been nipped in the bud. I walked back towards my lodgings and gradually as my boldness decreased I began to feel grateful for the thug's audacity.

*

Craving the water around, apples above his head,
   Poor Tantalus[4] can neither drink nor eat.
This is the rich man's image: in plenty dogged by dread
   To drink dry-mouthed, to choke and starve on meat.

*

One should not rely a great deal on one's plans as fate has a way of her own.

*

83. I went into an art-gallery, which had a wonderful variety of of paintings. For instance, I even saw work by Zeuxis[5] still unaffected by the ravages of time. And I examined, not without a certain thrill, some sketches by Protogenes,[6] so life-like they were a challenge to nature herself. I practically worshipped that masterpiece of Apelles[7] that the Greeks call The Goddess on One Knee. The lines of the paintings were so subtle and clear-cut that you could see them as expressing the subjects' very souls. Here

the eagle, way up on high, was carrying off the Idaean youth,[8] there a dazzling white Hylas repulsed the lascivious Naiad. Apollo cursed his murderous hands and decorated his unstrung lyre with a new flower. Surrounded by the faces of these lovers, I burst out as though I were alone:

'So love affects gods too. Jupiter didn't find anything to love in heaven, but at least when going to sin on earth he injured no one. The nymph that snatched Hylas away would have controlled her passion if she had thought Hercules would come to restrain her. Apollo called back the boy's soul into a flower – all of them enjoyed embraces free from rivalry. But I took to my heart a crueller friend than Lycurgus.'[9]

All of a sudden, however, as I was arguing with the wind, a white-haired old man entered the gallery. His face was lined and seemed to have in it a promise of something impressive. But his clothes were shabby and this made it clear that he belonged to the class of intellectuals so hated generally by the rich. He came and stood by my side.

*

'I am a poet,' he said, 'and a poet of no mean ability, I like to think, at least if bardic crowns are to be trusted when favouritism confers them even on mediocrity. "Why," you ask, "are you so badly dressed then?" For this one reason – concern for the arts never made anyone rich.

> I see the merchant fat from trade,
> On a belt of gold I see
> The soldier hang his blade.
> On purple sheets I see
> Cheap flatterers sprawl drunkenly,
> Gigolos and lovers all well-paid
> For their wealth and want of parts.
> Only a poet is a tattered thing,
> Cold scarecrow, eloquent and sighing,
> For the lonely and abandoned arts.

84. 'No doubt about it. If a man sets his face against every temptation and starts off on the straight and narrow, he's immediately hated because of his different ways. No one can approve of conduct different from his own. And secondly, those who are

interested in piling up money don't want anything else in life regarded as better than what they have themselves. So lovers of literature are sneered at[10] by whatever means possible to show that they too are inferior to wealth.'

*

'I suspect somehow that poverty is the twin sister of intelligence.'

*

'I'd like to think that the man who hounds me in my hard life were honest enough to be conciliated. As it is, he's hardened in crime and cleverer than the very pimps.'

*

85. (*Eumolpus*) 'When I was taken out to Asia on the paid staff of a treasury official, I accepted some hospitality in Pergamum.[11] I was very pleased to accept the invitation not only because of the smart house but also because my host had a very handsome son and I thought up a way to prevent his father becoming suspicious of me. Whenever any mention was made at the table of taking advantage of pretty boys, I flared up so violently and I was so stern about my ears being offended by obscene talk that the mother especially regarded me as a real old-world philosopher. From then on I escorted the young lad to the gymnasium, I organized his studies, I taught him and gave him good advice. After all, we didn't want any seducer admitted to the house.

*

'One holiday, when the festivities had cut short his schoolwork, we were lounging in the dining-room, as the long day's enjoyment had made us too lazy to go to bed. About midnight, I realized the boy was awake. So in a very nervous whisper I breathed a prayer.

' "Dear Venus," I said, "if I can kiss this boy without his knowing it, I'll give him a pair of doves tomorrow."

'Hearing the price of my pleasure, the boy started snoring, and I therefore went to work on the faker and kissed him several times. Content with this beginning, I rose early next morning and brought him the choice pair of doves he was expecting and fulfilled my vow.

86. 'Next night, given the same opportunity, I altered my prayer.

' "If I can run my hands all over him," I said, "without his feeling anything, I'll give him two really savage fighting cocks for his patience."

'At this offer the boy moved over to me of his own accord. I think he was getting afraid I might fall asleep. Naturally I dispelled his worries and his whole body became a whirlpool in which I lost myself, although I stopped short of the ultimate pleasure. Then when day came, I brought the delighted boy what I'd promised.

'The third night offered similar opportunities, and I got up, came close to his ear, as he tossed restlessly, and said:

' "O eternal gods, if I can get the full satisfaction of my desires from him, for this happiness tomorrow I shall give the boy the finest Macedonian thoroughbred – but with this proviso, he must notice nothing."

'The lad had never slept so soundly before. First I filled my hands with his milk-white breasts, then I clung to his lips, and finally I reduced all my longings to one climax.

'In the morning he sat in his room and waited for me to follow my usual practice. Of course, you know how much easier it is to buy doves and cocks than a thoroughbred, and besides, I was nervous in case such an extravagant gift should make my kindness suspect. So after walking round for a few hours, I returned to my host's house and gave the boy nothing more than a kiss. He looked round, as he threw his arms about my neck, and said:

' "Please, sir, where's my thoroughbred?"

*

87. 'This offence had lost me the headway I had made, nevertheless I returned to my old ways. A few days later when a similar chance left us in the same position, hearing the father snoring, I began asking the boy to become friends with me again and allow me to satisfy my desire for him – and I said all the other things that a strong physical urge dictates. But clearly annoyed, he only said:

' "Just go to sleep or I'll tell father."

'Nothing is too difficult if you're prepared to be wicked. Even while he was saying, "I'll wake father", I slipped into the bed and despite his ineffectual struggles, I took my pleasure by force. Actually he was not displeased that I'd been so naughty and after complaining for a long time that he'd been tricked and that he'd been laughed at and talked about among his schoolfriends because he had boasted to them of my wealth, he said finally:

' "But you'll see I'm not like you. Do it again, if you wish."

'Well, I was back in the boy's favour with all his hard feelings gone, and after taking advantage of his kindness, I fell asleep. The boy, however, being fully mature and of an age very much able to take it, was not content with the repeat performance. He woke me up from my sleep saying:

' "Don't you want anything?"

'Of course it wasn't a tiresome job yet, so somehow, riding out the panting and sweating, he got what he wanted and I fell back asleep, exhausted with passion. Less than an hour later he began pinching me and saying,

' "Why aren't we getting on with it?"

'Being woken up so often, I really flared up. I turned the tables on him:

' "Just you go to sleep or I'll tell your father." '

*

88. Cheered by the conversation, I began to ask my mentor . . . about the age of the pictures and the subject of some of the obscure ones, at the same time pressing him for reasons for the present decadence, when the loveliest of the arts were dying out, not least painting, which had vanished without the slightest trace. His reply was:

'Financial greed has caused this revolution. In former days when mere merit was still sufficient, the liberal arts flourished and there was great competition to bring to light anything of benefit to posterity. Democritus for instance distilled all forms of vegetable life and spent his days in scientific experiments to discover the properties of minerals and plants.[12] Eudoxus grew old on the top of one of the highest mountains to further his knowledge of astronomy, and Chrysippus purged his brain three times with hellebore to allow himself to continue his investigations.[13]

'To turn to the plastic arts, Lysippus [14] was so preoccupied with the lines of one statue that he died of starvation, and Myron, who almost captured the souls of men and animals in his bronzes, left no heir. But we, besotted with drink and whoring, daren't study even arts with a tradition. Attacking the past instead, we acquire and pass on only vices. What has happened to dialectic? [15] Astronomy? Or the beaten road of wisdom? Who has ever gone into a temple and prayed to become eloquent – or to approach the fountainhead of philosophy? People do not even ask for a sound mind or body, but before they touch the threshold one man immediately promises an offering if he can arrange the funeral of a rich relation, another if he can dig up some treasure, another if he can come into a safe thirty million. Even the senate, the standard of rectitude and goodness, habitually promises the Capitol a thousand pounds of gold, and to remove anyone's doubts about financial greed, tries to influence [16] even Jove with money.

'So don't be surprised that painting is on the decline, when a lump of gold seems more beautiful to everybody, gods and men, than anything those crazy little Greeks, Apelles and Phidias, [17] ever made.

89. 'But I notice you can't pull yourself away from that painting of the Fall of Troy. [18] Well, I'll try and interpret its subject in verse:

'The tenth harvest, tenth year of the Troy-siege,
The Phrygians forlorn, doubt-fraught and frightened,
Calchas the soothsayer downcast,
A dark daunting upon him.
The Delian doled his destinies
And tall trees toppled on Ida,
Their boles borne from the mountain;   5
Trunks trimmed, massed for its making,
For hewing the horse, shaping the fell shape.
A cave is uncovered, a cavern to capture the foe-camp.
Herein taut from the ten-year taking,
Their valour is hidden, deep in the gods' vail;   10
Doughty Danaans crouch in the depths of it.
    The thousand-fold fleet we felt was in full flight,
      Your fields, O my fatherland, freed from the fighting.
Words on horse side said it,

Sinon, steady in death's sight, said it,   15
Steady in deceit that dealt us destruction.
Uncaged, careless of combat, the crowd came,
Eager to acquit them of oaths made.
Joy in the faint heart, tears trickling –
Terror retrieves them.   20
                              Priest of the sea god,
Loud Laocoön, locks lank, hails the assemblage,
His flung spear wounding the full womb:
Fate slows his sinews; blade-point rebounding
Tells us only of truth in the treachery.   25
Yet again Laocoön, hardening his halt hands,
Aims at the sheer side his axe-stroke.
At the cry of captives, lo, at their murmuring
The oak-bulk breathes of an alien faintness –
The captured chiefs move to Troy's capture.   30

'Other prodigies press us and portents,
Where tall Tenedos breaks back the billows,
Swollen the straits surge up in motion,
And the waters, broken, wince back, breaking the sea-calm.
As in the nightwatch oars sound from far-off,   35
Of fleets faring through sea foam, sea face
Groaning of grazes from fir-keels coursing.
Back stare we.
Waves speed snakes, sinuously doubling, rockwards;
As tall ships, their breasts scatter spindrift;   40
Tails tolling thunder, head fringes foam-freed
Shine as their eyes shine. Thundery skin-sheen
Shines on the water, as waves hiss and tremble.
Men stand mindless. Laocoön's loved ones,
In sacred ribbons and Phrygian tiring, his twin sons,   45
Are suddenly twined in the twinkling snake-coils.
They lock little fingers into the snake-jaws,
Each for the other, neither from self-love –
Brother for brother, their love is requited,
Death a deliverance from mutual mourning.   50
Added unto their doom is the old one,
Helpless to aid them.
The serpents, sated from slaying
Beset him, bear to the earth his body,
He lies on his own altars, a priestly victim,   55
Striking the soil there.

So by its sins Troy
Doomed to destruction destroyed first its godhead.

'Full moon had lifted its white refulgence,
Leading the lesser lights with radiant torchbrand :   60
The sons of Priam were sleeping and wine-soaked –
"Undo the bolts, ye Danaans, bring out your brave ones!"
Chieftains acquitting themselves in combat,
As in Thessalian hills a horse out of halters
Shakes its neck, its mane, for the onrush.   65
Swords unsheathed, hefting their bucklers,
They fly to the fray : here dealing death to the drunken,
Sent in their sleep to the death-sleep;
Here brands are brought from the altars
To turn against Troy town the worship of Trojans . . .'   70

90. Some of the people walking about in the colonnades interrupted Eumolpus's recitation with a shower of stones. Being
familiar with this sort of appreciation of his genius, he covered
his head and fled from the sanctuary. I was nervous myself in
case they should tear me to pieces for being a poet. So I followed
his fleeing figure and arrived at the seafront. As soon as we were
out of range and could stop, I said :

'Listen, what's wrong with you? You've been with me for less
than two hours and you've spoken more often like a poet than
a human being. I'm not surprised people chase you with stones.
I'm going to fill my pockets with rocks and whenever you start
taking wings, I'll let some blood from your head.'

He shook his head :

'My lad, today is not the first time I've tested the air like that.
In fact I've never gone into a theatre to give a recitation without
getting this sort of strange reception from the spectators. But I
don't want to quarrel with you as well, so I'll keep off the stuff
for the whole day.'

'Right,' I said, 'if you swear off this madness for today, we'll
dine together.'

*

I gave the landlord of my little place the task of preparing a
simple meal.

*

91. I saw Giton leaning against the wall with towels and scrapers, and looking depressed and confused.[19] You could tell he didn't like his menial position. To test what I observed ...

*

He turned towards me, his face softening with pleasure:

'Don't be hard on me, my dear. Where there are no weapons around, I can speak freely. Take me away from this bloody criminal and punish me as savagely as you like for the decision I've been regretting. I feel so bad about everything, it will be a sufficient consolation to die because you wanted me to.'

I told him to stop complaining in case someone should guess our plans, and abandoning Eumolpus, who was reciting a poem in the main bath, I dragged Giton through a dark and sordid exit and flew hastily to my lodgings. Then, with the doors barred, I rushed to take him in my arms and press my cheeks to his tearful face. For a long time neither of us recovered his voice. The boy's lovely breast heaved with a succession of sighs.

'Oh, this shouldn't happen,' I said, 'for me to love you, though I was deserted, and for there to be no scar on my heart from that great wound. What have you to say after giving yourself to another lover? Did I deserve this treatment?'

When he realized he was still loved, he raised his eyebrows a little higher ...

*

'I left the decision about our love to no other judge but you. But I won't complain of anything any more, I won't remember anything any more, if you restore your credit by your repentance.'[20]

As I poured all this out with sobs and tears, he wiped my face with my cloak and said:

'Encolpius, please, I appeal to your memory to be honest. Did I desert you or did you betray me? I admit this and I'm not ashamed of it – when I saw two armed men, I went to the stronger.'

I kissed that wise little breast and threw my arms round his neck, and to let him fully realize that I was reconciled and I was renewing our friendship as sincerely as ever, I hugged him to my heart.

92. It was well into the night and the woman had taken care of our orders for dinner, when Eumolpus hammered on the door.

'How many of you are there?' I asked, and meanwhile began peeping carefully through a chink in the panels to see if Ascyltus had come with him. Then seeing my guest by himself, I let him in immediately. As he threw himself on the bed and saw Giton in full view fixing the table, he nodded his head, saying:

'There's a pretty Ganymede. It should be a nice day.'

Such a studied opening did not make me happy and I was afraid I had joined up with someone just like Ascyltus. Eumolpus pressed on, and when the boy gave him a drink, he said:

'I prefer you to the whole bathful of them,' and after greedily emptying the glass, he said he had never had such a disagreeable time and he explained:

'You see, I was almost beaten up while I was having my bath, just because I tried to recite a poem to the people sitting round my tub. After I'd been thrown out of the bath, I began going round every nook and cranny and calling out 'Encolpius' in a loud voice. And somewhere else a naked young man, who had lost his clothes, was demanding someone called Giton with equally indignant shouts. And while the boys just ridiculed me for a lunatic with the most impudent imitations, a huge crowd surrounded him with applause and the most awestruck admiration. You see, he had such enormous sexual organs that you'd think the man was just an attachment to his penis. What a man for the job! I think he starts yesterday and finishes tomorrow. So he found help in no time. Someone or other, a Roman knight and notorious for his tastes, the loungers said, covered him with his own clothes as he went wandering round and took him off home – to enjoy such a piece of luck on his own, I suppose. Whereas I wouldn't have got even my own clothes back from the sneaky attendant there if I hadn't produced someone who knew me. A polished wick is much more profitable than a polished wit.'

While Eumolpus was telling us this, my expression kept changing all the time, now through amusement at my rival's misfortunes, now through annoyance at his successes. But all the

same, I said nothing and passed the food, pretending the story
had no personal interest for me.

*

93. 'There are no attractions in anything legal; our wayward
and obstinate hearts prefer to go outside the law.[21]

> 'Pheasants snared in Colchis, in Africa game-birds,
> These are the rarities that have to be chased;
> White goose and duckling,
> Gaudy in their gay plumes,
> Are left to the populace, not to our taste.

> 'Parrot-wrasse from far shores, haul from Syrtes,
> Bought at the price of some great shipwreck,
> These are for the table –
> Mullet's indigestive –
> Don't ask the cost: you can pay by cheque.

> 'Wives are out of fashion. Better get a girl friend –
> A little more expensive but really very nice.
> Rose leaves are out of date,
> Cinnamon's the thing now.
> Anything hard to get is well worth the price.'

'Is this how you keep your promise,' I said, 'not to produce
any verse today? As a favour, at least let *us* off – we never threw
stones at you. Because if anyone drinking in the house we're in
smells the suggestion of a poet, he'll rouse the whole neighbourhood and finish us all off for the same reason. Have some
thought for us and remember the art-gallery or the public baths.'

Giton, being a very gentle boy, remonstrated with me for this
way of speaking, and said it wasn't right for me to abuse someone older than myself, while forgetting my obligations and let-
ting my insults spoil the meal I had provided in all kindness.
And there was a lot of other moderate and courteous things he
said, which came very well from his pretty lips.

*

94. 'What a lucky mother,' said [Eumolpus], 'to have such a
child! Good boy! Your good looks and your good sense make a

rare mixture. Don't think you've wasted all that breath: you've found someone who loves you. I'll fill poems with your praises. I'll follow you as your teacher and guardian, even when you don't ask me to. And Encolpius is not losing, he's in love with someone else.'

That soldier who took away my sword was a piece of luck for Eumolpus too. Otherwise I would have cooled the spleen I'd felt against Ascyltus in Eumolpus's blood. Giton was not unaware of this. He went out of the room on the pretext of getting some water and by his prudent withdrawal damped my anger. Then a few moments later, as my fury rekindled, I said:

'Eumolpus, I prefer you even speaking in verse to the sort of thoughts you are having. Now I'm a hot-tempered man and you are a lecherous one. You can see how these temperaments don't go together. So you have to regard me as a madman and give in to my insanity – now get out quick!'

Confused by this outburst, Eumolpus did not ask the reason for my anger, but going straight out over the threshold, suddenly slammed the door of the room, and, as I was expecting nothing of the sort, shut me in; he swiftly removed the key and ran off to look for Giton.

Shut up inside like that, I decided to finish everything by hanging myself. I had already put the bed frame against the wall, tied a belt to it and was inserting my neck in the noose when the door was unlocked and Eumolpus came in with Giton and in a race against death brought me back to life. In his grief Giton, unlike Eumolpus, went mad with rage; he raised a great outcry and pushing me with both hands precipitated me on top of the bed.

'You're wrong, Encolpius,' he said, 'if you think by any possible chance you can die before me. I tried first: I looked for a sword in Ascyltus' rooms. If I had not found you, I was going to throw myself to my death. To make you realize death isn't far away if you look for it, see in your turn what you wanted me to see.'

With this he snatched a razor from Eumolpus' hired servant and slashing his throat once and once again, collapsed at our feet.

Thunderstruck, I let out a cry and following his collapsing body to the floor, I looked for a way to die with the same instrument. But Giton showed not the slightest suspicion of a wound nor could I feel any pain myself. It was a practice razor and blunted for the purpose: to give apprentices courage, it had a sheath fitted round it. This was the reason why the servant had not panicked at his snatching the razor and why Eumolpus had not intervened in this fake death scene.

95. While this love drama was being played out, the landlord came in with the rest of our little dinner and at the sight of the disgraceful sprawling heap on the floor, he shouted:

'Hey, are you people drunk or runaway slaves? Or both? Who turned that bed up? What's the meaning of all this undercover behaviour? But of course – you were going to do a moonlight flit to avoid paying your room rent. But you're not getting away with it. Because I'll have you know the place doesn't belong to some helpless widow but to Marcus Mannicius.'

Eumolpus yelled back: 'Are you threatening us?' and at the same time he hit the man hard in the face with the flat of his hand. Reckless from so much drinking with the guests, the fellow hurled an earthenware pot at Eumolpus' head, split his forehead in mid-shout, and flung himself out of the room. Eumolpus was not standing for this insult; he snatched up a wooden candlestick, followed him as he made off and avenged his pride with a tremendous shower of blows. The whole household came rallying round, as well as a crowd of drunken guests. I however took this opportunity for my revenge by shutting Eumolpus out. Having put paid to the bastard, I was of course without a rival and I went on to put the room and the evening to their full use.

Meanwhile the kitchen staff and the people who lived in the building were beating up Eumolpus now that he couldn't get inside – one was aiming for his eyes with a spit covered with sizzling tripes, while another went through his battle-drill with a butcher's hook. One old woman in particular, a bleary old hag, dressed in the filthiest clothes and wearing odd wooden clogs, came dragging along an enormous dog on a chain and set him on Eumolpus. But he defended himself from all these threats with his candlestick.

96. We were watching everything through a hole left in the door when the handle had been pulled off a little while ago,

and I was cheering every blow that reached Eumolpus. Giton however with his usual compassion pressed me to open the door and rescue him. As my resentment was still with me, I didn't restrain myself but smashed him on the head with my clenched fist for his pains. He sat down on the bed in tears while I applied each eye alternately to the hole and feasted my eyes on the sight of Eumolpus in trouble – this was rich food indeed! I was recommending him to a good lawyer when the manager of the lodging house, Bargates by name, who had been disturbed at his dinner, was carried into the centre of the brawl by two porters – he had bad feet, it seems. After coming out with a long and furious diatribe in a foreign accent about drunken sots and runaway slaves, he then looked at Eumolpus and said:

'It was you, was it, you wonderful poet? Now why don't these no-good slaves get off quick and stop fighting? The woman I'm living with is acting high and mighty with me. So be a friend and write some dirty verses about her so she'll know her place.'

*

97. While Eumolpus was talking privately to Bargates, a town-crier entered the hotel accompanied by a policeman and quite a number of other people. Waving a torch that gave out more smoke than light, he made the following announcement:

'LOST, a short while ago in the baths, a boy aged about sixteen. He is curly-haired, soft-skinned, good-looking, and goes by the name of Giton. There is a reward of one thousand sesterces for anyone who will bring him back or give any information of his whereabouts.'

Not far from the announcer stood Ascyltus, wearing a multi-coloured shirt and displaying the description and the reward on a silver plate.

I ordered Giton to get immediately under the bed and tie his hands and feet to the webbing and so stay out of the hands of the searchers.

Giton was not slow and in a moment he inserted his hands in the fastenings and beat Ulysses with his own tricks. To avoid leaving any room for suspicion, I filled the bed with clothes and made up the shape of a man about my size.

Meanwhile Ascyltus after going round all the occupied rooms, came to mine and became more hopeful because he found the doors more carefully bolted. The policeman however, inserting an axe where the doors joined, loosened the bolts from their hold.

I fell at Ascyltus' knees and appealing to the memory of our friendship and our companionship in misfortune, I begged him at least to let me see my little friend. In fact to lend some sincerity to my hypocritical appeals, I said:

'I know you've come to kill me, Ascyltus. Why else have you brought an axe? Well, vent your rage on me. Look, I'm showing you my neck, spill the blood you really came for under the pretence of a search.'

Ascyltus denied any malice on his part and assured me he was only looking for the runaway who belonged to him and didn't want to kill a helpless man, least of all a man he regarded as a very dear friend once the fated quarrel[22] was over.

98. The policeman on the other hand did not take things so easily. Snatching a rod from the innkeeper he pushed it under the bed and even tried all the cracks in the wall. Giton pulled himself away from the poking, and holding his breath in a great panic, pressed his mouth to the very bedbugs.

*

But as the broken door could keep no one out of the room, Eumolpus burst in excitedly:

'I've got the thousand sesterces,' he said. 'I'm going after the advertiser now – he's only just leaving. I'm fully justified in betraying you; I'll explain that Giton is in your possession.'

He was determined about this even as I clasped his knees and begged him not to kill two dying men.

'You would be quite right to be flaming mad,' I added, 'if you could bring forward your prisoner. The boy just got away among the crowd and I haven't a suspicion where he's going to. For pity's sake, Eumolpus, bring the lad back. I'd even rather Ascyltus had him.'

While I was persuading him till he almost believed this, Giton through holding his breath to bursting point, sneezed three times in rapid succession, so hard that the bed shook. At the noise Eumolpus said: 'God bless you, Giton!'

When the mattress was pulled back too, he saw our Ulysses, and even a hungry Cyclops would have had pity on him. Turning to me, he said:

'What's this, you thief? You didn't have the courage to tell me the truth even when you were caught. Why, if the god in charge of human destinies hadn't forced a sign from the lad as he hung there, I'd have been wandering round the public bars like a fool.'

*

Giton, far more conciliatory than I, first of all bound up the cut on his forehead with cobwebs soaked in oil; then he replaced his tattered clothes with his own little cloak, and embracing the now mollified poet and pressing kisses on him like poultices, said to him:

'My dear, dear father, we are all completely in your hands. If you love your little Giton, now is the time to save him. I wish some terrible fire would burn me up, just me, or some freezing sea would cover me. I'm the object of all these crimes, I'm the cause. If I were to die, it would reconcile the people at each other's throats.'

*

99. (*Eumolpus*) 'Always and everywhere I have lived as though each day were my last and would never return.'

*

With tears flowing from my eyes, I begged him to become my friend again too: the madness of jealousy was not in a lover's control. Nevertheless I would take great care never to say or do anything again that could offend him. Only let him, as befitted a poet and scholar, smooth away all the rancour festering in his heart, leaving no scar.

'The snows cling longer in rough and uncultivated regions, but where the ground has come under the plough, the light frost vanishes from its bright expanse even while you are speaking.

In the same way anger chokes an untutored heart, but falls smoothly away from a cultivated mind.'

'What you say is true,' said Eumolpus, 'and to prove it, look, I'll even kiss you and put an end to our quarrel. Well now, I hope everything will be all right. Get your things together and follow me, or if you prefer, you lead the way.'

He was still talking when the door was pushed and creaked open, and a rough-bearded sailor stood in the doorway.

'You're late, Eumolpus,' he said. 'You'd think you didn't know we have to hurry.'[23]

We all got up without delay, and Eumolpus ordered his servant, who had been asleep for some time, to start moving with his baggage. Giton and I got together what we had for the sea-voyage,[24] sent up a prayer to the stars and passed aboard.

*

100. 'It's annoying that our new acquaintance likes the boy. But aren't the best things in life free to all? The sun shines on everyone. The moon leads even the beasts to pasture. What can you think of lovelier than water? But it flows for the whole world. Is love alone then to be something furtive rather than something to be gloried in? Exactly, that's just it – I don't want any of the good things of life unless people are envious of them. One man, and old at that, will be no trouble: even if he wished to try something, he'll give himself away through panting.'

I put forward these considerations with something less than confidence and managed to overcome my inward disagreement. Then, with my head buried in my tunic, I began pretending to sleep.

But suddenly as though fortune were determined to take all the heart out of me, a voice on deck could be heard complaining:

'So he made a fool of me, did he?'

It was a male voice that sounded to my ears like an old friend and sent me into palpitations. Then a woman, apparently cut to the quick and equally indignant, blazed out with even greater vehemence:

'If only some god would put Giton into my hands, what a welcome I'd have for the wanderer!'

Both of us were so shaken by these unexpected sounds that the blood drained from our faces. Myself in particular, as though caught up in some distressing nightmare, found my voice only after a long interval and with trembling hands I pulled at Eumolpus' cloak, just as he was falling off to sleep.

'For heaven's sake, sir, can you tell us whose ship this is and who are aboard?'

He was annoyed at being awakened.

'Was this the reason why you wanted us to occupy the most secluded place on the ship, so that you could stop us sleeping? Anyway, suppose I told you that Lichas of Tarentum was the owner of the ship and that he was taking Tryphaena to Tarentum, what does it matter?'

101. Thunderstruck by this, I broke out trembling and baring my throat, I said:

'Fate has utterly defeated me at last.'

Giton indeed fainted across my chest and went on lying there. When the sweat broke out and revived us, I gripped Eumolpus by the knees.

'Show some pity for us,' I said, 'we're as good as dead. In the name of our common education, lend us a helping hand. Our last hour has come and unless you prevent it, it can only be a blessing.'

Overwhelmed by this bitterness, Eumolpus swore by all the gods and goddesses that he neither knew what had happened nor had he planned any deliberate treachery – with the most straightforward of intentions and in all good faith he had brought his friends to the boat he'd long before planned to take.

'Anyway,' he said, 'what is the trap here? Who is the Hannibal sailing with us? It's just Lichas of Tarentum, a very respectable man, who is not only the owner of this boat which he's in command of, but also of a number of farms and a trading company. He's carrying a commercial cargo to some trading centre. This is your pirate-captain, and we owe our passage to him. And as well as this man, there's Tryphaena, the loveliest woman in the world, who travels from place to place in the service of pleasure.'

'These are the people we're running away from,' said Giton and went on to explain briefly to the frightened Eumolpus the reasons for their hatred and the seriousness of the danger.

Confused and not knowing what to do, Eumolpus suggested we each put forward our ideas:

'You have to imagine we've got into the Cyclops' cave. Some way of escape has to be found, short of involving ourselves in a shipwreck [25] and extricating ourselves from every possible risk.'

'No,' said Giton, 'better get the pilot to take the ship back into some port – not for nothing, obviously – and tell him your brother is not a good sailor and is at his last gasp. You can cover up the deception by looking worried and shedding some tears, so the pilot will be touched and do what you want.'

Eumolpus argued that this wasn't possible. 'You see,' he said, 'large ships don't put into a harbour off their course,[26] and it is not likely that my brother could have fallen ill so quickly. And another thing, perhaps Lichas will want to look at the sufferer out of a feeling of duty. You can see how very useful that would be to us, deliberately summoning the captain to the very ones running away from him. But suppose the ship could be diverted from its long voyage and suppose Lichas did not specially go round the sick-beds, how could we leave the ship without being seen by everyone? With heads covered or bare? Covered? Then everyone would want to give a hand to the invalids. Bare? Then that would be simply advertising ourselves.'

102. I interposed: 'Why don't we rely on really bold measures, slip down a rope, get into the ship's boat, cut the painter, and leave the rest to fortune? Not that I'm calling on Eumolpus to share this risk. I'm satisfied if he helps us.'[27]

'Not a bad plan,' said Eumolpus, 'if it were practicable. But everyone will notice you leave, especially the pilot, who stays on watch all night and observes the movement of the stars. Now you might trick him somehow, if you were taking your leave by another part of the ship. As it is, you have to slide down by the stern, by the very steering gear. Besides, I'm surprised, Encolpius, that it hasn't occurred to you that one sailor stays in the boat on continuous day and night watch and you couldn't get rid of him without killing him or throwing him overboard by brute force. For this you must ask yourselves how brave you are. As for my coming with you, I shirk no danger that offers any hope of safety. I presume that not even you would want to risk your lives for nothing as though they were trifles. See whether you like this idea: I'll drop you into two leather bags, tie them up with straps and put you among my clothes, leaving the tops a little way open of course, so you get air and food. Then I'll tell everyone loudly that my two slaves have thrown themselves in the sea during the night through fear of worse punishment. Then when we arrive in port, I'll carry you off like luggage without any suspicion.'

'Oh, really,' I said, 'you'd tie us up as though we were solid right through and our insides couldn't give us any trouble, or as though we didn't ever sneeze or snore? Or just because this type of trick did work once? But suppose we could stand being tied up for one day. What happens if either a calm or bad weather holds us up longer? What would we do? Clothes tied up too long get ruined by creases and papers tied together lose their shape. We're young and not used to hard work. Can we stand being tied up in covers like statues?'

*

'Some safe way still has to be found. You look at my idea. Eumolpus as a literary man naturally has some ink. So let's use this as a dye and change our colour – hair right down to fingernails. Disguised as Ethiopian slaves, we can wait on you quite happily without any chance of being tortured and at the same time we can trick our enemies by our change of colour.'

Giton added: 'Why not circumcise us too, so we look like Jews, and bore holes in our ears to imitate Arabs, and whiten our faces so Gauls would take us as fellow-countrymen. As though this colouring by itself could change our shapes. A lot of details have to be consistent to keep up the deception! Suppose a face could stay stained for some time. Suppose no drops of water produce spots on our skins and our clothes don't cling to the ink. Well then, can we also puff out our lips into that hideous swollen look? Can we change our hair with a curling-iron? Can we cut our foreheads with scars? Can we open our legs till they're bandy? Can we touch the ground with our ankles? Can we produce foreign-looking beards? Artificial dye stains your body, it doesn't change it. Listen to my coward's way out – let's tie our heads in our clothes and throw ourselves to the bottom.'

103. 'Gods and men forbid,' Eumolpus exclaimed, 'that you

should end your lives in so ugly a fashion. Better do what I tell you. My hired man, as you know from the razor, is a barber. Let him shave the hair off both of you right away, not just your heads but your eyebrows too. I'll follow up by marking your foreheads with an artistic inscription, so you'll appear to have been punished with branding. The letters will simultaneously lull the suspicions of the people looking for you and hide your faces under cover of the punishment marks.'

No time was lost working the trick. We went stealthily to the side of the ship and presented our heads to the barber to be shaved. Eumolpus covered both our foreheads with the huge letters and with a liberal hand extended the notorious inscription put on runaway slaves over the whole of our faces.

As it happened, one of the passengers who was leaning against the side of the ship and emptying his sick stomach noticed in the moonlight the barber bent over his unseasonable office. Swearing at the bad omen which was reminiscent of a last offering in a shipwreck, he flung himself back to bed. Pretending to ignore the sea-sick man and his curse, we returned to our melancholy coiffure[28] and, wrapped in silence, spent the remaining hours of the night sleeping fitfully.

*

104. (*Lichas*) 'I dreamt Priapus said to me: "Since you are looking for him, I want you to know that Encolpius has been brought aboard your boat by my agency." '[29]

Tryphaena shuddered and said:

'You would think we'd slept in the one bed. I dreamt that a statue of Neptune that I'd noticed in a shrine at Baiae spoke to me too – "You will find Giton on Lichas' ship." '

'You should realize from this,' said Eumolpus, 'how godlike a man Epicurus was.[30] He condemned this sort of nonsense in a very humorous way.'[31]

*

But Lichas took Tryphaena's dream seriously. 'Who's going to stop us searching the boat?' he said. 'That way we'll avoid any appearance of damning the workings of the divine mind.'

*

The man who had noticed our furtive and worried behaviour in the dark (Hesus was his name) suddenly shouted:

'Then those are the ones who were being shaved in the dark – and that's a terrible thing to do, by god! I'm told no mortal soul should cut his nails or hair on a ship unless the wind and the sea are at odds.'[32]

105. Lichas, shocked by this report, started blazing:

'Is it true that someone cut his hair on the ship, and in the dead of night at that? Bring the culprits out here immediately, so I'll know whose heads should roll to purify the ship.'

'I gave the orders,' said Eumolpus. 'And as I was going to be on the same ship I didn't intend any bad omen for myself, but since they had long shaggy hair, in case I appeared to be making a prison out of the ship, I gave orders for the condemned men to be cleaned up. Another reason was to allow the marks of the letters to be entirely visible to readers and not hidden by their covering of hair. Among other things they spent my money on a whore the two of them kept, and I dragged them from her last night soaked in wine and scent. In fact they still smell of what was left of my inheritance.'

*

So to appease the guardian deity of the ship, it was decided to give each of us forty lashes. There was no delay. The raging sailors laid into us with ropes and tried to placate the ship's god with our worthless blood. I personally absorbed three lashes with Spartan fortitude. But Giton after one blow cried out so loudly that Tryphaena's ears could hear nothing but that well-known voice. And it was not merely the mistress who was thrown into confusion; her maids too, under the impulsion of the familiar tones, rushed to the victim. Giton with his marvellous body had already made the sailors drop their whips and his silent appeal had even begun working on their savage hearts before the maids cried out in chorus:

'It's Giton, Giton! Keep your cruel hands off him. It's Giton, lady. Help him!'

Tryphaena lent an already believing ear to their cries and flew quickly to the boy's side. Lichas, who knew me best, as though he too had had vocal testimony, ran to me and without considering my hands or face but immediately stretching out an investigating hand to my private parts, he said:

'How are you, Encolpius?'

Will anyone now be surprised that Ulysses' nurse after twenty years found a scar sufficient identification[33] when this shrewd man so cleverly went straight to the one thing that identified the runaway?

Tryphaena began to cry, for she believed that the marks really had been branded on our foreheads, and in a rather subdued manner she began to ask what prison had got hold of us in our travels, and whose hands had been cruel enough to carry out this punishment, making it clear, however, that some of the maltreatment had been richly deserved by us for running away and for hating a situation where we were so well off.

106. Highly irritated, Lichas leapt forward:

'You simple-minded woman! As though the scars and the letters had sunk in under iron. I wish they *had* branded themselves with the inscription. We would have had this consolation at the very least. As it is we have been the victims of a pure farce and made ridiculous by a mere outline.'

Tryphaena was prepared to be more merciful, seeing she was not debarred from her pleasures, but Lichas, still remembering his wife's seduction and the affronts he had received in the colonnade of Hercules,[34] exclaimed with contorted face:

'You've realized, I suppose, Tryphaena, that heaven takes some interest in human affairs. It brought the culprits unawares to our ship and warned us what they'd do in a pair of corroborating dreams. So think, what possibility is there of pardoning men that the god himself has handed over for punishment? As for me, I'm not a cruel man, but I'm afraid I'd suffer whatever penalty I remitted.'

Swayed by so superstitious an argument, Tryphaena said she would not interfere with the punishment; on the contrary, she was even in favour of such richly deserved reprisals. She had suffered no less serious an injury – her reputation as a decent woman had been publicly blackened.

*

107. (*Eumolpus*) 'They chose me for this task, I suppose, because I'm well known and they asked me to reconcile them to their one-time dearest friends.[35] Unless perhaps you think the young men fell into this trap accidentally, even though the first thing every traveller asks is into whose care he is committing himself. So let your hearts be softened now reparations have been made and allow these free citizens to go where they are bound without interference. Slave owners who are brutal and unrelenting actually hinder the satisfaction of their sadistic impulses if conscience is ever likely to bring runaways back. And we don't kill enemies who are handed over to us. What more are you after? What more do you want? Lying before your eyes, begging for mercy, are two young men, respectable, honest, and, what is more important than either of these things, once bound by friendship to you. For god's sake, if they had run off with your money or had betrayed your trust, you might still be well satisfied by the punishment-marks you see. Look, you can trace the brand of slavery on their foreheads and their respectable faces have voluntarily undergone a penalty that puts them outside society.'

Lichas interrupted this plea for mercy and said:

'Don't confuse the issue, but deal with each item. And first of all, if they came of their own accord, why did they cut all the hair from their heads? Anyone who disguises his face is planning deception, not satisfaction. And another thing, if they were trying to ingratiate themselves through an intermediary, why did you do everything you could to keep your protégés out of sight? It is obvious from this that the culprits fell into the trap through sheer chance and you looked for a way to baffle our revenge. As for the odium you are bringing on our heads by shouting about their respectability and honesty, watch you don't damage your case through over-confidence. What should the injured parties do when the guilty come running to be punished? They were our friends, of course! Then they deserve all the greater punishment. A man who attacks strangers is called a criminal, a man who attacks friends, a monster.'

Eumolpus refuted this unjust attack.

'I see,' he said, 'that the greatest objection to these poor young men is the fact that they cut off their hair during the night. Now

I'd like you to hear an account as frank as the matter was simple. Before they embarked, they wanted to rid their heads of a troublesome and superfluous burden, but the unexpectedly favourable wind caused them to delay carrying out their intention. However they didn't think it mattered when they began carrying out their purpose, because they didn't know about sailors' superstitions and the code of the sea.'

To this Lichas said:

'What use was it in their position to shave their heads? Unless perhaps bald men tend to be more pitiful objects? In any case what use is it looking for the truth from an intermediary?

'What have you to say, you criminal? Did a salamander burn your eyebrows off? What god did you dedicate your hair to? Speak up, you poisonous creature!'

108. I simply gaped, terrified by the thought of being punished. I could find nothing to say, the case was so open and shut. I was such a confused and ugly object[36] – for besides the disgrace of my shorn head, my eyebrows were as bare as my forehead – it didn't seem right for me to say or do anything. But once a dripping sponge had been wiped over my tearful face, and the wetted ink, streaming over it, reduced all my features to a dark cloud, anger turned to hatred . . .

Eumolpus however[37] said he would not allow anyone to outrage respectable people contrary to all moral and legal principles, and he not only verbally but bodily interposed himself between us and their threatening temper.

His servant was there to help him in his intervention[38] as well as one or two very feeble passengers – giving moral support in the dispute rather than any physical aid. And I was not asking anything for myself – holding my fists before Tryphaena's eyes I said loudly in firm clear tones that I would resort to what force I had, if that criminal woman, the only one who deserved a thrashing on the whole ship, did not leave Giton alone. At my boldness Lichas blazed up into further anger: he was indignant with me for forgetting my own situation to shout so loudly for someone else. Tryphaena, blazing at the insult, was in just as much of a rage and she forced the whole ship's company to take sides. On our side Eumolpus' man armed himself and distributed razors amongst us. On their side Tryphaena's entourage put up their bare fists. There was only the navigator, who threatened to abandon steering the ship if this madness provoked by the lust of the dregs of society did not stop. But the struggle continued raging nonetheless, they fighting for revenge, we for our lives.

A good many went down on both sides without any fatalities. Even more retreated bleeding from their wounds. And yet neither side's anger abated. Then Giton, like the hero he was, held his menacing razor over his genitals and threatened to cut off the cause of all our misery. Tryphaena averted this extreme action by an unambiguous pardon. Several times I myself put the barber's razor to my throat with no more intention of killing myself than Giton had of carrying out his threat. But he played his tragic role more boldly because he knew he had the razor he'd already cut his throat with.

Both sides stood there ready for the fight. So when it was obvious that it was going to be no ordinary battle, the navigator managed with difficulty to persuade Tryphaena to accept the role of ambassador and make a truce. The requisite promises were solemnly offered and accepted. Tryphaena then extended an olive-branch plucked from the ship's figurehead and boldly began the negotiations.

> 'Under stress of what madness peace becomes war?'
> She cries. 'What guilt on our hands?
> No hero Trojan[39] elopes on this ship
> (Menelaus tricked of his bride);
> No maddened Medea
> Makes her brother's blood a weapon.
> Rejected love is the driving force.
> O, god help us!
> Who takes to arms and calls for death
> Amid these waves?
> Or finds one death inadequate?
> The sea's savagery is enough –
> Send no fresh floods to swell
> The savage waves.'

109. As the woman poured all this out in shrill distressed tones, the lines hesitated a moment and our hands dropped

peaceably to our sides – the fight was over. Eumolpus took command and made full use of this change of heart. Prefacing it with a violent attack on Lichas, he wrote out and signed a treaty, the formula of which was:

'You, Tryphaena, sincerely undertake not to complain of any past injury done to you by Giton or to bring up, avenge, or by any other method attempt to pursue any action committed before today. You undertake not to impose any service on the boy against his will, whether it be an embrace, kiss, or sexual intercourse, unless for each service you pay one hundred denarii in cash.

'Secondly: you, Lichas, sincerely undertake not to persecute Encolpius with insulting words or looks or make any inquiries as to where he sleeps at night. Otherwise you are to pay two hundred denarii in cash for each separate offence.'

Once the treaty was concluded on these terms, we put away our weapons and to avoid any lingering resentment after the ceremony, we agreed to put the past behind us with an exchange of kisses. Amid the general encouragement our hatred simmered down and a feast was spread out on the battlefield, which restored everyone's high spirits. The whole ship rang with the songs and as a sudden calm had interrupted the voyage, we had one man trying to harpoon the fish as they jumped out of the water and another trying to drag the struggling catch aboard with baited fishhooks. Sea-birds had even perched along the yard and a clever bird-catcher got at them with reeds woven together. They stuck to the limed twigs and were brought down into his hands. The air took hold of the floating plumes and the light spray whirled the feathers over the sea.

Lichas was beginning to be friendly to me again, Tryphaena was splashing Giton with the dregs of her drink, when Eumolpus, being well into his cups, got the idea of throwing out some quips about bald heads and brandmarks, until exhausting his weak witticisms he went back to his poetry and began reciting a little elegy on hair:

'Your hair has fallen out – your only good feature;
A cruel storm has stripped the foliage of spring.
Each temple misses its natural shade
And a bare expanse grins under worn stubble.

Oh, the gods, the gods cheat us!
Our Youth's first glories are Youth's first forfeits.

*

'Poor boy,
One moment your hair
Was shining gold
And you were more beautiful
Than Phoebus or his sister.
Now you are shinier
Than a bronze
Or the round cap
Of a mushroom after rain.
You run nervously
From the laughter of ladies.
Death's sooner than you think,
You realize now –
See, Death has begun at the top.'

110. He was ready to give us more of the same, I think, or worse, but Tryphaena's maid took Giton down to the lower half of the ship and dressed the boy's head in one of her mistress's curly wigs. In fact, she even produced eyebrows from a box and by cunningly following the outlines of the missing features, entirely restored his appearance.

Tryphaena recognized the real Giton and, moved to tears, gave the boy this time a really sincere kiss.

For myself, although I was delighted to see the boy restored to his pristine glory, I began covering my face more than ever. I realized how bizarre my deformity was – not even Lichas thought me worth talking to. But the same girl got me out of my depression by taking me to one side and fixing me up with an equally handsome head of hair. In fact, my face was brighter and more attractive, because mine was a yellow wig.

*

However, Eumolpus, our champion in time of trouble and the author of the present harmony, to prevent the general merriment lapsing into silence without a few stories, began a succession of gibes about feminine unfaithfulness – how easily they fell in love, how quickly they forgot even their children. There was no woman so modest that she could not be driven crazy by some stranger's physical attractions. He wasn't thinking of old tragedies or famous historical names but of something that happened in his own recollection, and he would tell us about it if we wanted to hear it. So when everyone's eyes and ears were turned to him, he began the following story.

III. 'There was once a lady of Ephesus[40] so famous for her fidelity to her husband that she even attracted women from neighbouring countries to come just to see her. So when she buried her husband, she was not satisfied with following him to his grave with the usual uncombed hair or beating her breast in front of the crowd but she even accompanied the dead man into the tomb, and when the corpse was placed in the underground vault,[41] she watched over it from then on, weeping day and night. Neither her parents nor her relations could induce her to stop torturing herself and starving to death. Finally the magistrates were repulsed and left her, and this extraordinary example to womankind, mourned by everyone, was now spending her fifth day without food. A devoted servant sat with the poor woman and added her tears to the lady's grief, and filled the lamp in the tomb whenever it began to go out. Naturally there was only one subject of conversation in the whole town: every class of people admitted there had never been such a shining example of true fidelity and love.

'About the same time the governor of the province ordered the crucifixion[42] of some thieves to be carried out near the very chamber where the wife was crying over the lately deceased. Next night the soldier who was guarding the crosses to prevent anyone removing one of the corpses for burial noticed a light shining clearly among the tombs and, hearing the sounds of someone mourning, he was eager to know – a general human failing – who it was and what was going on. Naturally he went down into the vault and seeing a beautiful woman, at first stood rooted to the spot as though terrified by some strange sight. When he observed the dead man's corpse and noted the woman's tears and scratched face, realizing rightly that here was a woman who could not bear her intense longing for the dead man, he brought her his bit of supper and began pleading with the weeping woman not to prolong her hopeless grief and break her heart with useless lamentation. The same end, the same resting-place awaited everyone, he told her – along with all the other things that restore grief-stricken minds to sanity. But in spite of his consoling words, which she refused to hear, the woman only tore at her breast more violently and draped her mangled hair over the body of the dead man. The soldier still refused to withdraw; instead, using the same arguments, he tried to press food on her servant until the girl, seduced by the smell of the wine and the food,[43] first gave in herself, stretched out her hand to his tempting charity, and then, refreshed by the food and drink, began to lay siege to her mistress's resolution.

' "What good is it," she said to her, "for you to drop dead of starvation, or bury yourself alive or breathe your last innocent breath before fate demands it?

> Believe you that ashes or the buried ghosts can know?[44]

Won't you come back to life? Won't you give up your womanly error and enjoy the advantages of life as long as you can? That very corpse lying there should be your encouragement to live."

'No one is ever reluctant to listen when pressed to eat[45] or stay alive. Dry-mouthed from taking nothing day after day, the woman allowed her resolution to be sapped and filled herself with food no less avidly than the girl who had given in first.

112. 'But you know what temptations follow on a full stomach. The inducements the soldier had used to persuade the lady into a desire to live became part also of an attempt on her virtue. For all her chastity the man appealed to her : he was neither un-pleasing nor ill-spoken, she thought. Moreover, her maid spoke on his behalf and quoted the line :

> Would you fight even a pleasing passion?[46]

'Need I say more? The woman couldn't refuse even this gratification of the flesh and the triumphant soldier talked her into both. They then slept together, not just the night they first performed the ceremony but the next night too, and then a third. The doors of the vault were of course closed, so if a friend or a stranger came to the tomb, he thought that the blameless widow had expired over her husband's body.

'Actually the soldier, delighted with the lady's beauty and the whole secret liaison, had bought whatever luxuries he could afford and carried them to the tomb on the very first night. As a result, the parents of one of the crucified men, seeing the watch had been relaxed, took down the hanging body in the dark and gave it the final rites. The soldier, tricked while he lay enjoying himself and seeing next day one of the crosses without a corpse, in terror of punishment, explained to the woman what had happened. He would not wait for the judge's verdict, he said – his own sword would carry out sentence for his dereliction of duty. Only let her provide a place for his body and let the tomb be the last resting-place of her lover and her husband. The woman's pity was equal to her fidelity:

' "Heaven forbid," she said, "that I should see simultaneously two funerals, for the two men I hold dearest. I'd rather hang the dead than kill the living."

'Suiting the deed to the word, she told him to take the body of her husband from the coffin and fix it to the empty cross. The soldier followed the sensible woman's plan, and next day people wondered how on earth the dead man had managed to get up on the cross.'

113. The sailors greeted the story with roars of laughter; Tryphaena blushed rather and laid her cheek affectionately on Giton's neck. Lichas however was not amused. Shaking his head angrily he said:

'If his commander-in-chief had been an honourable man, he should have put the husband's body back in the tomb and nailed the woman to the cross.'

No doubt he had remembered Hedyle and the robbery on his ship before the elopement. But the terms of the treaty did not permit him to recall this and the prevailing high spirits left no room for bad temper. Tryphaena meanwhile was settled on Giton's lap, covering his chest with kisses and occasionally titivating his depilated appearance. Being depressed and annoyed with the recent treaty, I took nothing to eat or drink, but looked at both of them with oblique and hostile glances. All the kisses and all the endearments that the lecherous woman thought up wounded me deeply. Yet I still wasn't sure whether I was more angry with the boy for stealing my mistress or with my mistress for seducing the boy. Both acts were offensive to my eyes and more saddening than my past captivity. Added to this was the fact that Tryphaena would not talk to me like an old friend and once pleasing lover, and Giton did not regard me as worth even the usual toasts – at least he didn't address me in the general conversation, which was the least he could do. He was nervous, I imagine, of opening some fresh scar in the initial stages of the reconciliation. Tears of vexation choked me, and my groans, which I smothered into sighs, almost made me faint.

*

Lichas tried to get invited to the party, putting on no lordly airs but acting like a friend asking a favour.

*

'If you had any decent blood in your veins, you wouldn't regard her as anything more than a whore. If you were a man, you wouldn't go to such a perverted creature.'[47]

*

Nothing embarrassed me more than the possibility of Eumolpus' realizing what had gone on then and with his usual fluency taking revenge in verse.

*

Eumolpus swore in the most solemn terms . . .

*

114. While we were talking about this and similar things, the sea grew rough; clouds gathered from all directions and turned the day into darkness. The sailors dispersed nervously to their duties and took down the sails before the storm. But the wind had not set the waves running in any particular direction and the helmsman did not know which way to head the ship. First the wind came from Sicily, then time and again the north wind from the Italian shore would take over and turn the helpless ship this way and that.[48] And what was far more dangerous than all the gales of wind, the sudden pitch-black darkness had quenched the light so completely that the navigator could not even see the length of the prow. When the storm was at its height and death

stared us in the face,[49] Lichas, trembling, stretched out his hands to me pleadingly and said:

'You're the one, Encolpius. Save us from this danger. Just restore to the ship that sacred robe and the goddess's rattle. In heaven's name, have some pity for us, as surely you used to.'

And then in mid-shout the wind flung him into the sea. He was caught up in a raging whirlpool and the blast whirled him round and sucked him under. Loyal servants however caught hold of Tryphaena, who was almost lifeless, put her in a boat with most of the luggage and snatched her from certain death.

*

Clasping Giton to me with a cry, I wept and said:

'Did we deserve this of heaven – is death alone to unite us? But our cruel luck does not allow it. Look, the waves are already overturning the ship. Look, the angry sea is trying to break our affectionate embraces. If you ever really loved Encolpius, kiss him while you can and take this last pleasure from the jaws of death.'

As I said this, Giton took off his clothes and, covered in my tunic, brought up his head for a kiss. And in case the envious waves should drag us apart even when clinging together like this, he tied his belt round both of us and said:

'If nothing else, we will float longer if we are tied together in death, or if out of pity the sea is likely to throw us up on the same shore, either some passing stranger will throw stones over us out of common humanity, or, as a last favour that even the angry waves cannot refuse, the drifting sand will cover us.'

For the last time I felt bonds about me and as though laid out on a bier I waited for death – no longer an enemy. Meanwhile the storm executed the commands of fate and carried away all that was left of the ship. No mast, no helm, no rope or oar was left, but like a rough and shapeless log it went with the waves.

*

Fishermen came hurrying out in little boats to do some looting. When they saw there were people to defend their property, their greed was replaced by the wish to help.

*

115. We heard a strange murmur or moaning from the captain's cabin, as though an animal were trying to escape. We followed the sound and found Eumolpus sitting there and turning out verses on a great sheet. Surprised that he had leisure in the fact of death to write poems, we dragged him out protesting and told him not to worry. But he was blazing with anger for being interrupted, and said:

'Allow me to get this line right. The poem is almost finished.'

I grabbed the lunatic and told Giton to come and drag the bellowing poet to land.

*

Finally the job was done and we sorrowfully entered the fisherman's cottage. Satisfying ourselves somehow with spoilt food from the wreck we passed a very miserable night. Next day, when we were discussing where we had got ourselves to, I suddenly saw a body turning in a gentle eddy and drifting to the shore.

I stopped sadly and began gazing at this example of the sea's treachery with moist eyes.

'Perhaps somewhere,' I said aloud, 'a carefree wife waits for him, perhaps a son, not knowing about the storm. Or perhaps it was his father he left, at least someone he kissed[50] when he set out. So much for mortal schemes and mortal desires. Look at him – how the man floats!'

I was still mourning for what I supposed was a stranger, when the tide turned his undamaged face to the shore and I recognized almost underneath my feet what had been a little while ago the terrible and implacable Lichas. I could hold back my tears no longer. In fact, I beat my breast again and again and said: 'Where are your bad tempers and your ungovernable rages now? You have been at the mercy of fishes and other horrible creatures. A little while ago you boasted of your power and your position, but you haven't even a plank left from the wreck of your great ship. Go now, mortals, and fill your hearts with great schemes. Go and carefully invest your ill-gotten gains for a thousand years. Yesterday he must have looked at the accounts of his investments, he must have imagined the day he would reach his home town. O heavens, how far away he lies from his destination! Yet it is not only the seas that serve mortals like this. Weapons play a man false in wartime; the collapse of his family shrine buries a man giving thanks to heaven; a man falls from his carriage and hastily gasps his last. Food chokes the glutton, abstinence the abstemious. If you think it over properly, there is shipwreck everywhere. Mind you, a man drowned at sea does not get buried – as though it matters what destroys a perishable corpse – fire, water, or time! Whatever you do, all these things come to the same thing. But of course, wild beasts will mangle the carcass. As though it were better that fire should have it – and yet we consider this the severest possible punishment when we are angry with our servants. So what is the point of this craze to make sure that no part of us is left behind after burial?'

*

And the pyre, built by his enemies' hands, reduced Lichas to ashes.

While Eumolpus was composing an epigram on the dead man, he gazed into the distance in search of inspiration.

*

116. We gladly performed this duty and then we took the road we had decided on and in a short time we were sweating our way up a high hill, from which we saw in the near distance a town situated on a great height. Being lost, we did not know what town it was until we learnt from a farmer that it was Croton,[1] a very ancient city, once the foremost in Italy. We then inquired most carefully what sort of people lived in this noble area and what type of business they particularly favoured, since their wealth had been diminished by a long series of wars.

'My dear sirs,' he said, 'if you are businessmen, change your plans and look for some other source of livelihood. If, however, you are a more sophisticated type and you can take incessant lying, you are following the right road to riches. You see, in this city no literary pretensions are honoured, eloquence has no standing, sobriety and decent behaviour are not praised and rewarded – no, whatever people you see, you must regard as divided into two classes. Either they have fortunes worth hunting or they are fortune-hunters. In this city no one raises children because anyone who has heirs of his own is not invited out to dinner or allowed into the games; he is deprived of all amenities and lives in ignominious obscurity. But those who have never married and have no close ties, attain the highest honours – only these have real courage, or even blameless characters. You are on your way to a town that is like a plague-ridden countryside, where there is nothing but corpses being pecked and crows pecking them.'

*

117. Eumolpus, turning his thoughts more carefully to this novel situation, confessed that this method of hunting for profit[2] appealed to him. I imagined that the old man was joking and showing the lack of seriousness typical of poets, until he said:

'I wish we had more elaborate stage-properties, more civilized costumes, and a more splendid set-up to give plausibility to the imposture. I wouldn't postpone the robbery,[3] by god! I'd lead you straight to a fortune. Even so, I promise. ...'

*

... whatever he should ask for, provided that our old companion in crime, the robe I'd stolen, would do and also whatever Lycurgus' burgled villa had yielded.[4] The mother of the gods with her usual good faith would send us money for immediate use.

*

'Why delay the start of the show then?' said Eumolpus. 'Make me your master, if you think the idea is a good one.'

No one dared condemn a scheme that would cost nothing. And so to safeguard the imposture in which we were all involved, we swore an oath dictated by Eumolpus, that we would be burned, flogged, beaten, killed with cold steel or whatever else Eumolpus ordered. Like real gladiators we very solemnly handed ourselves over, body and soul, to our master. After swearing the oath we saluted our master in our role as slaves, and we were all instructed that Eumolpus had buried his son, a young man of great oratorical abilities and high promise, and that the unhappy old man had therefore left his native city so that he should not have daily cause for tears at the sight of his son's followers and friends or his tomb. Shipwreck was next added to this grief, in which he had lost more than twenty million sesterces. But he was not worried by the loss, except that being deprived of his servants, he did not see about him what was proper to his rank. Besides he had thirty million invested in Africa in farms and loans; in fact, he had such a large number of slaves spread among his estates in Numidia that they could even capture Carthage.

Following this outline, we told Eumolpus to cough a lot, cultivate a weak stomach, and curse all his food openly. He was to talk about gold and silver, false returns from his farms and his invariably unproductive lands. Moreover he was to sit down every day at his accounts and renew the terms of his will every *month*. And to complete the setting, whenever he tried to call one of us, he was to call out the wrong name, to make it very clear that their master remembered even the ones who were no longer with him.

After making these arrangements, we prayed that it would all turn out well and happily, and set off down the road. Giton however, could not manage the unaccustomed pack and Corax the hired man, a constant grumbler in his job, kept putting his bag down, hurling insults at us for hurrying, and vowing that he'd throw away the bags and run off with his load.

'What *is* this, you people?' he said. 'Do you think I'm a beast of burden or a ship for carrying stones? I contracted for a man's job, not a dray-horse's. I'm a free man as much as you are, even if my father did leave me poor.'

Not content with cursing, every so often he lifted his leg right up and filled the road with obscene sounds and smells. Giton laughed at his bad behaviour and followed each of his farts with an equally loud imitation.

*

118. 'Poetry[5] has deluded many a young man,' said Eumolpus. 'As soon as each of them has made his lines scan and wrapped up some half-baked inspiration in roundabout words, he thinks he's gone straight up Helicon. Tired by their bar practice they often fly to the calm waters of poetry, as though it were a port in a storm, believing it must be easier to construct an epic poem than a speech that glows with scintillating epigrams. But noble inspiration hates empty verbiage and a mind cannot conceive or bear fruit unless it is soaked in a mighty flood of great works. One must avoid all vulgarity of language and one must select expressions not in common use. Besides this, one must be careful that witty lines are not made to stand out from the body of the narrative, but add their colour and brilliance to the texture of the poem. Witness Homer and the lyric poets, Roman Virgil, and Horace's careful felicity. Other poets either have not seen the way to approach poetry, or if they have seen it have been frightened to take it. Above all, whoever attempts the great theme of the Civil War without being full of the great writers, will fail under the task. For it is not historical fact that has to be handled in the poem – historians do this far better. No, the unfettered inspiration must be sent soaring through riddles and divine

interventions and strange stories, driven by the weight of its language as though from a catapult,[6] so that it gives the impression of prophetic ravings rather than the accuracy of a solemn speech before witnesses.

'As an example, see if you like this hurried attempt, even though it has not received the final touches:[7]

I

119. 'All-conquering Rome was mistress of the globe,
By land and sea an empire to the poles,
        but still unsatisfied.
Sea-lanes battered by heavy hulks;
A hidden bay, a gold-producing region –   5
        this was the ENEMY
The Fates are bent on war
And the search for wealth continues.
Ordinary pleasures,
        plebeian enjoyments   10
            are tedious,
Soldiers connoisseurs of Corinthian bronze.
Gems from deep mines
        flash challenges to purple
From Numidia inlays of ivory   15
        From China new silks
The Arabian countryside
        stripped bare for export.
Further disasters, more stabs at a stricken Peace (hear ye!):
High profits available in the wild beast trade,   20
Ammon in darkest Africa
        flushed for the monster
"which is slain
        because his tooth sells dear".
Starvation in strange forms   25
        weighs down the ships;
The prowling tiger hauled in a golden cage
To gorge on human blood for the PLEBS
        (loud cheers).
Shame chokes my spleen and voice.   30
How can I reveal these doomed lives?
The genitals removed
Organs mutilated under the knife
And broken into the services of lust.

The solemn march of time is checked,   35
The speeding years retarded,
Nature seeking herself
Finds nothing.
Each man has his catamite
(The soft enervated gait,   40
The floating hair,
The fashions in clothes,
Tokens of absent virility.)

'Eye-catching tables of citron-wood from Africa
Mirror the splash of purple and lackeys;   45
Imitate in mottled surfaces disvalued gold.
About the useless wood, the pride of fools,
The mob moves tipsily.

'Footloose, the soldier hefts his tackle,
                          an esurient mercenary.   50

'The Belly, miracle of ingenuity,
Brings the parrot-wrasse,
Submerged in Sicilian water,
Alive to the table;
Pulls oysters from the Lucrine Lake,   55
To make a sale to the palate
The high price most of the flavour.

'The Phasian Lake emptied of birds,
Along that silent shore
Only the wind breathes upon the deserted leaves.   60
The same madness in politics:
A bribed electorate changing sides for silver.
On sale: one people and one senate

CHEAP!
  (*Political support: consult the price list*)   65
Even old men forget
                    the strenous requirements of freedom.
A change of government for small change,
Auctoritas corrupt and humiliated.
        Cato is defeated,   70
                  rejected by the electorate;

The victorious candidate is embarrassed,
Ashamed to snatch
          the *fasces* from Cato.
Not the defeat of a candidate   75
The death-blow of a great people –
Rome a lost city,
          merchant and merchandise,
          plunderer and plundered.
A vile vortex, a gaping whirlpool   80
The people drowning.
    With *Usura*
    Merdery in the absolute rottenness,
    With usura hath no man a house
    With usura hath no man a hand free   85
    A canker born in the hidden marrow,
    A madness raging in the limbs of the body politic
    And wandering with its sorrows
    Like a pack of hounds.
    And out of this revolution   90
    Revolution from poverty.

'War tempts the poor.
Dissipated finances are recouped by murder,
Boldness with nothing has nothing to lose.
Drowned in this filth, sodden with this sleep,   95
What practitioner's skill can rouse Rome surely?
Furor militaris
None but the soldier's, *furor militaris*,
          desire pricked by the sword.

II

120. 'Fortune produced three captains.   100
Enyo, murderous goddess of War,
Crushed each on different battlefields.
Parthia kept Crassus,
In the Libyan Sea lay Pompey (surnamed Magnus)
And Julius –   105
        his blood incarnadined ungrateful Rome.
The earth,
Intolerant of so many tombs together
Divided their ashes.
Such are fame's privileges.   110

The scene:
Deep in a hollow cleft
Between Neapolis and Puteoli,
A cleft awash with water from Cocytus,
Hot with eternal exhalations,   115
Damp with a deadly dew.
No autumn green here,
No green fields of pleasant turf,
No echoing thickets
      Or sweet discords of spring song.   120
 But CHAOS,
     foul black pumice rock,
In triumphant isolation,
And a ring of depressed cypresses above.
Father Dis, appearing from below,   125
Head powdered with white ash
And flames from funeral pyres,
Sardonically to Fortune, winged goddess:
 "Divine-and-human-things-commanding-Power,
 Hater of all security of power,   130
 Lover of the new, forsaker of triumphs,
 Art thou not crushed
 By the weight of Rome?
 Canst thou raise higher that doomed mass?
 The new generation frets at its strength,   135
 Burdened by accumulated wealth.
 See, everywhere rich pickings of victory,
 Prosperity raging to its ruin.
 They build in gold and raise their mansions to the stars.
 The seas are dammed by dykes of stone   140
 And other seas spring up within their fields –
 A rebellion against the order of all things.
 The tunnelled earth yawns under insane buildings;
 Caverns groan in hollowed mountains;
 As long as frivolous employments are found for stone, 145
 My ghosts confess their hopes of heaven.
 On then, Fortune –
 Change thy looks of peace for the face of war.
 Rouse Rome and give my kingdom its dead.
 I have felt no blood on my face,   150
 My Tisiphone has not bathed her parched limbs,
 Since Sulla's sword drank deep
 And the bristling earth produced its bloody crops."

121.   '(He tries to take her right hand,
         But the ground breaks into a yawning chasm.)   155

'Fickle-hearted Fortune thus replies:
     "Father, lord of inmost Cocytus,
     If I may with impunity reveal
                         what must come to pass,
     Thy wishes are granted.   160
     The mad rage inside me no less than thine,
     A more wayward fire eats my heart.
     All I have heaped upon the Roman citadels
     I now detest,
                    resenting my generosity.   165
     The same power that built
                         will destroy their mighty works.
     I have in mind
                    to immolate their warriors,
     Choke their decadence with blood: 170
     Now the clang of arms beats in pricking ears,
     I see Philippi strewn with double slaughter,
     Thessalian pyres, Spanish and Libyan dead;
     I see Nile's barriers groaning,
     The bays of Actium,   175
                    warriors terrified of Apollo's
                              martial port.
     Go then, open the thirsty territories of thy kingdom
     To beckon in new ghosts.
     The ferrying Charon will be too weak   180
     To ferry the shades in his boat –
                    there will be want of a fleet.
     Glut thyself on the great disaster, pale Tisiphone,
     Bite into the open wounds.
     The torn world is led to the Stygian shades."   185

122. 'As she finished a cloud shook
     And with abrupt flashes of fire
     Broke apart for a gleaming thunderbolt,
     Closing behind the jetting flame.
     The father of the shades retreated,   190
     Pater umbrarum
     Closed the gaping breast of the earth
                                   in panic,
     Paling before fraternal bolts.

III

'At once mankind's disaster, *venturaque damna*   195
Are revealed by heavenly omens.
Hyperion, ugly with bloody face,
       hid himself in darkness,
(You might think he saw civil war already).
Elsewhere Cynthia dimmed her full face,   200
Withdrew her light from the scene of the crime.
Mountain ridges thundered into fragments,
  As peaks collapsed,
And rivers wandered no longer free
      dying slowly between familiar banks. 205
Heaven a pandemonium of military excursions;
A tremulous trumpet from the stars
  took Mars by the ears.
Etna, eaten by strange fires,
  flung its eruptions into the skies.   210
Amid the tombs and unburned bones
  the faces of the dead appear
With terrible menacing shrieks.
A comet trailing new stars, bearing fire;
Recens descendit Iuppiter   215
A new sky descending in bloody rain.
Portents soon clarified by God.

'Caesar brooks no delay,
Pricked by lust for revenge
He abandons the Gallic,   220
   begins the Civil
     War.

IV

'In airy Alps
Where the rocks once pounded by a Greek divinity
Slope softly to let men enter   225
Est locus
    a holy place with altars there to Hercules.
Winter blocks it with tight-packed snow
And lifts it to the stars with a blanching peak.
The heavens might have fallen from its top. 230
It does not melt in midsummer rays, spring breezes,
Its packed surface stays stiff with ice and winter frost,
It could carry the globe on its threatening shoulders.

When Caesar tramped these ridges with his exulting
                              soldiers and chose his site,   235
He looked out
              over the wide Italian plains from the summit,
Hurled both hands to the stars:
     "*Iuppiter omnipotens,*
     Saturnian land once glad of my armies,   240
     And loaded down with my triumphs,
     I call you to witness:
     Mars summons me to war
                              an unwilling warrior.
     I bring unwilling hands to the execution,   245
     Forced by my grievances,
     Driven from my city
                    while I reddened the Rhine with blood
     And blocked the Gauls from the Alps
     (Their second attempt on the Capitol).   250
     Exile the surer for my victory.
     In German blood my guilt is rooted,
                              in a hundred triumphs.
     Yet who are they my glory terrifies?
     Who are they who would put an end to war?   255
     Cheap operators bought and sold,
                              mercedibus emptae
     My Rome their step-mother.
     But not with impunity, nor without revenge, I think,
     Shall a coward tie my hands.   260

     'Run mad, my victorious ones!
     Go, comrades, plead my case with a sword!
     The same charge laid at all our doors,
     The same disaster over us all.
     I owe you thanks –   265
                    I did not win alone.
     So, since there are penalties
                    for the acquisition of trophies,
     And victory celebrations see us in convicts' dress,
                              indice fortuna cadat alea   270
     'Let the die be cast.'
     Begin the war and try your mettle.
     Yet my case is already won –
     With so many brave around me
     I do not know the meaning of defeat."   275

'At the trumpet of his voice
A raven, *Delphicus ales*,
Was a glad omen in the sky,
Cleaving the air.
From the left of the dread grove   280
Strange voices sounded
                              and flames rose.
The brightness of the Sun grew brighter than its wont
And set a burning halo of gold about its face.

123. Caesar deployed his standards of war,   285
     Fortior ominibus
     First to attempt these new audacities.
     The icy surface and frost-hard ground
     Made no resistance,
                              lay quiet, crunching gently. 290
     But the squadrons shattered the bound clouds,
     The horses panicking unfettered the ice,
                              the snow melted.
     Rivers of sudden origin ran from the mountain heights,
     Yet these too (as at a command)   295
     Halted and the flow was still,
                              (chained downpour).
     One moment a mire, then a hardened floor.
     Treacherous before, it now mocked at their steps, deceived
                              each foot. 300
     Men, horses equally, arms and armour
     Lay piled in sorry confusion.
     Now the clouds, hit by the cutting wind,
     Let fall their loads,
     Winds torn by whirlwinds,   305
     Skies rent by swollen hailstones.
     The very clouds were tatters
                              and fell about their armour.
     The frozen ice heaved like ocean waves.
     The earth was covered by the storm of snow,   310
     The stars were covered
     And the rivers stuck to their banks
                              covered too.
     Only Caesar above it –
     Leaning on his great spear,   315
     With sure strides breaking across the cracking fields,
     Like Hercules, Amphitryonides, striding, head-high,

From the Caucasian peak,
Or like a frowning Jupiter,
Rushing *verticibus Olympi*   320
Hurling his bolts at the doomed Gigantes.

V

'While Caesar angrily trod underfoot
                the haughty pinnacles,
Winged Rumour, wings fluttering in terror,
Took flight to the high ridges of the Palatine,   325
And with this thunder of rumours smote
Every statue in the city:
    "The fleets are on the sea,
      The whole Alps a blaze of squadrons
      Spattered with German blood."   330
Armies, *cruor*, *caedes*, fire, whole wars
Flit before their eyes.
Their hearts battered by this din
Were torn in two and much afraid.
Flight by land, said one –   335
The sea is better, said another:
The sea is now safer than our country.
Not wanting were those who favoured fight,
Accepting the command of Fate.
The people trailed from the desolate city,   340
To wherever their stunned minds moved,
                    miserabile visu.
Rome's heart is in the flight,
Beaten already the Quirites
Leave their sad homes when they hear the rumour.   345
One clutches his children in trembling hands,
One hides his family gods beneath his coat,
Leaving the sad hallway
                cursing to death the distant enemy.
Some clasp wives to their sad breasts   350
And young men who never felt a load
Clasp aged fathers,
Carrying only what they fear for most.
Others unwarily take all they have,
Carrying booty to battle.   355
In a storm at sea,
When great Auster starts to roughen the sea

And sends the driven waves toppling,
When rigging and rudder fail,
One man battens down,   360
Another looks for safe harbour, tranquil shore,
And another hoists sail to fly the storm,
Trusting his all to Fortune.

'An end to these minor catastrophes:
Pompeius Magnus with both consuls,   365
Pompey, *tremor Ponti*
Explorer if *saevus Hydaspes*,
The rock that wrecked the pirates,
For all his three triumphs that made Jupiter tremble,
For all the veneration of Pontus   370
After he sheered through its maelstrom,
And the submission of the waves of the Bosphorus,
Took to flight,
                    (*pro pudor!*)
His titles to power forgotten,   375
So fickle Fortuna might see the back
                    Of even Pompeius Magnus.

VI

124. 'Such a great Calamity overcame even the gods:
The timorousness of heaven set the seal on flight.
And through the world a gentle host of gods,   380
Abominating earth's madness, abandoned earth,
Avoiding the armies of the doomed.
First Pax, first of them all,
Bruising her white arms, hid her defeated head
In her dress, left earth in haste   385
For the implacable kingdom of Dis.
Submissive Honour her companion,
And Justitia, *crine soluto*,
Concordia sobbing in her torn dress.
The flight not all in one direction: 390
Where the realm of Erebus yawned,
Emerged in broad array the troop of Dis:
Bristling Erinys, Bellona *minax*,
Megaera with her armoury of torches,
Doom, Treachery and the pale image of Death,   395
                    lurida mortis imago.

In their midst went Furor,
Like a horse trailing broken reins,
Her bloody head held to the world
Her face pitted with a thousand wounds   400
Hid in a bloodstained helmet:
The battered shield of Mars,
                        heavy with innumerable arrows,
Gripped in her left hand,
In her right the threat of a burning torch   405
Carrying fires to earth.

VII

'The earth feels the weight of the gods,
Stars shifted, losing equilibrium,
The whole kingdom of heaven divided.
Dione first heads the armies of her Caesar,   410
Pallas moving to her side and Romulus (Mavortius)
                        beating his great spear.

Phoebus and Phoebus' sister,
And Mercury, *Cyllenia proles*, took Pompey away,
And Hercules Tirynthius like him in all his deeds.   415
        The trumpets sounded.
Discordia with her torn hair,
Raised to the gods above her Stygian head.
Clotted blood in her mouth,
Tears in her battered eyes,   420
Her teeth mailed with a scurf of rust,
Her tongue dripping with foulness,
Her face in a ring of snakes;
With bosom convulsed beneath her tattered dress,
She waved in a shaking hand a bloody torch.   425
Left Tartarus, *tenebrae Cocyti*,
Striding up to the high ridges
Of the lordly Appennines,
Vantage-point for all lands, all seas,
And the forces flooding the world.   430
From her mad breast these cries erupted:
    "To arms, ye nations – now your hearts are on fire.
    Sumite arma and throw your torches
                        into the hearts of cities.
    Whoever hides will be defeated.   435
    Let no woman lag behind, or child,
                        Or age-torn man.

Earth trembles, the ripped houses revolt.
Legem tene, Marcellus.
Concute plebem, Curio.   440
Lentulus, quench not that brave and martial ardour.
And you, son of heaven,
Why do you delay with your armies?
Why are you not battering at gates,
Tearing away town walls, hauling off treasure?   445
Can you not guard the Roman fortress, Pompey?
Look then to the walls of Epidamnus,
And dye Thessalian bays with human blood."

'All that Discordia commanded

                       came to pass on earth.'

CROTON

By the time Eumolpus had poured this out in loud tones,[1] we had finally entered Croton. We stopped at a little inn and next day, looking for a house on a larger scale, we fell in with a crowd of legacy hunters, who asked us what sort of people we were and where we came from. Following our concerted plan we told them with excessive volubility where we were from and who we were, and there was no doubt that they believed it all. Immediately they did their best to outdo each other in putting their financial resources at Eumolpus' service.

*

All of them vied with each other to get into Eumolpus' good graces with presents.[2]

*

125. While all this was taking place in Croton over a considerable period of time . . . Eumolpus, full of happiness, forgot the earlier state of his fortunes to such an extent that he boasted to his entourage that no one in the place could stand up against his influence; with the good offices of his friends they would get off scot-free for any crime they committed.

Personally, although I fattened myself up every day with more and more of these over-abundant luxuries and thought Fortune had taken her eyes off me, yet quite often I was worried not from any real cause, but from thinking of my usual luck: 'What if some shrewd legacy-hunter sends a spy to Africa and uncovers our whole plot? What if Eumolpus' servant gets tired of our present happy position, produces evidence for our friends, and exposes the whole scheme by his envy and treachery? We'll obviously have to run away again and just when we were rid of it, we'll reduced to poverty again for a fresh period of beggary. Heavens above, how awful it is to live outside the law – one is always expecting what one rightly deserves.'[3]

*

126. *(Circe's maid, Chrysis, is talking to Polyaenus, i.e. Encolpius)*

'You know you're attractive, so you put on an arrogant air and sell your favours instead of giving them free. Otherwise what's the point of your combed wavy hair, the heavy make-up, the soft sulkiness in your eyes, the self-conscious walk, the carefully measured steps? What's the object unless you're prostituting your good looks for money? You look at me – I'm no fortune-teller, and I don't go in for astrology, but I tell people's characters from their faces, and now I've seen your walk, I know what you have in mind.[4] If you're selling what I've come for, there's a customer waiting. Or if you're giving it free – which is nicer – put me under an obligation for your kindness. You say you're just a poor slave, but you're only exciting her desire to boiling point. Some women get heated up over the absolute dregs and can't feel any passion unless they see slaves or bare-legged messengers. The arena sets some of them on heat, or a mule-driver covered with dust, or actors displayed on the stage. My mistress is one of this type. She jumps across the first fourteen seats from the orchestra and looks for something to love among the lowest of the low.'[5]

I said in a voice full of sweetness: 'Tell me, are you the one who is in love with me?'

The maid laughed heartily at such an unlikely notion.

'I wouldn't make you so pleased with yourself. I have never yet gone to bed with a slave, and heaven forbid I should ever see a lover of mine crucified. That's for ladies who kiss the whip-marks. Even though I'm a servant, I've never sat anywhere except in the lap of knights.'

I couldn't help some surprise at such contrasting sexual desires. I thought it very strange that the maid should cultivate the superior outlook of a lady and the lady the low taste of a maid.

Then as the joking continued, I asked her to bring her mistress to the copse of plane-trees. The girl agreed to the suggestion. She tucked up her tunic and turned into the laurel grove bordering the avenue. In a very short time she brought out of the shadows a woman who was lovelier than any work of art, and led her to my side.

No words could do justice to her charms – whatever I said

would not be enough. Her curls flowed naturally over the whole
breadth of her shoulders and waved back at the hairline from
her exquisitely narrow brow. Her eyebrows ran down to the
contour of her cheeks and almost met over the bridge of her nose.
Her eyes were brighter than stars shining in a dark sky. Her
nostrils curved in a little, and her little mouth was as Praxiteles[6]
imagined Diana's.[7] Her chin, her neck, her hands, the pearly
lustre of her feet clasped by a thin gold chain – each in turn
would have put Parian marble[8] to shame. Then for the first time
I despised my old passion for Doris.[9]

*

What has happened, Jove, what has happened
To make you throw down your arms,
To become an old story in heaven,
To disdain these terrestrial charms?

Now here was a worthy occasion
To beetle your brows and put on
Two horns or cover your white hair
With the feather and beak of a swan.[10]

Here is a real Danaë –
She would kindle your lust even higher.
One touch, one mere touch of her body
And your limbs would melt in the fire.

*

127. She was delighted and smiled so sweetly I thought the full
moon had shown her face out of a cloud. Modulating her voice
to her gesture, she said:

'If you don't find a lady distasteful, one who had a man for
the first time only this year, let me recommend myself as your
girl-friend, young man. Of course, you have a boy-friend too – I
wasn't ashamed of making inquiries, you see – but what's to
stop you adopting a girl-friend as well? I shall come on the same
footing. You have only to agree to put up with my kisses as well,
whenever you like.'

'On the contrary,' I replied, 'I must beg you, you beautiful
creature, not to disdain to take on a poor stranger as one of your
adorers. You will find him religiously devoted if you permit him

to worship you. And don't imagine I am entering this temple of Love without making an offering. I shall sacrifice my boy-friend for you.'

'What?' she said. 'Are you making me a sacrifice of the boy you cannot live without, the lips you cling to, the one you love the way I want to love you?'

As she said this, there was such charm in her voice, such a sweet sound caressed the enraptured air that it was as though the song of the Sirens sang through the breezes. And then in my amazement – the whole sky seemed somehow brighter – it occurred to me to ask the goddess her name.

'So my maid hasn't told you,' she said, 'that I'm called Circe? Not that I am the child of the Sun – my mother never stopped at will the course of the revolving heavens. Yet if the fates unite us, I shall have something to thank heaven for. A god, in fact, is already working his mysterious purposes to some end. It is not by chance that Circe is in love with Polyaenus – a great flame is always kindled between these names.[11] Take me in your arms, if you wish: there is no reason to fear any prying eyes. Your beloved boy is a long way from here.'

Saying this, Circe drew me, entwined in arms softer than swans-down, on to the grassy mound.

> Flowers such as the Earth Mother spread on Ida's top
> When Jove and his legitimate love united [12]
> (His breast one raging fire).
> Roses, violets, soft rushes glinting there
> And the white lilies smiling
>   from the green meadows.
> Such a place cried for love on its soft grass
> The day brightened like a blessing
> On our secret amours.

Side by side there in the grass we kissed a thousand times in our love-play as the prelude to more strenuous pleasures.

*

128. (*Circe to Polyaenus*) 'What is it?' she said. 'Do my kisses offend you in some way? Does my breath smell through not eating? Have I neglected to wash under my arms? If it's not these, am I to suppose you're somehow frightened of Giton?'

Flushed with obvious embarrassment, I even lost whatever virility I had. My whole body was limp, and I said:

'Please, my queen, don't add insults to my misery. I've been bewitched.'

*

(Circe) 'Tell me Chrysis – but the truth, mind! Am I somehow unpleasant? Am I untidy? Am I somehow ruining my beauty because of some natural defect? Don't deceive your mistress. I've done something wrong.'

Then as Chrysis remained silent, she snatched a mirror from her and after trying every expression that lovers usually put on to amuse each other, she threw off her dress, rumpled from contact with the ground, and rushed into the shrine of Venus. Like a guilty thing, trembling as though I'd seen a horrible vision, I began asking myself mentally whether I had been robbed of the chance of true pleasure.

> Any soporific midnight an instance,
> When the unfocused eyes are dream-deluded:
> The spaded earth exposing gold,
> Guilty hands fingering criminal gains
> And a deep fear in the mind
> That mere awareness of gold about the person
> May dislodge it
>   even from the breast pocket.
> The images of joy recede from the mocked brain;
> Reality returns
> To a heart longing for lost pleasures
> Lingering in old illusions.

*

(Giton to Encolpius) 'So thank you for loving me in such an honourable Platonic way.[13] Alcibiades himself couldn't have been safer when he slept in his teacher's bed.'

*

129. *(Encolpius to Giton)* 'Honestly, dear lad, I can't realize I'm a man, I don't feel it. The part of my body that once made me an Achilles[14] is dead and buried.'

*

The boy was frightened of being detained privately and giving rise to gossip, so he rushed off and took refuge in the inner part of the house.

*

Chrysis entered my room and gave me a letter from her mistress, which read as follows:

Dear Polyaenus,

If I were a sensual woman, I would complain I had been tricked. As it is, I am positively glad of your impotence. I've played too long in the mere shadows of pleasure. However what I want to know is how you are and whether you got home on your own feet. Doctors say a man can't walk if he has no strength. I'll tell you something, my young friend – beware of paralysis. I have never seen a sick man in such great danger – you are as good as dead, for heaven's sake. If that same chill got into your knees and hands, you could send for the undertaker. To come to the point: although I was deeply offended, still I don't begrudge a sick man his prescription. If you wish to get better, consult Giton. You will get your strength back, I can tell you, if you sleep without your darling boy for three days. As far as I am concerned, I'm not afraid of meeting someone who will like me less. The mirror doesn't lie, nor does my reputation.

Get well soon – if you can.

Circe

When Chrysis saw I had read the whole insulting screed, she said:

'These things tend to happen, particularly in this part of the country, where women even drag down the moon. ... This problem will be taken care of too. Just write a soothing reply to my mistress and restore her good spirits with a frank and natural answer. If the truth must be told, from the moment she was so insulted, she has not been her usual self.'

130. I gladly took the maid's advice and wrote some such letter as this:

My dear Circe,

I admit I have done many bad things. After all, I am a man and still young. But I have never till today committed a really deadly sin. You have the culprit's confession. Whatever you order, I deserve it. I have been guilty of treachery, I've killed a man, and I've robbed a temple – find a punishment for these crimes. If you wish to kill me, I'll come and bring my sword. If you are content with just whipping, I'll run naked to my beloved. Remember this one thing, not I but my instruments were at fault. The soldier was ready, but I had no weapons. Who caused this trouble I don't know. Perhaps my thoughts ran ahead of my lagging body; perhaps in my keen desire to enjoy every last thing, I used up the pleasure in dallying. I have not discovered what I did. Still, you tell me to beware of paralysis – as though it could become any worse now, now it has deprived me of the ability to possess you of all women. However this is what my excuses come to: I will give you satisfaction, if you allow me to atone for my fault.

Your slave,
Polyaenus

*

I sent Chrysis off with this promise and carefully attended to my treacherous body. Omitting a bath, I used a very moderate amount of oil to rub myself down, then dining on more solid dishes than usual, onions and the heads of snails without seasoning, I drank a sparing quantity of wine. After this, setting myself up with a very gentle stroll before bed, I went to my room without Giton. So great was my anxiety to placate her that I was afraid my boy-friend might impair my virility.

131. Getting up next day without any mental or physical strain, I went down to the same grove of plane-trees, although I was nervous of such an inauspicious place, and began waiting among the trees for my guide, Chrysis. I walked round for a short while and I had only just sat down where I had been the day before when she arrived bringing a little old woman with her. When she greeted me, she said:

'How are you, my fine friend? Have you begun to feel in better spirits?'

The old woman brought out of her dress a string consisting of various coloured threads twisted together and bound it round my neck. Then mixing some dust with spittle, she took it on her middle finger and ignoring my repugnance, marked my forehead with it.

*

After completing this spell, she instructed me to spit three times and drop down my chest, again three times, some pebbles which she had charmed and wrapped in purple. Then she began to test my virility with her hands. Faster than you could speak, the nerves obeyed the command, and the little old woman's hands were filled with a mighty throbbing. Highly elated, she said: 'Do you see, my dear Chrysis, do you see how I've started a hare for others to hunt?'[15]

*

The tall plane-tree disposes summer shade,
Metamorphosed Daphne[16] nearby, crowned with berries.
Cypresses tremulous, clipped pines around
Shuddering at their tops.
                              Playing among them
A stream with wandering waters,
Spume-flecked, worrying the stones
                              with a querulous spray.
                                        A place fit for love.
Witness the woodland nightingale,
                    and Procne[17] turned urban swallow –
Everywhere amid the grass and soft violets,
Their woodland homes a hive of song.

*

She lay relaxed, her marble neck resting on a golden couch, and she beat the tranquil air[18] with a branch of flowering myrtle. When she saw me, she blushed a little. Then when everyone had gone, and I had sat down beside her at her invitation, she placed the branch over my eyes, and with this wall between us she became bolder.

'How are you, you paralytic? Have you come intact today?'

'Why ask me?' I said. 'Try me!' and I threw myself bodily into her arms and kissed her till I could kiss no more – no magic spells there.

*

132. Her physical charms were so inviting she impelled me to make love to her. Our lips ground greedily together in kiss after kiss. Our locked hands discovered every possible method of making love. Our bodies wrapped in a mutual embrace united even our very breaths.[19]

*

Smarting from these open insults, the lady finally rushed to have her revenge. She called her attendants and had them beat me. And not content with such a drastic punishment she called all her wool workers and the lowest types of servant and had them spit at me. I put my hands over my eyes, and without any begging for mercy because I knew what I deserved, I was flung through the door. Proselenus was thrown out too, Chrysis was beaten, and the whole household gloomily muttered to each other and wondered who had lowered their mistress's high spirits.

*

This was some compensation for my misfortunes and encouraged me a little. I concealed the marks of the whips with some doctoring so that my ill-treatment would neither amuse Eumolpus nor sadden Giton. Then I did the only thing possible to save my face, I feigned weariness; and wrapped up in bed, I directed the whole blaze of my anger on what had been the cause of all my troubles.

> Three times I took the murd'rous axe in hand,
> Three times I wavered like a wilting stalk
> And curtsied from the blade, poor instrument
> In trembling hands – I could not what I would.
> From terror colder than the wintry frost,
> It took asylum far within my crotch,
> A thousand wrinkles deep.
> How could I lift its head to punishment?
> Cozened by its whoreson mortal fright
> I fled for aid to words that deeper bite.

And so leaning on my elbow I made quite a speech, abusing it for its disobedience. 'What have you got to say?' I said, 'you insult to mankind, you blot on the face of heaven – it's improper to give you your real name when talking seriously. Did I deserve this from you – that you should drag me down to hell when I was in heaven? That you should betray me in the prime of life and reduce me to the impotence of the last stages of decay? Go on, give me my death certificate.' As I poured this out angrily:

> She held her eyes averted and down-cast,
> Nor altered aught her face at this address
> Than supple willow or drooping poppyhead.[20]

Once this vile abuse was finished, I began to regret talking like this, and I blushed inwardly for forgetting my sense of shame and bandying words with a part of the body that more dignified people do not even think about. Then after rubbing my brow for some time, I said to myself: 'Still, where's the harm in relieving my feelings by some natural abuse? Anyway, how is it we curse such parts of the body as the stomach or the throat and even the head, when we have the occasional headache? In fact, didn't Ulysses have an argument with his heart, and don't some tragic heroes abuse their eyes as though they could hear them? People with gout curse their feet, people with arthritis their hands, people with ophthalmia their eyes, and when people stub their toes, they often blame the pain on their feet.

The Censor[21] frowns and knits his brows,
The Censor wants to stop us,
The Censor hates my guileless prose,
My simple modern opus.
My cheerful unaffected style
Is Everyman when in his humour,
My candid pen narrates his joys,
Refusing to philosophize.

Find me any man who knows
Nothing of love and naked pleasure.
What stern moralist would oppose
Two bodies warming a bed together?
Father of Truth, old Epicurus[22]
Gave philosophy a soul
And taught, his followers assure us,
Love is Life's sovereign goal.

There is nothing on earth more misleading than silly prejudice and nothing sillier than moral hypocrisy.

*

133. After finishing this speech, I called Giton and said:
'Tell me, my dear, but on your honour. That night Ascyltus stole you away from me, did he stay awake and do anything bad to you or was he content with a lonely and honourable night?'

The lad touched his eyes and solemnly swore that Ascyltus had offered him no violence.

*

Kneeling on the threshold, I offered up a prayer to the hostile god:

'Comrade of Nymphs,[23] comrade of Bacchus,
Deity of the rich forests
          whom fair Dione appointed,
Famed Lesbos, green Thasos obey your wishes
And the Lydians spread over the seven rivers
Bow before you –
They built you a temple in your own Hypaepa –
Come to me, protector of Bacchus, darling of Dryads,
Hear my timid orisons.
I come before you –
          unsaddened by my blood-soaked hands.[24]
I was no enemy of religion
          when I robbed that temple.
Need and the attrition of poverty,
          these were the agents –
Not my true self.
The man who sins through poverty
          is a venial offender.
My prayer is:
    Relieve my mind,
    Forgive the venial sin.
When fortune smiles,
I shall not let your glory go unthanked –
A horned goat, sire of his herd,
Will come to your altars,
The farrow of a grunting sow, a milky victim,
Will come to your altars.
Wine of the most recent vintage will foam in the chalices
And inebriated young men
Will march in triumph
Three times around your shrine.'

*

While I was doing this and keeping a close eye on the dear departed, the old woman entered the temple. She looked a sight with her torn hair and black clothes. She put a hand on me and led me outside the vestibule.

*

134. (*Proselenus to Encolpius*) 'Were they witches who enervated you? Did you tread on some filth in the dark at a crossroad? Or a corpse? You haven't even redeemed yourself with the boy. You're soft, weak, and tired, like a cart-horse on a slope; you just wasted your efforts and sweated for nothing. And not content to be a sinner on your own, you've put heaven against me too.'

*

And without any protest from me, she led me back and through into the priestess's room where she threw me on a bed, and snatching a rod from behind the door, still without a murmur from me, gave me a thrashing. If the rod had not shattered at the first stroke and lessened the force of the blows, she might perhaps have broken my arms and head as well. I howled particularly at the cuts aimed at my groin. With my tears flowing freely I leant my head on the mattress and covered it with my right hand. She was equally upset and tearful. She sat on the other side of the bed and complained in tremulous tones of living too long, until the priestess came in and found us.

'Why have you come to my room like mourners to a funeral?' she said. 'Especially on a holiday, when even miserable people show a smile.'

*

'Oh, Oenothea,[25] it's this young man you see here,' she said, 'he was born under an evil star. He can't make a sale to boy or girl. You've never seen a man so unlucky – he's got a piece of wet leather, not a penis. In fact, what do you think of someone who could get out of Circe's bed without having had any enjoyment?'

Hearing this, Oenothea sat down between us and shook her head for a time.

'I'm the only one who can cure that trouble,' she said. 'And don't think I'm working in the dark – I want the young man to sleep a night with me . . .

*

'. . . if I don't make it as stiff as a horn :

All visible things obey me. At my wish
The flowering earth grows dry, the sap sluggish.

At my wish its benisons spill forth.
Rocks and jagged cliffs gush out Nile waters;
For me the ocean flattens its white tops;
The zephyrs lay their blasts hushed before my feet.
The rivers obey me, Hyrcanian tigers,[26] and dragon sentinels.
These are but minor accomplishments –
The orbed image of the moon descends
At the pull of my spells.
                    The Sun-god
Turns round his foaming horses
And fear-driven retraces his orbit.' *

135. I shuddered: I was terrified by such a fabulous promise and I began scrutinizing the old woman very warily.

*

'Well,' cried Oenothea, 'now do what I tell you both.'

*

And carefully washing her hands she lay on the bed and kissed me a couple of times.

*

Oenothea placed an old table in the middle of the altar and heaped red-hot coals on it. She took down an old broken cup and repaired it with some warmed pitch, then she replaced a wooden nail in the smoky wall which had come out with the wooden cup as she took it down. Wearing a square cloak, she placed a great kettle on the hearth and drew out from her larder with a fork a bag containing beans and an ancient piece of pig's cheek, very knocked about and with a thousand bruises on it. When she unfastened the string of the bag, she poured part of the beans on

---

* The MSS have also the following verses:
    Such power have words.
    The hot breath of bulls is quenched
                            by the rites of virgins;
    Sun-child Circe transformed the companions of Ulysses[27]
                            with magic spells.
    Proteus becomes what he likes.[28]
    Expert in magical experience,
    I will root Idaean trees in the sea,
    Plant rivers instead at the summit.

the table and ordered me to shell them carefully. I obeyed her instructions and with meticulous fingers separated the beans from their filthy pods. But with some caustic comments on my slowness, she took them herself, stripped the pods off with her teeth and spat them to the ground like dead flies.

*

I was amazed at the ingenious shifts of poverty and the methods followed with each individual thing:

No gleam of Indian ivory and inlaid gold,
No radiance of marble underfoot,
The earth not mocked by the earth's profusion;
Rather a thicket of husked straw on a willow frame,
New ... clay pots,
                the hasty products of cheap wheels.
A tank for the soft water-drops,
Tough platters of wicker work,
A wine-stained cup.
The walls around were a stiffness
Of dry straw and random mud –
On them a scattering of rustic nails,
And hanging there a slim broom of green rushes.
The provisions of the humble place
Hung from its smoky beam:
Bland sorb-apple
Dried savoury and raisins in bunches,
Twined in sweet-smelling wreaths.

*

In such a hut on Attic ground
Lived Hecale,[29] hostess worthy of heaven,
Whom in the years of eloquence
The Muse of old Battiades described
For posterity's admiration.

*

136. She also cut off a small piece of the meat, ... and as she put back the cheek, which was as old as she was, into the cupboard with the fork, the rotten stool, which she had used to give her the necessary height to reach, broke and the weight of the old woman sent her sprawling into the hearth. The neck of the

kettle was broken and put out the fire, just as it was beginning to blaze up. She burnt her elbow on a blazing piece of wood and blackened the whole of her face in the cloud of ashes she stirred up. I got to my feet in alarm and set the old woman on her feet, not without some amusement ... To prevent anything delaying the sacrifice, she immediately rushed off to some place in the neighbourhood to relight the fire ...

I went to the door of the cottage ... when all of a sudden three geese – I suppose they generally got their daily rations from the old woman at midday – made a rush at me and to my alarm surrounded me with an obscene and infuriated hissing. One tore my tunic, another undid my shoe-laces and tugged at them, and the ring-leader in this savage assault went so far as to peck at my leg with its serrated beak. Without any further trifling, I tore a leg off the table and with this weapon began hammering at the most ferocious of the birds. And not content with a quick stroke, I avenged myself by killing the goose:

> They fled like the heavenward flight
> Of Stymphalian birds [30]
> Under Hercules' coercion;
> Like the dribbling Harpies,
> > foilers of Phineus
> (his banquet drenched in poisonous bile);
> The aether tremulous and afraid,
> The heavenly kingdoms confused
> At the strange wailing ...

*

The rest had already snapped up the beans, which had rolled over the whole floor; and now, deprived, I suppose, of their leader, they had returned to the temple.

Pleased by my profitable revenge, I threw the dead goose behind the bed and bathed the wound in my leg, which was not deep, with vinegar. Then fearing a scene, I made up my mind to leave. Collecting my clothes I made my way out of the cottage, but I had not crossed the threshold when I noticed Oenothea on her way with a potful of fire. I naturally retreated, threw off my clothes and stood in the doorway as though waiting for her impatiently.

She placed the fire in the hearth – it was in some dry reeds – and after putting a lot of sticks on top, she started to explain her delay. Her friend had not let her go without her getting through the usual three drinks.

'Here,' she said, 'what have you done while I was away? Where are the beans?'

I thought I'd done something to be proud of, so I gave her the whole battle in detail, and to cheer her up I offered her the goose as compensation for the loss. When the crone saw it she raised such a loud shrill shriek[31] that you'd have thought the geese were back in the place again. Naturally confused, in fact thunderstruck, as though my action was some strange crime, I asked her why she was so furious and why she was more sorry for the goose than for me.

137. She beat her hands together:

'You criminal,' she said, 'why go on talking? You've no idea of the great offence you've committed. You've killed Priapus' darling, the pet goose of all the ladies. Don't think it's a mere nothing you've done. If the authorities knew of this, you'd be crucified. You've polluted my house with bloodshed – the first time it's ever happened, and you've given any enemy who likes an opportunity to expel me from my post as priestess.'

*

'Please don't shout,' I said, 'I'll give you an ostrich in place of the goose.'

*

While I stood stupefied at all this, and she sat on the bed and wailed over the fate of the goose, Proselenus arrived with the provisions for the sacrifice. Seeing the dead goose, she asked how it happened and then began to cry copiously herself, and said she was deeply sorry for me – as though I'd killed my father, not a communal goose.

So, bored and tired of it all, I said:

'Tell me, can one pay compensation for sacrilege?

*

... even if I insulted you, even if I'd committed a murder. Look, here are two gold pieces – you can buy gods and geese with this.'

When Oenothea saw them, she said:

'I apologize, young man. I'm worried for your sake. It's a sign of friendship, not vindictiveness. We'll do our best to prevent anyone knowing. You just pray heaven forgives you for what you've done.'

> With money you've a yacht with a following breeze;
> With money you've got Lady Luck on her knees;
> You could marry Danaë [32] with cash on the nail
> And make her and her father believe the same tale.
> If you're poet or speaker, the crowd thinks you're great,
> If you plead at the bar, Cato [33] sounds second-rate.
> You can prove and disprove, be a lawyer of note,
> Whose cases are vital for textbooks to quote.
> Whatever you wish for, if you can disburse,
> Will be there – you've a Jupiter locked in your purse.

*

She put under my hands a cup of wine and after rubbing my outstretched fingers clean with leeks and garlic, she threw some filberts into the wine, murmuring a prayer. She made various deductions from whether they came to the top or settled, but I didn't fail to notice that the air-filled nuts naturally stayed on the surface of the liquid, while the heavy nuts with an unrotted kernel were carried to the bottom.

*

Cutting open the goose's breast, she extracted a massive liver and foretold my future from it. And more, to get rid of every trace of the crime, she cut up the whole goose, spitted the pieces and prepared an elegant feast for a man who a little while ago, by her account, was doomed.

*

Cups of strong wine passed quickly round as this went on ...

*

138. Oenothea brought out a leather dildo: this she rubbed with oil and ground pepper and crushed nettle seed, and began inserting it gradually up my anus.

*

The vicious old woman then sprinkled my thighs with this liquid.

*

She mixed the juice of cress with some southern-wood, and after soaking my genitals in it, she took a green nettle-stalk and slowly began whipping me everywhere below the navel.

*

Although staggering with drink and desire, the old crones took the same route and followed in my tracks for several streets, shouting 'Stop thief!' But I got away, my toes bleeding through my headlong rush.

*

'Chrysis, who detested your earlier position, intends to follow you in your present situation even at the risk of her life.'[34]

*

'What did Ariadne or Leda[35] have to compare with her loveliness? What could Helen or Venus do against her? Paris himself, judge in the contest of goddesses, if he'd seen her with his roving eyes when making his comparison, he would have given up Helen *and* the goddesses for her. If I were allowed just to take a kiss, or embrace that divine and heavenly breast, perhaps my body would recover its strength and the parts that I'm positive are drugged by some witches' brew would revive. It's not her insults that make me reluctant. I overlook the whipping. I was thrown out, but I regard that as a joke. Only let me back into her good graces . . .'

*

139. I tossed and turned in bed, groping continually and pretending it was my beloved.

*

Others have been hounded by gods and implacable fate,
Not I alone.[36]
Hercules hounded from Argos,
And propping heaven on his shoulders.
Impious Laomedon
And those two angry immortals:
He paid the price of his offences.
Pelias felt the weight of Juno.
Then there was Telephus –
He took up arms in his ignorance
Even Ulysses went in fear of Neptune's power.
Now I too take my stand among these –
Over land and white Nereus' sea, I am hounded
By the mighty rage of Priapus of Hellespont.

*

I started by asking dear Giton whether anyone had been looking for me.

'No one today,' he said, 'but yesterday quite an elegant lady came to the door and after a long conversation, when she wore me out with irrelevant chatter, she finally said you ought to be punished and you would suffer as a slave should if you took offence and persisted in your ill-feelings.'

*

I had not yet finished when Chrysis arrived and clasped me in a most effusive embrace, saying:

'I've got you just as I'd hoped. You are my only desire, my only pleasure in life. You will never put out the fire I feel unless you quench it with my blood.'

*

One of the new servants hurried up and swore that our master was furious with me because I'd been absent from my duties for over two days. I'd be well advised to prepare some suitable excuse, as it was highly unlikely his rage would simmer down without someone getting the whip.

*

140. There was one highly respectable matron, Philomela by

name, who had extorted a great many legacies while she had the advantages of her youth. By now she was an old woman and her bloom had gone, so she forced her son and daughter on childless old men and by means of these deputies managed to continue her profession. Naturally she came to Eumolpus and entrusted her children to his firm and upright nature. She told him she was putting herself and her dearest wishes in his care. He was the only one on earth who could manage every day to instil sound principles into young people. In fact, she was leaving her children in Eumolpus' house so that they could listen to his talk – which was the only legacy that could be given to young people.

She was as good as her word. She left the very pretty daughter with her young brother in his room and pretended she was going off to the temple to say her prayers.

Eumolpus, who was such a sexual miser that he even regarded me as a boy, did not hesitate a moment to invite the girl to be initiated in certain matters in which she was backward. But he had told everyone that he had gout and a weakness in the loins, and if he did not keep up this pretence, he would be in danger of ruining the whole show. So to ensure that the lie was not discredited, he actually asked the girl to sit on top of the upright nature to which she had been entrusted, and ordered Corax to get under the bed he was lying in and with his hands placed on the floor to move his master with his own thighs. He followed these orders gently and the expertise of the girl responded with similar movements. When things were looking forward to the desired result, Eumolpus called loudly to Corax to hurry. Placed in this way between his servant and his lady friend the old man looked as though he was enjoying himself on a swing. Eumolpus repeated this performance amid howls of laughter, including his own.

Not unnaturally I for my part, not to get out of the habit through lack of practice, approached the brother, as he admired his sister's tricks through the key-hole, and tried to see if he would accept my advances. The well-trained little fellow did not withdraw from my caresses but divine hostility dogged me in this situation too.

*

'There are mightier gods who have restored me to full health. Mercury,[37] who leads souls away and leads them back, by his kindnesses has returned me what was cut off by the hand of vengeance. So you may take it that I am more favoured than Protesilaus[38] or anyone like him in history.'

With this I lifted my tunic and showed all I had to Eumolpus. At first he was horrified, then to convince himself fully, he held in both hands the gifts of the gods.

*

'Socrates, the glory of gods and men,[39] used to boast that he had never visited a tavern and never allowed himself to look in on a crowded assembly. There is nothing more helpful than words of wisdom.'

*

'All of this is true,' I said, 'no one should come to grief quicker than those who are after what belongs to others. How would a confidence man or a pickpocket survive, if he didn't drop little boxes or chinking bags into the crowd to hook his victims? Dumb animals are snared with food and men can't be caught unless they are nibbling hopefully at something.'

*

141. 'The ship with your money and servants has not arrived from Africa as you promised. The legacy-hunters are already drained dry and are cutting down their liberality. So if I'm not mistaken, fortune is beginning to have her regrets again.'

*

'All those who have legacies in my will, except for my freedmen, will receive them only on this condition – that they cut up my corpse and eat it in front of the people.'

*

'We know that among certain races the custom of the dead being eaten by their relations is still observed. In fact, sick people are often reproached for causing their flesh to deteriorate. I therefore advise my friends not to shrink from my request, but eat my body in the same spirit as they damned my soul.'

*

The enormous reputation of his money blinded the eyes and hearts of the poor fools.

Gorgias was ready to carry out the terms.

*

'I see nothing to fear in your stomach revolting. It will obey your command if you promise it a lot of luxuries as compensation for one hour's disgust. Just close your eyes and pretend you are eating a million sesterces, not human offal. Then for another thing, we'll find some seasonings to change the taste. After all, no meat is pleasant by itself; it's adulterated in some way and made acceptable to the reluctant stomach. And if you want your determination to be justified by examples, there are the Sanguntines,[40] who ate human flesh when they were hard pressed by Hannibal – and they weren't expecting a legacy. The Petelians did the same in the last stages of a famine and all they were after in eating this dish was to avoid dying of starvation. When Numantia was captured by Scipio, there were some mothers found carrying around with them the half-eaten bodies of their own children.'

*

THE FRAGMENTS

THE FRAGMENTS

I

Servius ad Vergili Aen. III 57: *auri sacra fames*] *sacra* means accursed. The expression derives from a custom of the Gauls. Whenever the inhabitants of Massilia suffer from a plague, one of their poor people offers himself to be fed at the public expense for a whole year on special religious foods. Afterwards he is dressed in sprigs of sacred foliage and certain ritual clothing and led round the whole city with curses, so that the ills of the whole city will fall upon him. He is then cast out. This is in Petronius.

II

Servius ad Vergili Aen. XII *159* (on the feminine gender of nouns ending in -tor): If, however, the nouns are not derived from a verb, they are of common gender. Both the masculine and feminine end similarly in -tor, e.g., a male and a female *senator*, a male and female *balneator* (bath attendant), although Petronius employs a form *balneatrix* in his writings.

III

Pseudacro ad Horati epod. 5. *48*: *Canidia rodens pollicem*] he has described the bearing and movements of Canidia in a fury. Petronius, to describe someone in a rage, says 'with her thumb bitten to danger point'.

IV

Sidonius Apollinaris carminis XXIII:

145. What shall I say to you, glories of Latin eloquence,
     Cicero of Arpinum, Patavinian Livy, and Mantuan Vergil. . . .
155. And you, Arbiter, worshipper of the sacred stump
     Amid the gardens of Massilia,
     A match for Priapus of the Hellespont.

V

Priscianus institutionum VIII *16* (GL II *381*) *et* XI *29* (*ibid.* *567*) (among examples of past participles of deponent verbs with passive meaning): Petronius 'soul embraced to our breast'.

VI (= Vb)

Boethius in isagogen Porphyrii commentorum editionis primae, lib. II 32 (CSEL 48 p. 132 Brandt) 'I will do that very willingly,' I said, 'but since the morning sun, as Petronius has it, has smiled upon the roofs, let us get up and if there is anything in that matter, it will be looked into later with more careful consideration.'

VII (= VI)

Fulgentius mythologiarum I p. 12 sq. Helm: You do not know ... how much ladies shrink from satire. Although even lawyers give way under a woman's flood of words and schoolteachers do not even mumble, although oratory is silent and auctioneers hush their noise, there is one thing alone that imposes some moderation on their rage; Petronius' character Albucia comes to mind, however.

VIII (= VII)

Fulgentius mythologiarum III 8 p. 73 (on the extreme heat of myrrh resin): So Petronius Arbiter too tells us he drank a draught of myrrh to arouse his sexual desires. [This is in Book XIV. Where Quartilla is in the company of Ascyltus and Encolpius and, to allow the latter to drink a second toast, gave him Ascyltus' portion to drink. Then Quartilla says 'Has Encolpius drunk all the satyrion there was?']

IX (= VIII)

Fulgentius in expositione Virgilianae continentiae p. 98 sq.: Now we earlier explained the fable of the three-headed Cerberus by way of a quarrel and litigation in court, cf. Petronius' description of Euscios – 'he was a Cerberus in court'.[1]

X (= VIIII)

Fulgentius in expositione sermonum antiquorum 42 p. 122: A mess of various meats is called a course or dish (*ferculum*), cf. Petronius – 'after the course was brought to the table'.[2]

XI (=X)

Fulgentius in expositione sermonum antiquorum 46 p. 123:
valgia (wry twists) are contortions of the lips due to vomiting,
cf. Petronius 'with his lips wryly twisted'.

XII (=XI)

Fulgentius in expositione sermonum antiquorum 52 p. 124:
alucinare (to have hallucinations) is the term for dreaming false
dreams. It derives from *alucitae*, which we call gnats. So Petronius says, 'for the gnats (*alucitae*) were bothering my companion'.

XIII (=XII)

Fulgentius in expositione sermonum antiquorum 60 p. 126:
manubies (booty) means the ornaments that kings wear, cf.
Petronius, 'the *manubies* of so many kings found in the possession of a runaway slave'.

XIV (=XIII)

Fulgentius in expositione sermonum antiquorum 60 p. 126:
Aumatium (little eye) is the term for a public privy of the sort
found in theatres or in the circus, cf. Petronius, 'I flung myself
into a privy'.

XV (=XIIII)

Isidorum originum v 26. 7: *dolus* (guile) is mental cunning, so
termed because it beguiles (*deludat*): it does one thing and feigns
another. Petronius thinks otherwise for he says: 'What is guile,
gentlemen of the jury? Surely when something has been done
which guys the law. You have your guile, now let me tell you
about an offence (*malum*).'

XVI (=XV)

Glossarium S. Dionysii – Daniel: *petaurus* (=*petaurum*, a
spring-board or see-saw) is a kind of game, cf. Petronius, 'and at
the demand of the spring-board now higher <now lower>.[2]

XVII (=XVI)

Glossarium S. Dionysii – Daniel: Petronius, 'there was general agreement that they did not usually go through the Neapolitan tunnel without bending'.

XVIII

[*Nicolaus Perottus Cornucopiae p. 200, 26 editionis Aldinae anni 1513*: Cosmus was also an excellent manufacturer of perfumes and Cosmian perfumes are named after him. The same author has 'and though he be smothered in a whole jugful of Cosmus (Juvenal 8, 86). Petronius, 'bring us, he said, a box of Cosmian'.]

XIX

Terentianus Maurus de metris (GL VI *p. 399*):

> We see that poet Horace
> Nowhere used such verses
> In regular succession
> But the Arbiter (of eloquence)
> Packs them in his writings.
> You can recognize them
> In lines we like to chant, as:
> 'Girls of Memphis origin,
> Trained for godly services'
> 'Tinged with darkness' colouring,
> Boy with hands loquacious'.

Marius Victorinus III. 17 (GL VI *p. 138*): We know that certain lyric poets inserted some verses of this metre and form in their poems, as we find also in the Arbiter. An example of his is:

> 'Girls of Memphis origin,
> Trained for godly services'

and again,

> 'Tinged with darkness' colouring
> Choruses Egyptian.'

XX

Terentianus Maurus de metris (GL VI *p. 409, 2849-2858, 2861–2865*):

The division which we speak of
Gives the metre old Anacreon
Used in his sweet singing.
We find Petronius used it,
When he says that lyric poet
Sang songs befitting Muses
(And many others used it).
But that verse of our Petronius –
iuverunt segetes meum laborem:
(The harvest helped my labour)
I'll show you its caesura –
iuverunt starts as hexameter ...
What's left, *segetes meum laborem*
Is like *triplici vides ut ortu*
'Seest thou with triple rising
The Moon's radiance revolving
And Phoebus with swift axle
Traverse the rapid globe.'

Marius Victorinus IV I (GL VI *p. 153*): ... The metre will be Anacreontic, inasmuch as <Anacreon> used it most frequently, but many poets used it in our literature, among them the Arbiter has this in the *Satyricon*:

> 'Seest thou with triple rising
> The Moon's radiance revolving
> And Phoebus with swift axle
> Traverse the rapid globe.'

XXI

Diomedes in arte (GL I *p. 518*): From this comes also that metrical division, an example of which Petronius offers in:

> 'An old woman soaked in wine,
> A trembling on her lips.'

XXII

Servius in artem Donati (GL IV *p. 432, 22*): Again, he uses *Quirites* [citizens] only in the plural. But we read in Horace '*hunc Quiritem*' as though the nominative were this *Quiris*. Again Horace also writes '*quis te Quiritem?*' where the nominative would be *hic Quirites*, a form used by Petronius.

Pompeius in commento artis Donati (GL v *p. 167, 9*) : No one says '*hic* (this) *Quirites*' but *hi* (these) *Quirites*', although we will find the former. Look in Petronius and you will find this done with the nominative singular, and Petronius says '*hic Quirites*'.

XXIII

grammaticus de dubiis nominibus (GL v *p. 578, 23*) : *Fretum* (sea-strait) is neuter and its plural is *freta*, cf. Petronius '*freta Nereidum*' (straits of the sea-nymphs).

XXIV

Hieronymus in epistula ad Demetriadem CXXX *19* : curled and waved boys, their skins smelling of exotic musk, the virgin should avoid like some plague and poison of chastity. The Arbiter's line refers to them:

['he who always smells nice has not a nice smell'][3]

XXV

Fulgentius mythologiarum II *6 p. 45 sq. Helm (on Prometheus)* : although Nicagoras[4] tells us that his subject first gave rise to the image and describes the exposure of his liver to the vulture as a representation of spite, cf. also Petronius Arbiter's lines:

> Of the vulture's victim the poet writes,
> At the liver, clawing the lights,
> Devouring each inward part,
> But Prometheus is not his name –
> Debauchery and spite
> Are the cankers of the heart.

XXVI

So the crow flies against Nature's way
By laying eggs when the corn is high;

So the bear gives birth, then licks its cub
Into shape; fish spawn, uncoupled in love;

So Apollo's tortoise, free of parental pangs,[5]
Cares for its eggs with warm nostrils in the sand;

So the sexless bee is roused from its web of wax,
Swarms and refills its empty ranks.

Nature's not happy with a limited range,
But delights in all variety and change.

XXVII[6]

Fear invented the gods.
Lightning flashing from a high heaven,
Walls riven by the flame,
Athos kindled beneath the blow,
Phoebus descending beneath the traversed earth
For his new risings,
The decay of the moon and its glory recovered,
Stars scattered over all the world,
And the year divided into changing months.
The vice took hold – vain superstition
Bade farmers offer first fruits to Ceres,
Bind Bacchus with full palms,
Let Pales rejoice at the shepherds' hands.
A hazard to every sailor,
Neptune from the depths claims the waters,
Pallas the streets and inns.
Every guilty wish, every venal instinct
Invents its own gods in greedy competition.

XXVIII

People would rather swallow a lighted candle
Than keep a secret that smacks in the least of scandal.
The quietest whisper in the royal hall
Is out in a flash buttonholing passers-by against a wall;
And it's not enough that it's broadcast to the nation –
Everyone gets it with improvement and elaboration.
So the servant, not being sufficiently stealthy
To play the gossip and stay alive and healthy,
Dug a hole and spilt the news into that
About the ears His Majesty was hiding under the royal hat.
The hole took the story to its bosom and in less time than
    it takes to utter,
The reeds started to mutter
And begin
To let out the whole story that Midas was trying to keep in.

XXIX

Our eyes deceive, the vagrant senses lie,
When reason's overborne. Yon tower hard by
Rises four-square, but from the distant ground
Looks circular, its angles worn and round.
Full stomach shrinks from honey, often the nose
From cinnamon. No degrees of taste could interpose
Did not the senses in predestined suit
Wrangle their old continual dispute.

XXX

Dreams,
The fleeting shadow-play that mocks the mind,
Issue from no temples,
No heavenly power sends them –
Each man creates his own.
When prostrate limbs grow heavy
And the play of the mind is unchecked,
The mind enacts in darkness
The dramas of daylight.
    The shatterer of cities in war,
    Who fires unlucky towns,
    Sees flying spears, broken ranks, the death of kings,
    Plains awash with spilt blood.
    The barrister pleads again in nightmare,
    Sees the twelve tables, the court, the guarded bench.
    The miser salts away his money
    To find his gold dug up.
    The hunter flushes the woodland with his hounds.
    The sailor dreams he is doomed,
    Drags out of the sea the upturned poop,
    Or clings to it.
    The mistress scribbles a note to her lover;
    The guilty lover sends a gift . . .
    And the hound in his slumbers bays at the hare's tracks.
    [The pangs of unhappiness last
    Into the watches of the night.]

XXXI

India bore me on shores purple as Tyre,
Where the white dawn rises in an orb of fire;
A creature born here, divine honours among,

I changed a barbaric noise for the Latin tongue;
Delphic Apollo, dismiss your every swan –
My parrot voice a worthier myrmidon.

XXXII

Shipwrecked, a sailor finds another
                stunned by the same blow
And tells his story.
Crops ruined by hail,
                a whole year's labour with them,
The farmer weeps out his troubles
On a breast similarly afflicted.
At funerals the bereaved weep in concert –
Death the leveller.
We too will hammer at the stars
                with antiphonal complaints.
I have heard that prayers
Fly more bravely linked.

XXXIII

You send me golden apples, Marcia dear,
You send me gifts of shaggy chestnut too;
For those I'm grateful, but if you came here,
You'd bring your choicest gift, my love, just you.
And if you wish, crab-apples you may bring,
Your honied lips would make them sweet to taste.
Yet if you must deny my welcoming,
Just kiss the fruit; I'll eat it up in haste.

XXXVI

In a soldier's bonnet there nested a dove
To prove the alliance of Mars and of Love.

XXXVII

A Jew may adore his god in the sky
And pour out his woes in the ears of the sky,
But unless he will shorten his scabbard to see
That the tip of his penis will always hang free,
He'll be driven from home to a city in Greece[7]
And spend all his Sabbaths – eating in peace.

*

Brave hands are the one nobility,
Sole sign of a heart that is free.

XXXVIII

My bed was soft, the early night was bliss.
My drowsy eyes surrender – Love broke my rest
And shook me by the hair in wild protest.
Nails ripped my flesh. 'To waste a night like this!
You're mine,' he said, 'You broke a thousand hearts,
Can you, hard-hearted, lie alone and rest?'
I leap from bed, barefoot and barely dressed;
I try each road, but all roads are false starts.
I run, but hate to go or to retreat,
Then stand ashamed to halt, so late abroad.
No song of birds, no watchdog even roared,
No human voice, no bustle in the streets.
Alone of all, I fear my bed and sleep:
At your command, great Love, your watch I keep.

XL

Each to his taste: for what she scorns
He likes; roses *she* plucks, *he* thorns.

XLI

Autumn had shattered the shadows' glowing line,
The slack-reined sun looked for colder skies,
The plane-tree's leaves were falling and the vine
Had stripped to count its grapes: before our eyes
The old year's promises were redeemed.

XLIII

I should love my wife like my income:
But I must confess to my shame
That I wouldn't love my income
If I thought it would stay the same.

XLIV

Hero, leave your home for newer worlds.
For you now dawns a mightier day;
Be strong and the Danube, that last boundary,
The icy North and the peaceful Egyptian realms,
The nations of the rising and setting suns,
Will all greet you by name: Ithacan, descend
A greater Ithacan, upon those foreign sands.

XLV

There's some use in everything, sometime, somehow –
In trouble, what you've thrown away seems so useful now;
When the boat goes down and the strongroom bullion too,
It's the floating oars that save the drowning crew;
When the trumpet sounds, the sword's at the rich man's throat,
And the poor man, watching the battle, sneers in his ragged coat.

LIII

Beauty is not enough; who wishes to be fair
Must not content herself with average care.
Talk, be witty and smile to show your wit –
If Nature's unaided, nothing comes of it.
Art is Beauty's aid, her finest dress:
Beauty, if scornful, dies of nakedness.

LIV[8]

Its joys are short and nasty
And end in quick disgust
So let us not be hasty:
In blind and beastly lust
Love wanes, its glow departing –
So let's be slow in starting;
Let's lie here sharing kisses
On an endless holiday.
There's no sweeter rest than this is
(Without a blush to pay),
An endless new beginning
That never dies away.

LV

Before my birth the gods, they say,
Discussed what sex I'd be.
'Boy!' said Phoebus; 'Girl!' said Mars;
Said Juno, 'I disagree.'
So I was born hermaphrodite,
But how was I to die?
The goddess was first with the answer:
'The sword!' Said Mars, 'The cross!'
But Phoebus decided on drowning,

So I had to die of them all.
A tree hung over a stream,
Wearing my sword, I climbed –
A slip, we were driven together:
My feet caught in a branch,
My head dipped into the stream –
Not woman, not man, yet both:
River and Sword and Cross.[9]

LIST OF CHARACTERS*

AGAMEMNON: Professor of Rhetoric at Puteoli, with whom Encolpius is arguing at the opening of the work. He takes the three heroes to dinner with Trimalchio. He is named after Agamemnon, leader of the Greek expedition to Troy, and his assistant is appropriately named Menelaus after Agamemnon's brother, the husband of Helen.

AGATHO: A cosmetician (74. 15).

ALBUCIA: An unknown woman (Fgt VI).

ASCYLTUS: Encolpius' companion and later enemy. In Greek his name means 'untroubled' or 'unmolested' or perhaps, as Ernout suggests, 'indefatigable'.

BARGATES: A landlord and friend of Eumolpos. The name is Semitic.

CARIO: A slave of Trimalchio. The name signifies a Carian and was a common slave name.

CARPUS: Another common slave name. Here it is the name of Trimalchio's carver (36 ff.). Literally, it means *harvest* in Greek.

CERBERUS: The three-headed watchdog of Hades. Used metaphorically in Fgt. VIII.

CHRYSANTHUS: A lately dead friend of Seleucus and others in Trimalchio's circle (42. 3).

CHRYSIS: Circe's supercilious maid (128 ff.). Literally, 'golden girl'.

CINNAMUS: Trimalchio's steward.

CIRCE: The would-be mistress of Encolpius, named after the famous witch of Colchis, wife of Jason.

CORAX: Eumolpus' hired servant. The name, often given to slaves, means literally 'raven'.

CORINTH: Trimalchio's manufacturer of Corinthian ware (50. 4).

CROESUS: Trimalchio's little favourite (64. 5). The name of a wealthy king of Lydia.

DAEDALUS: Trimalchio's ingenius cook. In mythology Daedalus was the prototype of the great inventor.

DAMA: A friend of Trimalchio's (41. 10). The name is Greek.

DIOGENES: C. Pompeius, a friend of Trimalchio's (38. 10).

* I have listed the main characters in the *Satyricon* and the 'Fragments', giving where requisite, the literal meaning of the names, which, no doubt, Petronius chose deliberately.

DIONYSUS: A young slave of Trimalchio's. In mythology, the great god of wine and ecstasy.

DORIS: Apparently a former mistress of Encolpius. Literally, 'a Dorian woman'.

ECHION: A friend of Trimalchio's, a rag-collector. Literally, a sort of plant.

ENCOLPIUS: The hero (or anti-hero) of the work. In other authors, such as Martial, his name is given to homosexual favourites. Literally, the name means 'embraced'.

ENDYMION: A mysterious boy who appears in the novel, probably due to an interpolator. In mythology, he is a beautiful and eternally sleeping youth, beloved by the moon-goddess, Selene.

EUMOLPUS: Homosexual poet, critic, and fraud, who befriends Encolpius and masterminds the affair at Croton. In Greek the name means 'sweet singer'.

EUSCIOS: A vague character mentioned in Fgt IX. Literally in Greek, 'pleasantly shadowy'.

FORTUNATA: Trimalchio's wife. Literally in Latin, 'blessed by fortune'.

GAIUS: See TRIMALCHIO.

GANYMEDES: A guest of Trimalchio's. In mythology Ganymede became cup-bearer of Zeus.

GITON: Encolpius' beloved. His name is Greek for 'neighbour'.

GORGIAS: A Crotonian legacy-hunter, who seems to stop at nothing. His famous namesake was a great orator and Sophist.

HABINNAS: Close friend of Trimalchio's, a monumental mason and one of the more important men at Puteoli.

HEDYLE: Apparently the wife of Lichas, whom Encolpius seems to have seduced (113. 3).

HERMEROS: A guest of Trimalchio's. He seems to be sitting next to Encolpius and takes exception to Ascyltus' sneers.

HESUS: A superstitious passenger on board Lichas' ship.

JULIUS PROCULUS: A guest of Trimalchio's (38. 16).

LICHAS: A ship captain from Tarentum and an old enemy of Encolpius.

LYCURGUS: A mysterious figure from some missing portion of the work; he had been a cruel host to Encolpius, who has apparently murdered him. His villa may have been the source of the trio's gold.

M. MANNICIUS: Owner of the block of flats in which Encolpius and Eumolpus are staying.

MASSA: A favourite young slave of Habinnas.

MENELAUS: Agamemnon's second in command at his school.

MENOPHILA: The mate of Philargyrus, one of Trimalchio's slaves.

NICEROS: One of the more interesting guests of Trimalchio.

OENOTHEA: A dissolute priestess of Priapus at Croton. Her name means literally 'wine-goddess'.

PANNYCHIS: An immature slave-girl, belonging to Quartilla.

PHILARGYRUS: A slave belonging to Trimalchio.

PHILEROS: A guest of Trimalchio.

PHILOMELA: A corrupt matron at Croton, who sells her children for legacies.

PHILEROS: A guest of Trimalchio.

PLOCAMUS: A guest of Trimalchio.

POLYAENUS: Encolpius' pseudonym at Croton. An Homeric epithet of Ulysses.

C. POMPEIUS: See DIOGENES.

PRIAPUS: The god of fertility who hounds Encolpius through the book and whom he constantly and inadvertently offends.

PROCULUS: See JULIUS PROCULUS.

PROSELENUS: An old bawd adept at magic.

PSYCHE: The maid of Quartilla.

QUARTILLA: Priestess of Priapus.

SCINTILLA: The wife of Habinnas.

SCYLAX: Trimalchio's dog.

SELEUCUS: A guest of Trimalchio.

SERAPA: Trimalchio's astrologer.

STICHUS: A slave of Trimalchio, who is in charge of Trimalchio's funeral arrangements.

TRIMALCHIO (the name means literally 'thrice-blessed' and is basically Semitic): The great vulgarian ex-slave, whose dinner occupies most of the extant fragments of the work.

TRYPHAENA (the root of the name is 'luxury'): A prostitute from South Italy with whom Encolpius and Giton had had dealings in some lost part of the work and who figures in 100. 7 following.

NOTES ON THE TEXT

1. Petronius' complaints in these chapters are echoed by Quintilian and Tacitus among others. The prestige of oratory under the Republic made higher Roman education primarily a training in rhetoric. Under the Empire political conditions reduced the importance of oratory enormously, but education continued in the same set mould, becoming progressively more remote from everyday life. The unreal topics of the school, briefly enumerated here by Petronius, left room only for ingenious argumentation and epigram and attention to sound and cadence. The lack of subject matter is paralleled by the attention paid to formulae and arrangement. It should be remembered, however, that Eucolpius is putting forward these criticisms for his own selfish purposes and the discussion between him and Agamemnon should not be taken as proposals for serious educational reform.

2. < *homines* >. Petronius seems here to be referring to the linguistic and thematic realism of Sophocles and Euripides, which he attributes to fifth-century Greek education. This was certainly more literary than rhetorical (the art of rhetoric was just coming in with the Sophists and was studied at a much later stage). In fact Euripides does show many signs of Sophistic rhetoric, but Petronius is right in making the point that it is at the service of real problems and not artificial set themes.

3. The nine lyric poets normally include Pindar. The others are Bacchylides, Sappho, Anacreon, Stesichorus, Simonides, Ibycus, Alcaeus, and Alcman. Corinna is sometimes added to the list and would give us the required total here. Although these lyric poets often drew extensively on the Homeric *Iliad* and *Odyssey* for both subject matter and language, yet Petronius is here probably referring to their great contributions in style and form to the development of Greek poetry. The lyric age of Greece was in its way as impressive and inventive as the age of the Homeric epics.

4. This sort of training: i.e., training in declamation on sterile themes, either in the form of *controversiae*, the ingenious discussion of complicated or unreal legal or moral problems (e.g., should sons provide for their parents, no matter what the parents have done?) or *suasoriae*, speeches recommending some course of action to an historical or fictitious character (e.g., advice to a dictator to retire into

private life). Plato's philosophical style and Demosthenes' oratorical style are in their different ways the greatest of Greek prose styles. Both belong to fourth-century Greece and of course would have had the traditional Greek literary training.

5. Petronius is here making the traditional distinction between the Attic and the Asianic styles. The first was simple and natural; the second was flowery and appealing to the emotions. Asianism proper began in the middle of the third century B.C., and thereafter the debate between the rival protagonists of the two main styles continued. There was a strong Atticist movement about the middle of the first century B.C. which looked back to the great period of Attic oratory for its models, and there was a revival of Asianism at the beginning of the second century A.D. But the struggle was perennial and sometimes resolved by compromise as with Cicero. The debate extended to more than oratory proper. Petronius' own style is clearly intended as Attic by contrast, for example, with Seneca's (cf. c. 132). In view of the perennial nature of the controversy there is no need to decide which particular period Petronius had in mind for the coming of Asianism to Athens.

6. Thucydides was the great fifth-century historian of the Peloponnesian War; Hyperides, a fourth-century Greek orator, was regarded as second only to Demosthenes. Although their styles are radically different, the one being tortuous and highly individual in style, the other being much more in touch with ordinary speech, Petronius obviously has in mind their grasp on real life and their imperviousness to sterile and academic formulae.

7. The exact technique involved here is still mysterious despite certain puzzling references in Pliny the Elder. As far as we can see, it seems to be a method of rapid sketching which allowed of easy reproductions.

8. Cicero, *Pro Caelio* 17. 41.

9. i.e., parasites who live off rich men. They are familiar characters in comedy and are credited with great shrewdness as flatterers.

10. I see no objection to the metaphor in *verba atroci stilo effoderent*, particularly if the *verba* are thought of as *lumina dicendi*.

11. C. Lucilius (*c.* 180–102 B.C.) was the earliest and most fearless Roman satirist. He boasted that he could improvise 200 verses an hour standing on one foot, a feat for which the more painstaking Horace reproaches him and his admirers.

12. The scheme of education Agamemnon offers in this poem begins with moralizing and then moves on to a more or less standard classical education in literature, and one which from all the evidence fits in with Petronius' own fairly conventional views on the right

authors and the right approach to literature. There is a certain incongruity in putting it in the mouth of Agamemnon, who seems from his behaviour at Trimalchio's house to be a fairly worthless sort of teacher, but then as Petronius has chosen his characters almost entirely from the lower and less reputable classes, he has no other mouthpiece available even for his own sincere views, and it seems part of his ironic intention that this should be so. The 'home of the Sirens' is roughly the Naples area, where Agamemnon now is, and the 'Lacedaemonian colony' may be Tarentum. The purpose of these lines is simply 'be you born in Greece or S. Italy'. Homer is to be the first author in accordance with Greek custom, then the various writers of Socratic dialogues (including Plato). Demosthenes is then followed by a course in Roman writers, probably the Roman orators, which will profit from the sound preliminary training in Greek literature. After this oratory should be left for a while in order that history may be studied, including military history and such events as Cicero's fight for the freedom of the Republic. With this training, the student may then begin writing himself.

13. I read [*quia*] *nec quo*. It is clear that Encolpius and his companions have but recently arrived in the town. Elsewhere in the work we discover certain facts about it, notably that it is near the sea and an important mercantile port. It was almost certainly Puteoli, the modern Pozzuoli.

14. I read *quosdam inter vetulas nudasque meretrices*.

15. This was *satyrion*, one of the best known of ancient aphrodisiacs. Pliny (NH 26. 10) describes its strange shapes and properties and distinguishes three kinds. It was supposed to be stimulating even if held in the hand – otherwise, as here, it was drunk in dry wine.

16. Lucretia was raped by Tarquin, son of the last Etruscan king of Rome. She was a model of wifely virtue. The story was the basis of Shakespeare's *Rape of Lucrece*. The relationship between Encolpius and Giton is of course clear. It is difficult to reproduce in translation the flavour of the words used by Encolpius, e.g., *frater*, which means literally *brother* but signifies a very different relationship.

17. This and the next episode with Quartilla occur after a lacuna. It is not unlikely that both of these episodes are misplaced in the text as we have it and perhaps came from a slightly earlier section of the work, perhaps their first arrival in Puteoli before they meet Agamemnon. In any case the present episode presupposes an adventure in the country where they steal the cloak, but through Encolpius's fault they also lose the gold which they have stolen (perhaps from the mysterious Lycurgus whom Encolpius murdered).

18. Cynics: followers of the cynical philosopher Diogenes, they professed to sneer at all normal human values, including money which they regarded as useless for happiness.

19. I retain *invidiam*.

20. Reading – *iam paene nox erat* – for *iam pene*.

21. Priapus: this is one of the many incidents involving Priapus in the extant fragments and the lost parts of the work. It is fairly clear that the general framework of the *Satyricon* is a sort of comic parody of the wrath of Poseidon against Odysseus, but with Priapus, the ancient god of sexuality and fertility, hounding Encolpius (cf. chs. 133, 139, and Fragment IV). In his more domesticated aspects in Rome he was a garden god, represented with a huge red phallus, who acts as scarecrow against birds and thieves as well as promoting vegetable fertility; in the novel, however, he is a slightly comic lord of sexuality and potency. He was originally worshipped in and around Lampsacus on the Hellespont (his sacrifice was an ass, the ancient symbol of lust), and he was a considerably more important deity than the tame Roman Priapus. For instance, legends made him the son of Dionysus and Aphrodite. His cult spread to Greece, Alexandria, and finally Rome in the period after the conquests of Alexander the Great, but he never matched his original local significance.

22. The text at this point becomes extremely fragmentary. It is quite likely that we have two collections of fragments or two recensions to deal with. The sequence of events is very confused and it is, for instance, unlikely that two *cinaedi* ('pansies', as I have translated) enter to harass Encolpius, particularly as they behave in much the same way and between each incident the atmosphere is one of jovial friendliness. It would be difficult and confusing in a translation such as this to reallocate the fragments, so I have translated them in the received order. The plot, such as it is, although jerky and repetitious, is fairly clear.

23. The Latin pun cannot be properly translated. In the original, *embasicoetas* (which I have translated 'night-cap') means both an obscene drinking-vessel and also an obscene bed-partner.

24. What follows is a sketchy parody of a Roman marriage, with veil, marriage torches, decorated marriage chamber, and even a matron of honour in the person of Quartilla.

25. This is the first obvious example of the scopophilic element that runs through the work.

DINNER WITH TRIMALCHIO

1. In Roman toasts a little wine was poured in the group as a libation to the gods. Trimalchio's pretensions to popularity with his household become even more absurd later. The masseurs, of course, are not drinking his health at all.

2. Such representations seems to have been common – mosaic examples may be seen in Pompeii and the Naples Museum. Life-like representations of the *trompe l'œil* sort was a main object of ancient art.

3. The allegory of the mural is fairly simple. Mercury as the god of trade (and thieves) is an appropriate patron for Trimalchio. Minerva as the goddess of general and technical wisdom is there to reflect Trimalchio's own high estimation of his education and capabilities. The platform or *tribunal* to which Mercury rushes him by the chin (the special bodily seat of power) is where the seats of magistrates are placed. In this case it would represent the position of *sevir*, one of the municipal officials who were in charge of the Imperial cult in the towns outside Rome. The rest of the symbolism is obvious and conventional. A line or two below, I read *multa iam* for *multaciam*.

4. The first shave was symbolic of a boy's reaching man's estate and donning the *toga virilis*. Cases are heard of, such as Nero's, where the trimmings are kept in a box. It was probably not customary and seems here a part of Trimalchio's self-importance.

5. The rods and axes were the Roman symbols of magisterial authority. Trimalchio has them as a *sevir*, a fact of which we are constantly reminded.

6. i.e. a *sevir* (see note 3 above).

7. The date of the action in Puteoli is some time in the summer. Trimalchio's lavish hospitality is such that he is boasting of being out to dinner only twice a year, which, therefore, has to be carefully noted as a reminder.

8. The first reference to Trimalchio's superstitious nature. The slave we find later warning guests not to step over the threshold on the wrong foot is another. The left was regarded by the Romans (and still is by moderns) as unlucky.

9. The seating arrangements at the dinner are confused and no satisfactory seating plan has been devised. At a Roman dinner normally three large couches were placed around a large central solid table, the diners reclining diagonally on their left sides and eating with their right hands. The fourth side was open to allow the slaves to serve the food. More than three could take their places on these couches, and it is clear from the number of guests that Trimalchio

had far more than the usual nine, the number of the Muses, even if we exclude *umbrae* (uninvited guests who would come with an invited friend), wives (e.g., Fortunata), who would just sit on the edge of a couch, and attendants such as Giton who would be at the feet of their masters. Trimalchio has also set out small tables to allow more room, and the traditional seating has been changed, Trimalchio reclining in the top place on the highest couch (no doubt in order to be nearer the bathroom). Encolpius is probably reclining below Hermeros and Habinnas will later take the honoured praetor's place on the middle couch. But the rest of the positions do not much matter.

10. This first course is typical of the rest of the dinner : elaborate servers of various precious metals; expensive delicacies such as dormice (European field-mice); and above all the attempt on the part of the cuisine to represent natural objects as something that they are not – here damsons and pomegranate seeds look like a fire beneath the griddle.

11. Trimalchio's appearance is rightly laughed at by the guests. The close crop is a sign of the slave or ex-slave; the napkin ostentatiously displays the broad purple stripe which was worn by the senatorial order on their togas; gold rings are the specific privilege of Roman knights, so Trimalchio wears a gilt ring and a gold ring studded with iron – thus sailing as close to the wind as he dares.

12. Probably the game called *latrunculi* – a game something between draughts and chess, although sometimes dice played a part in it. The object was to put an opponent's piece between two of one's own and so capture him. There is at least one Egyptian picture of a solo game, although normally it was played between two people.

13. This label has given commentators a lot of trouble. Opimius was consul in 121 B.C., but although this vintage produced long-lived wines (some bottles, almost undrinkable, surviving to the middle of the first century A.D., according to the elder Pliny), we cannot, therefore, date the time of this episode to 21 B.C. The point is that Trimalchio is trying to impress his guests with the age and quality of his wine, but no vintner puts a label like this on a bottle, unless he is trying to cheat a customer. Trimalchio does not know his dates – all he knows is that Opimian was the best (like Napoleon brandy). He is either lying or he has been cheated.

14. The skeleton is a frequent motif in fresco or mosaic on dining-room walls or house floors. Its purpose is to admonish the diners to eat, drink, and be merry, for tomorrow we die.

15. Each of the foods placed over the signs of the Zodiac is either

a sort of rebus, e.g., over Aries, *cicer arietinum* (chickpeas), or has some appropriate connexion with the sign in question, e.g., the goose is connected with rain and is placed over the rainy constellation of the Water-carrier. The rebuses will not always come through in translation, so I have substituted where necessary a reasonable English equivalent. I have made the following changes in the text: *super scorpionem* [*pisciculum marinum*] < *locustam marinam* > ... *super capricornum* < *cornutam marinam* > cf. Pliny NH 32. 11. 53. 145.

16. Pegasus was the winged horse of Bellerophon, on which he killed the Chimera.

17. The satyr Marsyas lost a musical contest with Apollo; for daring to challenge the god he was flayed alive.

18. 'Millions of millions' – the sums are generally given in sesterces, which are now calculated as worth about forty pence or fifty cents (1976). Even so the total sums, even Trimalchio's thirty million (approx. £12,000,000), will not seem impressive to us with our knowledge of modern millionaires. But we are dealing with a non-industrial, non-technological society and given this, Trimalchio is extremely rich.

19. A quotation from Vergil – *Aeneid* 2. 44. The original context was pejorative.

20. I read *talem* for *ta mel*. Trimalchio's explanation of the various types born under the different signs of the Zodiac is an amalgam of popular superstition and fairly obvious astrological symbolism. I have tried to make the connexions alleged by Trimalchio self-evident in the translation. The only ones which might cause difficulty are the following: 'those who find their own feed', i.e., independent people are generally associated with the Bull in other astrological authors; 'runaways' are born under the Virgin, because she is Astraea, who 'fled' the earth after the Golden Age and became the constellation; she is also associated with a certain astrological *nodus* or knot, hence the chain-gang association. A complete discussion may be found in J. G. W. M. de Vreese, *Petron 39 u. die Astrologie* (Amsterdam, 1927).

21. Hipparchus and Aratus: Aratus (c. 270 B.C.) was the author of two astronomical poems which survive; Hipparchus (c. 190–125 B.C.) was the greatest of the Greek astronomers.

22. Carver: I have deleted *qui altilia laceraverat*.

23. The set of puns on which this little farce depends is untranslatable. Dionysus or Bacchus, the Greek god of the vine and ecstasy, was identified by the Romans with their own god of the vine and agricultural fertility, Liber or Liber pater. The slave boy Dionysus, after imitating the various cult-aspects of Dionysus, is asked by

Trimalchio to be *Liber*, a request he takes as meaning that he is liberated (*liber* meaning free). Trimalchio goes along with this no doubt pre-arranged joke and so makes the unlikely claim that he has a *liber pater*, i.e., a free father, punning on the Italian god's name.

24. Reading with Bücheler *si simila siligine inferior esset, larvas sic.*

25. *Morra* is the modern Italian equivalent of the Roman game whereby two players put up a number of fingers and each tries to guess the total. 'Up-Jenkins' is the English term.

26. Reading *as <s>i<l>a<pi> dis*, cf. Pliny, NH 36. 17. 27. 131.

27. Reading *mentibus* with the MSS.

28. *Bestiarii*, the animal fighters, were generall put on in the morning shows and were of decidedly inferior status to the real gladiators.

29. This was one of the various types of gladiators. A 'Thracian' was comparatively lightly armed and was often matched against a 'Samnite', who was more heavily armed.

30. Read *venit < abit >.< scit qui > dem litteras.*

31. Tarracina, a town of Latium, is midway between Rome and Naples. Tarentum is at the top of the heel of Italy. The distance intervening would be about 200 miles.

32. Trimalchio's learning, like that of the Calvisius Sabinus described by Seneca, is defective and pretentious. Homer does not narrate the twelve labours of Hercules and the Cyclops did not tear off Ulysses' thumb, but had his own eye put out by that hero.

33. This is one of the famous Sybils of antiquity: she was Aeneas' guide to the underworld. Sybils were regarded as immortal, but unfortunately, grew old and withered like Tithonus, hence this reply. Cumae is just up the coast from Puteoli and, like Puteoli, it was a town colonized by Greeks.

34. Corinthian bronze was a special amalgam and highly prized, by the Emperor Augustus, for example. Trimalchio's history is as defective as his mythology. He is probably thinking of the false story that Corinthian bronze was discovered when Corinth was sacked in 146 B.C. by Mummius, but he confuses this sack with the sack of Troy (c. 1180 B.C.) and replaces Mummius by the great Carthaginian general Hannibal, who died about 183 B.C..

35. The Caesar referred to here is the Emperor Tiberius according to a similar story in Pliny.

36. Cassandra, of course, had no children; she was the Trojan priestess who became the concubine of Agamemnon and was killed by his wife Clytemnestra. Daedalus was responsible for many things,

including flying, but he did not build the Trojan horse. Niobe had twelve children, but they were killed by Apollo and Artemis because of her maternal boasting. Hermeros and Petraites were contemporary gladiators and cups like those described here have been found by archaeologists. (I read *patronus meus* for *patronorum meus*).

37. The *Cordax* was originally a coarse choral dance from old Greek comedy. It would correspond to our can-can or the bump-and-grind.

38. Atellan farces were at first improvised Italian character sketches in Oscan dialect; they revolved round certain stereotypes – Maccus, the clown, Bucco, the babbler, Pappus, the old man, etc. They had originally a certain refined and satirical humour, in fact certain Romans even wrote them, although they eventually degenerated and became more like mimes.

39. Reading < *in lectum* > *Trimalchionis*.

40. Mopsus is otherwise unknown and is perhaps an invention of Trimalchio's, unless he was some very minor writer of the period whom it is absurd to rate so highly. There is a similar absurdity in comparing Cicero, the great orator, to Publilius Syrus, his contemporary, who was only a writer of mimes. The fragment that follows is probably an imitation by Petronius.

41. The game was a great favourite with Augustus, according to Suetonius. It is impossible to translate the passage with absolute literalness, but I have kept as close to the Latin as possible. The poverty of the puns and the rebuses is equally apparent in the Latin as in the English.

42. Roman citizens did not pay tribute and manumission was a fairly common honour for a hard-working slave.

43. December was the month of the Saturnalia when a great deal of licence was allowed to slaves.

44. The liberation tax was 5 per cent of the slave's value, payable on manumission either by the master or the slave. In the next sentence I read < *nescit* > *quid faciat*.

45. The riddle has never been satisfactorily answered, despite many attempts. The most plausible answers are the shadow or the *membrum virile*.

46. Another mishmash of mythology. Diomede was a Greek hero at Troy, quite unrelated to the Cretan Ganymede, who became Jove's cup-bearer. Helen was, in fact, the sister of Castor and Pollux. Helen was stolen by Paris and Agamemnon, her brother-in-law, was trying to recover her. Trimalchio introduces also a half-memory of the story of the hind being substituted by Diana for Iphigenia, daughter of Agamemnon, who was to be sacrificed at Aulis to allow the Greek

fleet to sail. The Trojans, of course, were fighting against the Greeks, not the inhabitants of the Italian town of Tarentum. Iphigeneia was not given to Achilles, who died unmarried, while Ajax went mad over the award of the armour of Achilles to Ulysses. It would be difficult indeed to find more confusion in these very familiar myths.

47. The Lares were the household gods responsible for the prosperity of the house. They were generally depicted as young men in tunics and it was frequent practice to show with them a picture of the genius of the house who was usually shown with the master's face. Trimalchio has given appropriately commercial names to his Lares. It was customary to sacrifice to the Lares during the evening meal, generally just before dessert. Kissing the image of Trimalchio is, however, a little extreme.

48. Reading *matutinas* with Heinsius for *matavitatau*.

49. Encolpius seems to be getting drunk.

50. Apelles was a famous tragic actor of the time of Caligula (assassinated in A.D. 41), so Plocamus is referring to a period approximately twenty-five years before the date of the action.

51. The place of honour meant here is the praetor's seat at the lower end of the middle couch and usually next to the host's seat, which however in this case is occupied by Fortunata and Scintilla.

52. The ninth-day dinner was a regular feature of Roman funeral arrangements; it followed the ninth-day sacrifice to the dead to which Habinnas refers when deploring pouring half his wine over the wretched slave's bones. Such elaborate treatment for a dead slave was extremely uncommon and hints at a very special relationship between him and Scissa.

53. The original is *pax Palamedes*, an obscure exclamation, which probably derives from the story of Palamedes' death. He was killed out of jealousy by Ulysses, and the above remark is perhaps to be interpreted as Ulysses' happy exclamation when the deed was done.

54. Reading *babaecalae* for *barcalae*.

55. One tenth per cent to Mercury: paid by the month by the grateful merchant to the patron god of traders. The size of the bracelet indicates a high revenue.

56. Reading *indecentissimam* for *indecens imam*. The piece of horse-play here depends on the fact that Roman women usually sat rather than reclined at table.

57. The joke here depends on the slaves taking Trimalchio's order for dessert (*secundae mensae*) literally and bringing in a second set of tables (*secundae mensae*).

58. The opening line of *Aeneid* 5.

59. On Atellan verses see note 38 above.

60. Cappadocians were regarded as the slyest and most difficult slaves.

61. Daedalus was the legendary craftsman who built the Cretan labyrinth, etc., and invented wings to escape from that island; he was the standard prototype of inventiveness.

62. A practice introduced to Nero's court by the later Emperor Otho: its presence at Trimalchio's dinner might indicate that Petronius thought it vulgar.

63. It was bad manners to dance in public; the incident might indicate that the women are drunk.

64. The Greens were one of the chariot teams who raced in the Circus, the others being Red, White, and Blue, although other colours were added later. Partisanship ran high and bets such as that described below were a great feature of the sport.

65. Ephesus is otherwise unknown.

66. I would delete *monumenti mei*, following Mueller.

67. As a *sevir* Trimalchio would be entitled to such official dress; he would not however be entitled to the gold rings, which were the privilege of the knights.

68. Slaves generally adopted their master's family names. 'Pompeius' would suggest that Trimalchio once belonged to the family of the Pompeii. 'Maecenatianus' may have been ostentatiously adopted to suggest a connexion with the great Maecenas, Augustus' Minister of State; it is unlikely that he ever was a slave of Maecenas.

69. I would delete *angustum scilicet et cisternae frigidariae simile* which neither befits Trimalchio's wealth nor the description of the bath below, which makes it sound very spacious.

70. Presumably the Neronian harp-player mentioned in Suetonius and Dio. If so, it would be further evidence for the Neronian date of the work.

71. Cock-crowing is a well-known omen and the transference of the ring from one hand to the other is akin to the superstition of changing money from one pocket to another for luck.

72. Reading *non meminit, sed de machina illam sustuli*.

73. Cassandra gloomily prophesied the fall of Troy; here she stands for a spoil-sport of a very crude sort.

74. Reading *herae proximae* with Buecheler.

75. It was a common practice to list the Emperor as an heir, both as a compliment to him and as a precaution against his setting aside the provisions of the will and confiscating the legacy.

76. The evidence of Dio and Suetonius is conflicting, but the most reasonable theory is that Augustus fixed the senatorial census at 1,000,000 sesterces, at which it presumably stayed for the next few reigns.

77. Reading < *comparo* > *venalicia*.

78. Apulia is part of lower Southern Italy.

79. Reading *casa adhuc* with Corbett for *cusuc*.

80. One for each season of the year.

81. Scaurus is perhaps the famous Pompeian manufacturer of fish-sauce, rather than a member of the noble family of the Scauri.

EUMOLPUS

1. Reading *tabellarius* [*Trimalchionis*] . . . *ex vehiculo desiliens* (Mueller) and *tandem intrare permisit* (Rose).

2. The Theban brothers were Eteocles and Polyneices, the sons of Oedipus. Polyneices led an army against Thebes and in single combat the two brothers killed each other.

3. These lines seem to have been introduced from elsewhere in the work. They are singularly inappropriate here.

4. Tantalus, one of the great sinners in Hades. He was punished by being stood in a river whose water ran from his lips; while overhead branches with fruit on them always eluded his grasp.

5. Zeuxis (*fl.* 424 B.C.), a famous Greek painter renowned for the realism of his still lifes. His figure painting seems to have been rather idealized.

6. Protogenes (*fl.* 332 B.C.) a diligent and self-taught artist of Rhodes; his works were rare because of the time he took over them. Like most great Greek artists he was renowned for his accurate draughtsmanship.

7. Apelles was a contemporary of the above and regarded as one of the greatest of all Greek artists. One of his best works was Aphrodite rising from the sea (the Anadyomene). He prided himself particularly upon the *grace* of his paintings.

8. This was Ganymede, who became Zeus's cupbearer. Hylas was the beloved companion of Heracles; during the voyage of the Argo, while getting water, he was pulled in by an amorous Naiad. The boy accidentally killed by Apollo with a discus was a Spartan prince called Hyacinth: the flower of that name was supposed to have sprung from his blood.

9. Lycurgus is a mysterious character in the novel whom Encolpius seems to have killed after being entertained by him and, apparently, ill-treated. His villa may have been the source of the trio's mysterious gold.

10. Reading *detrectant* for *iactantur*.

11. Pergamum was the capital of the Roman province of Asia. A quaestor was in charge of the financial side of Roman provincial administration.

12. Democritus of Abdera (*c*. 460–370 B.C.), a voluminous writer on natural science and ethics, he elaborated the atomic theory and is important for his contribution to Epicureanism. He wrote a book on the powers of seeds, plants, and fruits, which Eumolpus may have in mind here.

13. Eudoxus of Cnidos (*c*. 408–355 B.C.) was a famous Greek mathematician and astronomer; far from growing old on a mountain, he engaged in politics in later life. Chrysippus (*c*. 280–207 B.C.) was the great systematizer of Stoicism and the author of innumerable works. Hellebore was a well-known purgative, supposedly effective against mental illness.

14. Lysippus of Sicyon (*fl.* 328 B.C.), the most famous sculptor of the time of Alexander, produced about 1,500 works according to one authority; he was noted for his fidelity to detail and for introducing new and more slender proportions to his figures. Myron of Eleutherae (*fl. c.* 480–445 B.C.) was a revolutionary Greek sculptor, especially known for the radically new postures of his works, which were made possible by the relatively new technique of bronze-casting. A copy of his Discobolus survives and well illustrates this tendency.

15. Dialectic by this time was probably very like our logic; in effect, the study of the laws of thought and argument.

16. Reading *exorat* for *exornat*.

17. Apelles (see n. 7 above); Phidias of Athens (*c*. 490–417 B.C.) is the great sculptor of the Elgin marbles, brought to England from the Parthenon. Two other great works of his were the chryselephantine statue of Athene Parthenos and the statue of Zeus at Olympia.

18. The Capture of Troy was a common subject of poetry; Nero wrote on the subject. Eumolpus' narrative is a pastiche in different metre of Vergil's account in the first half of *Aeneid* 2, and there are constant Vergilian echoes. The following notes on the classical allusions are keyed to the line numbers of the translation: line 1 – Calchas was the priest of Apollo who predicted the war would last ten years; l. 3 – the Delian is Apollo; one of his cult-sanctuaries was the island of Delos where he was born; through Calchas he urges the building of the Trojan horse out of hatred for Troy; l. 4 – Ida is a mountain in the Troad; l. 10 – god's vail: the Horse was supposed to be a Greek offering to the gods; l. 15 – Sinon pretended to be a deserter and told the Trojans that the Horse, if taken into Troy, would keep the city from capture; l. 22 – Laocoön's death with his two sons is the subject of the famous statuary group in the Vatican; l. 32 – Tenedos is a small island off the coast of the Troad; l. 45 – sacred ribbons: the boys are dressed as acolytes for a sacrifice.

19. Giton is carrying out his usual function of attending his lover. He is guarding Ascyltus' clothes in the public baths, holding the towels and scrapers for the oil.

20. Reading *bonam fidem paenitentia tua emendas*.

21. Eumolpus is clearly the speaker and is presumably responding to some moralizing from Encolpius.

22. Reading *nec mortem hominis concupisse [nec] supplicis, utique eius quem post fatalem rixam* . . .

23. Reading *properandum*.

24. Reading *in altum compono*.

25. Reading *naufragium proponimus*.

26. Reading *de cursu locatis*.

27. I would delete *descendentes* as well as *casus*.

28. Reading *ad ornationem tristitiae*.

29. Another example of the constant persecution of Encolpius by Priapus.

30. Epicurus of Athens (342–270 B.C.), the great founder of Epicureanism. He proposed pleasure as the sole good for man and tried to abolish all religious fear of the gods, of death, of omens, etc. Naturally he would discount oneiromancy as superstitious; in his system the gods lived in carefree happiness and did not interfere at all in the affairs of men.

31. It has been plausibly suggested that Fragment xxx was originally located here.

32. Consequently to do this when there was no storm was regarded as inviting disaster.

33. See Homer, *Odyssey* 19. 473.

34. Hercules: a reference to a missing part of the work. This episode probably took place in Baiae. Lichas' wife was named Hedyle.

35. Eumolpus offers here a parody of forensic oratory, just as later he will parody the language of treaty-makers.

36. Reading *turbatus et deformis. < ita enim me opprimebat > praeter.* . . .

37. Reading *negat < autem >*.

38. Reading *aderat interpellanti*.

39. No hero Trojan: a reference to Paris' abduction of Helen from Menelaus. Medea cut her brother in pieces and scattered them in the sea to delay her father's pursuit of Jason and herself.

40. Ephesus was a large Ionian city on the coast of Asia Minor. The story of the Widow of Ephesus has its parallels in many literatures and since its classic statement here has been the basis of many other versions.

41. I delete '*Graeco more*', following Fraenkel.

42. Crucifixion was the punishment of criminals and slaves.

43. Reading *cibique* for '*certum ab eo*'.

44. Vergil, *Aeneid* 4. 34.

45. '*aut cibum sumere aut*' should stand.

46. Vergil, *Aeneid* 4. 38.

47. Although the MSS attribute this fragment to Tryphaena's maid who is talking to Encolpius, it is more likely that it belongs to Encolpius who is jealously protesting over Giton's behaviour with Tryphaena, who as a prostitute is more likely to be described by him as *spintria* (an inventor of monstrous new sexual techniques). Tryphaena's maid in any case liked Giton, saved him from punishment and improved his appearance. The fragment following seems to support this view.

48. Reading *Sicilia modo ventos dabat, saepissime Italici litoris aquilo possessor convertebat huc illuc obnoxiam ratem*. The description of the winds and the storm makes it difficult to put the shipwreck in the Straits of Messina, as is generally done; more likely, it took place in the Gulf of Squillace or off Cape Rizzuto, which makes their landing near Croton more easily explicable. See *Latomus* 21 (1962), 372–3.

49. Reading *tempestas < morte > manifesta*. The robe and rattle which Lichas refers to would belong to the tutelary goddess of the ship, the Egyptian deity, Isis. Encolpius has apparently stolen them in the lost episode which deals with Lichas.

50. Reading *aut patrem reliquit aut utique aliquem*.

THE ROAD TO CROTON

1. Croton, the modern Crotone, on the coast of the toe of Italy, was colonized by Greeks about 710 B.C. The height of its power was marked by the defeat of Sybaris in 510 B.C., but thereafter its defeat by Locri and Rhegium in the fourth century, its capture by Dionysius of Syracuse, and a series of internal and external wars (the Lucanian, the Bruttian, the Pyrrhic, and the Hannibalic) ruined it. A Roman colony sent there in 194 B.C. failed to revive the town. This part of the work, whose theme is the common satirical topic of legacy-hunting, is placed in a less realistic setting than the events centring on Puteoli, presumably because Petronius was less familiar with the area and because his satire here is of a more literary and far-fetched nature than heretofore.

2. Reading *id venationis*.

3. Reading *rapinam*.

4. Further references to certain lost episodes. The robe is probably the robe of Isis which Encolpius had stolen from Lichas' ship and about which Lichas was so concerned during the storm. Lycurgus seems to have been a host of Encolpius, whose ill-treatment had driven Encolpius to kill him and then, with Ascyltus and Giton, plunder his villa.

5. This piece of literary criticism with its famous epigrammatic description of Horace gives us a very good idea of Petronius' views on literature. He is a traditionalist, an admirer of the standard classics such as Homer, the Greek lyric poets, Vergil, and Horace, and is opposed to the glittering epigrammatic style of such contemporary authors as Seneca and Lucan. His ideal is a smooth sober Atticism. In particular, his criticism of the innovations in the epic made by Lucan in his *Pharsalia* is clear from his insistence on wide reading in traditional authors and a retention of the divine machinery of Homer and Vergil which Lucan had dropped. Although Lucan is not mentioned by name, it is obvious that he is referred to, because the criticisms are appropriate only to the *Pharsalia*. No doubt Lucan was by now out of Nero's favour on account of the latter's jealousy, but the mention of Lucan would be inappropriate in the fictional situation, even if the purport of the criticism is plain. The poem that follows is full of reminiscences of Lucan Books I–III (which had probably been published by this time) and, to a lesser extent, of certain later books of Lucan (cf. the end of the *Pharsalia*). The purpose of the poem which follows has been long disputed. It has been regarded as a parody (but then why are there not hits at Lucan's Stoicism, the excessive use of portents, etc.?); or an attempt, particularly appropriate in Eumolpus' mouth, to show how easily it can be done; or a model for the proper handling of such an epic theme (but in this case by making it a very unfinished effort of Eumolpus', Petronius is certainly disclaiming much poetic responsibility for it), and other suggestions have been made. My own rather hesitant opinion is that Petronius has taken the subject matter of Lucan Book I and re-written it in the light of his own (and Eumolpus') strictures. He has expanded, combined, and changed some of the material – e.g., by substituting the crossing of the Alps for the crossing of the Rubicon and by introducing more deities in place of Lucan's portents – but he has kept Lucan before the reader's mind by the use of direct references and allusions and imitations of Lucan's frigid conceits (e.g., the statement that Charon's boat will be insufficient to carry over the ghosts of the dead, a fleet will be needed). Nevertheless, by giving the whole criticism and rehandling to the poetaster Eumolpus (who says the work is still unrevised), he disclaims any great responsibility

for its merits, although no doubt he thought it as good as Lucan's work. For the style of the translation, see the Introduction.

6. Reading *fabulas < pondere > sententiarum quasi tormento*.

7. The notes on the poem are given by the line numbers of the translation.

Line 21 – Ammon was the name of Jupiter, worshipped as a ram in Africa. The temple stood on the present oasis of Siwah. Here the name means little more than Libya.

l. 24 – Wild beasts for use in the amphitheatre commanded heavy prices.

l. 55 – Oysters from the Lucrine Lake were particularly valued.

l. 58 – These were pheasants.

l. 70 – Cato (the Younger) was the very type of stern unbending Roman virtue. He was one of Caesar's most vehement opponents and finally committed suicide when defeated by the Caesarian party in Africa. He was defeated by Vatinius for the praetorship.

l. 100 – The three captains were Julius Caesar, Pompey, and Crassus, who formed the first triumvirate until Crassus' death fighting the Parthians allowed the jealousy of Pompey to turn him against Caesar. Pompey was assassinated on the shore of Egypt, and Caesar, of course, was killed in Rome by the conspirators.

l. 111 – The scene takes place in the Phlegrean Fields, the modern Solfatara, a heavily volcanic region of mud-pits and hot sulphur holes and caves. Cocytus is one of the rivers of the underworld.

l. 125 – Dis is the lord of the underworld.

l. 151 – Tisiphone is one of the Furies, the avenger of murder.

l. 152 – Sulla was the last instance of civil war, when he proscribed and murdered hundreds of followers of Marius in order to become dictator in Rome. This was over thirty years before the civil war between Caesar and the senate began.

l. 172 – The battle of Philippi (42 B.C.) saw the defeat of Brutus and Cassius by Octavian and Antony. Although the battlefield is in Macedonia on the borders of Thrace, Roman poets sometimes wrongly locate it at Pharsalus, in Thessaly, where Caesar routed Pompey in 48 B.C. Hence the double slaughter. There is a reference here also to the battles that took place in Spain and in Africa.

l. 174 – Nile's barriers: reference to Caesar's Egyptian campaign.

l. 175 – Antony and Cleopatra were decisively defeated by the forces of Octavian at the Battle of Actium in 31 B.C. Apollo was on Octavian's side: Propertius has a laudatory poem describing the god's intervention.

l. 180 – Charon took souls across the River Styx in an old leaky boat.

l. 194 – The lightning bolts came from Jove, the brother of Dis.

l. 197 – Hyperion is the sun.

l. 200 – Cynthia is the moon.

l. 220 – Caesar has just pacified Gaul in a long and bloody series of battles. The civil war ostensibly began over the senate's refusal to prolong his command of an army.

l. 240 – Saturnus was, according to myth, the most ancient king of Latium and afterwards was honoured as the god of agriculture and civilization.

l. 250 – The Gauls were a constant fear to Romans; they had already sacked the Capitol in 390 B.C.

l. 252 – Caesar had also conquered a number of German tribes.

l. 277 – The raven was the bird of Apollo, who had a shrine at Delphi, and it was therefore considered prophetic.

l. 318 – Hercules, son of Amphitryon, had gone to the Caucasus to release Prometheus from his chains and shoot the vulture that perpetually devoured his liver.

l. 321 – This is a reference to the war between the Gods and Giants.

l. 325 – The Palatine Hill was one of the oldest and most important areas in Rome.

l. 344 – Quirites was the formal name for Roman citizens.

l. 357 – Auster is the South Wind.

l. 365 – The two consuls of the year 49 were C. Claudius Marcellus and L. Cornelius Lentulus Crus, both Pompeian supporters.

l. 366 – *tremor Ponti*: Pompey had conquered Mithridates of Pontus in 63 B.C.

l. 367 – Hydaspes is a river in India, the scene of a victory won by Alexander the Great. Pompey had never in fact gone so far.

l. 368 – Pompey had been charged with clearing the Mediterranean of pirates in 67 B.C. He effected this great task in three months.

l. 391 – Erebus, the god of Darkness.

l. 393 – Erinys, a Fury; Bellona, the goddess of War.

l. 394 – Megaera, another Fury.

l. 410 – Dione, a poetical name for Venus. She was the mythical ancestor of the Julian line.

l. 411 – Pallas Athene (the Roman Minerva) was, of course, notable for her martial abilities; Romulus, the mythical founder of Rome, was a son of Mars, hence his epithet Mavortius.

l. 413 – i.e., Apollo and Diana.

l. 414 – Mercury was born on Mount Cyllene.

l. 415 – Pompey is like Hercules both because of his extensive travels and because he freed Rome from so many perils, as Hercules freed Greece. Hercules was born in Tiryns.

l. 439 – 'Legem tene, Marcellus': the most appropriate person for this reference would be M. Claudius Marcellus, consul 51 B.C., who proposed to recall Caesar on 1 March 50 and certainly ensured that the question would be discussed on 1 March 49. Petronius may have confused him with his brother, C. Claudius Marcellus, consul in the fateful year of 49.

l. 440 – C. Scribonius Curio was tribune of the people in 50 B.C. and a staunch supporter of Caesar. Here he is called on to agitate the mob to ensure the advent of war.

l. 441 – Lentulus was a consul of 49 B.C. (cf. line 365 above). Lentulus was, in fact, a determined advocate of civil war, despite all the pleas of his friend, Balbus, one of Caesar's lieutenants.

l. 442 – Son of heaven: Julius Caesar, later the divine (*divus*) Julius.

l. 447 – Epidamnus (or Dyrrachium) in Epirus was Pompey's main base on the Adriatic after he left Rome, and he managed to ward off Caesar's first attack there. Later he moved into Thessaly for the disastrous battle of Pharsalus, where he was defeated.

[I adopted the following readings for the translation: line 9 (of the Latin text), *aes Ephyraeum tum laudabut miles*; *in ima*; l. 11, *crustas* (with Scaliger); l. 113, I have placed before l. 111 (following Bouhier); l. 212, *rumorum* for *Romano*; l. 250, *palla* (with Schrader).]

CROTON

1. Reading *voce* for *volubilitate verborum* (following Fraenkel).

2. This reduplication is probably due to an abbreviated text, which was then incorporated into the main text.

3. Possibly this fragment is out of place in its present position and should occur later in the Crotonian adventure.

4. Reading *spatiantem < te > vidi, quid cogites*.

5. This sort of lady is a fairly frequent type in ancient and modern satire. Similar examples may be found in Herondas, Juvenal, and Martial. Madame Philibert in Thomas Mann's *Felix Krull* is one of the latest examples in fiction. The fourteen rows referred to are those reserved for the Knights by the *Lex Roscia* of 67 B.C.

6. Praxiteles, an Athenian sculptor, (*fl.* perhaps 364 B.C.) was famed for his statues of Aphrodite. Unlike the earlier Athenian school, he produced statues which were full of emotion and sensuality.

7. Reading *Dianam* despite the difficulties. Diana, the puritanical goddess of the hunt, is hardly appropriate in an erotic context such as this. Possibly an allusion to Venus was originally intended, e.g., *Cnidiam* or *Dionen*, as Jahn suggested.

8. Parian marble from the island of Paros was renowned for its pure whiteness.

9. A reference to some lost episode in the work.

10. References to the rape of Europa by Jupiter in the form of a bull, Leda in the shape of a swan, and Danaë as a shower of gold.

11. Circe, the daughter of the Sun, was the name of the enchantress who turned the companions of Ulysses into swine, but fell in love with the hero (cf. *Odyssey* 10). Polyaenus is one of the epithets used by Homer to describe Ulysses (*Odyssey* 12. 184); it means muchpraised or, alternatively, with many a tale, a meaning which is more appropriate for Encolpius' assumption of it as a pseudonym.

12. A reference to Juno's distraction of Jupiter from the Trojan War, when they went to bed together on Mount Ida: the description roughly follows Homer's (cf. Homer, *Iliad* 14. 347 ff.).

13. Platonic way: *Socratica fide* in the original. A reference to Alcibiades' description in Plato's *Symposium* (217 ff.) of the chaste and honourable way Socrates treated him, even when he spent the night with him. It is almost certainly this passage which is the origin of our concept of Platonic love.

14. Achilles is the natural prototype of prowess. Encolpius seems however to have found his own Achilles' heel.

15. *quod ... excitavi* may be defended as a vulgarism.

16. Daphne, according to Ovid, was turned into a laurel to escape from Apollo's amorous pursuit.

17. Procne, the wife of Tereus, was turned into a swallow. Her sister Philomela was changed into a nightingale.

18. Reading *quietum < aera >*.

19. In the MSS this paragraph is prefaced by the words '*Encolpius de Endymione puero*', which are clearly an intrusion. The paragraph itself is not necessarily out of place. A close reading reveals that, however active their hands are clasping each other and however close their embraces and kisses, 'the right true end of love' is not to be inferred and the next paragraph comes as no surprise.

20. A pastiche of Vergil: *Aeneid* 6. 469–70 (a description of Dido on meeting Aeneas); the last line is half a line from *Eclogue* 5. 16, and half a line from *Aeneid* 9. 436.

21. The Censor – in the original *Catones*, those who were stern and censorious puritans like the elder Cato. The poem seems a key to the whole work. It pleads for naturalism of attitude, language, and subject-matter.

22. Epicurus (341–270 B.C.) admittedly held that pleasure was the only good, but his definition of pleasure would probably be such as to exclude the joys enumerated in the lines above. He advocated

moderate, non-violent pleasures, not such pleasures as involved as much pain as pleasure. Roman Epicureans however tended to interpret his doctrines more crudely.

23. Priapus, the divine antagonist of the novel, is being addressed. Bacchus was Priapus' father; Dione is poetic for Aphrodite, his mother. As a country god, he would be a natural companion of nymphs. The islands of Lesbos and Thasos would be cult-centres. The particular devotion of the Lydians 'spread over the seven rivers' (to adopt the reading *septifluus*) I find difficult to explain, but Hypaepa (-orum) is a small town in Lydia, now Bereki.

24. Encolpius' confessions refer to parts of the work now lost. He may refer to the slaying of his host Lycurgus, but the incident involving a temple (of Priapus or Isis?) is more obscure.

25. This fragment is prefaced in the MSS by the words *Proselenos ad Oenotheam sacerdotem Priapi de Encolpio*. Oenothea's name (Wine-goddess) refers clearly to her drinking habits.

26. Hyrcania was on the Caspian Sea. Hyrcanian tigers were no doubt familiar to Roman writers chiefly through the line of Vergil that mentions them (*Aeneid* 4. 367).

27. cf. note 11 above.

28. Proteus was the Old Man of the Sea and had the power to assume any shape he wished.

29. Hecale was a poor old woman who gave hospitality to Theseus when he was on his way to kill the Bull of Marathon. She was the subject of a small epic by Callimachus, the great Alexandrian poet and scholar (*c.* 305–240 B.C.); he is referred to a line or so later in the Latin text as Battiades (reading *Battiadae veteris mirandam*) because he was a native of Cyrene and Battus was the mythical founder of that city.

30. Stymphalian birds: rapacious birds, who were driven by Hercules from their original haunt near the Stymphalian lake in Arcadia to the island of Aretias in the Euxine. Harpies were winged creatures sent to punish Phineus for the ill-treatment of his sons by his first marriage; they swooped down and removed part of any food served to him and soiled the rest. According to some stories, he was rescued from them by the Argonauts.

31. Reading *acremque* for *aeque*.

32. Acrisius, king of Argos, shut up his daughter Danaë in a bronze tower because of a prophecy that a son of hers would kill his grandfather. Zeus nevertheless got to her in the form of a shower of gold and she gave birth to Perseus.

33. Marcus Porcius Cato Licinianus, son of Cato the Censor, was the most celebrated jurist of his time. The other 'lawyers of note'

specified in the original are Servius Sulpicius Lemonia Rufus, contemporary and friend of Cicero, who was a famous orator and jurisconsult, and M. Antistius Labeo, a learned and revolutionary jurist in the reign of Augustus.

34. The order of the fragments in this section (138-9) seems seriously dislocated. I have decided however to keep the order as found in the manuscript tradition, leaving it to the reader to work out a more satisfactory order of events.

35. Famous mythical beauties. Ariadne was a Cretan princess, the mistress first of Theseus, who abandoned her, and then of Dionysus. Leda was seduced by Zeus in the shape of a swan and became the mother of Helen, who ran off with the Trojan Paris and became the cause of the Trojan War. Paris was granted her as a reward for giving the prize of beauty to Venus in the contest of the three goddesses on Mount Ida.

36. This poem is the clue to one of the main motifs of the work – the wrath of Priapus. The mythical comparisons Encolpius adduces are all cases of divine hostility against some mortal. Hercules was hated by Juno and had the twelve labours imposed upon him, one of which entailed his taking the sky off the shoulders of Atlas for a time. Laomedon was king of Troy and took Apollo and Neptune into his service, but he cheated them of their pay and for that Neptune sent a sea-monster to ravage Troy. He is called impious because he broke his contract with the two gods. Pelias killed Sidero, the cruel stepmother of his mother before the altar of Juno. It may have been this piece of impiety which led eventually to his dismemberment by his daughters on the advice of Medea who had promised a method of rejuvenating him. Telephus was king of Mysia at the time of the Trojan War and in repelling the Greek invasion of his land, encountered Bacchus who was helping the Greeks. The god caused him to stumble over a vine root and he was then wounded by Achilles. The wrath of Neptune against Ulysses is of course a major theme in the *Odyssey*; Ulysses incurred this enmity for his blinding of the Cyclops Polyphemus, who was one of Neptune's sons. Nereus was the old man of the sea, father of the Nereids, and his domain was the Mediterranean, in particular the Aegean.

37. The Roman Mercury was identified with the Greek god Hermes; the latter did have a fertility aspect as well as being the god of sudden and unexpected gains. Here, however, Encolpius seems to be attributing his restoration to the god's power as the guide of the dead. Encolpius after all is dead in that part where he was once an Achilles.

38. Protesilaus was the first Greek killed at Troy. He was granted

a few hours of return from the underworld to visit his dearly beloved wife, Laodameia. Encolpius has come back from the dead too.

39. Reading *hominumque* < *decus* >.

40. Saguntum, a city in Spain, was captured by Hannibal in 219 B.C. after an eight-month siege. Petelia, a town in Southern Italy, was captured by Himilco, a lieutenant of Hannibal, after a siege of several months. Livy described the extremities the inhabitants were reduced to from lack of food, but makes no mention of cannibalism. Numantia, a Spanish town, was captured in 133 B.C. after an eight-month blockade by Scipio Aemilianus. Tales of cannibalism in times of siege are common in ancient literature and need not be taken literally. Josephus' description of the siege of Jerusalem is equally sensational.

THE FRAGMENTS

I have retained Ernout's numbering (giving Mueller's numbers in parenthesis) and used or adapted Ernout's text where Mueller's stops (i.e., at Fgt XXX). As the later fragments are very dubiously attributed to Petronius I have translated merely a selection of them; I have not tried to decide which are possibly Petronian and which not. The famous fragments XXXVIII and LIV, for instance, are almost certainly not by him.

1. Fgt IX – I delete *'causidicus'*.
2. Fgt XV – I read < *modo inferior* >.
3. Fgt XXIV – the line probably belongs to Martial (2. 12. 4) and has been mistakenly attributed to Petronius.
4. Fgt XXV – Nicagoras was an Athenian sophist who lived during the reign of the Emperor Philippus (244–249 A.D.) and wrote a series of biographies of famous men.
5. Fgt XXVI – I read *vinclo resoluta parentis*.
6. Fgt XXVII – Mount Athos is a mountain in Macedonia, now famous for its monastery. Pales was a Roman divinity of flocks and shepherds and was worshipped during the Palilia (21 April). I read *nautae obvius omni* for *nutat obrutus omnis*. Pallas claims the streets and inns perhaps because she was the goddess of all useful and domestic arts.
7. Reading *Graias ad urbes*.
8. A number of versions of this famous poem, including that by Ben Jonson, may be found in *Arion* 2 (1963), pp. 83–4.
9. Text in M. Rat's edition of Petronius (*Classiques Garnier*).

THE APOCOLOCYNTOSIS

OR

THE DEIFICATION OF CLAUDIUS THE CLOD

INTRODUCTION

THE following work, variously entitled in the MSS as *Divi Claudii Apotheosis per saturam, Ludus de morte Claudii*, or *Satira de Claudio Caesare*, or *Apotheosis Annaei Senecae per Saturam* and attributed to Seneca, was early identified with the *Apocolocyntosis* mentioned in the well-known passage of Dio Cassius (60. 35):

[Claudius] received the state funeral and all the other honours accorded to Augustus. Agrippina and Nero made a show of mourning for their victim and they elevated to heaven the man they'd carried out from the banquet in a litter. This prompted Lucius Junius Gallio, Seneca's brother, to a very pungent witticism. Seneca himself had written a piece he called the *Pumpkinification*, playing on the word *Deification*, and Gallio is credited with the following pithy remark. As the public executioners used to drag the bodies of those executed in prison to the Forum with large hooks and hauled them from there to the river, he commented that Claudius had been hauled into heaven on a hook.

There is little reason to doubt the identification of the Senecan authorship. The main objections are that the work is not given the title *Apocolocyntosis* in the MS tradition and that there is no mention in the text of Claudius' metamorphosis into a gourd (or pumpkin, as modern translators have preferred), although there should be on the strict analogy of the word *deification*. It has therefore been suggested that the last part of the work, where this might take place, is lost; that the gourd really refers to the broken dice box that Claudius is given; that Seneca wrote two works about Claudius' death or even that the work before us is by Petronius, the author of the *Satyricon*. None of these suggestions carry conviction. The traditions of contemporary Menippean satire and current colloquialisms may account for the resemblance between the language of the *Satyricon* and that of the *Apocolocyntosis*; again, Seneca would hardly write two similar pamphlets when the job would be effectively done by one; the dice box explanation is far-fetched even for a first-century joke, and it does not meet the point about the *gourd-ification*; and although the work ends fairly hastily and abruptly, the ending is satisfactory and final in terms of probability and plot. The best solution so far offered to the problem of the meaning of the title is that the pun, like many puns, is not an exact linguistic parallel to' its host word. *Apocolocyntosis* is not *transfiguration into a pumpkin*, but *transfiguration of a pumpkin-head*. Gallio's joke about Claudius 'playing hookey' involves a similar licence about the factual situation. The MS tradition might easily have changed the rare coinage *Apocolocyntosis* to the more understandable *Apotheosis*, and it would be equally literal-minded to protest that the whole point of the satire is that Cladius' claim to be made a god is rejected.

The piece has excited a certain amount of scepticism and distaste among scholars. Could this pamphlet be the work of the same author as the *Consolatio ad Polybium* with all its flatteries of Claudius and his entourage, or, for that matter, the work of the author of Nero's funeral speech over his predecessor? Could its humour spring from the same pen that wrote the humourless exhortations that fill the *Letters of Lucilius*? Seneca's defenders argue unconvincingly that the praise of Claudius in the *Consolatio* is insincere and satirical; his critics, when they do not deny the Senecan authorship of the *Apocolocyntosis*, find it a cruel and disgusting piece of work.

But there is no internal evidence against Senecan authorship and his is the most likely claim to the pamphlet. Seneca was a realist, as some of his advice to Lucilius on public life bears witness (cf., e.g., *Letters* 22. 6-8). His attitude to poverty was suitably stoic; his wealth proberbial. Yet he made no bones about surrendering the latter to Nero, when it looked as though it might save his life. Similarly, he had no cause to love Claudius, who had exiled him. His return was due to Agrippina, who desired him as a tutor and later counsellor for Nero. After Claudius' murder, he wrote the funeral laudation perhaps a little too zealously – hence the audience's laughter (Tacitus, *Annals* 13. 3), but the same opportunistic spirit that accepted the new emperor's vices as the protection against something worse (*Annals* 13. 2), might well welcome the chance of bolstering the new régime at the expense of the old and also working off a grudge against Claudius. Seneca's attitude to exile in the *Letters to Lucilius* (cf., e.g., 24. 17) does not correspond to his attitude in the epigrams of his exile.

On the question whether Seneca has a sense of humour enough to write such a work as the *Apocolocyntosis*, opinions must differ. It should however be pointed out that the works of Seneca which survive are predominantly philosophical: Seneca's contributions to the great Stoic tradition. Were it not for the anecdotes, we could never guess Cicero's wit from the *Tusculan Disputations* or the *De natura deorum*. But even in the *Letters to Lucilius*, Seneca shows that he has a taste for such absurd figures as Calvisius Sabinus; his fondness for witty epigram and philosophical point is equally apparent, although there they are at the service of philosophical moralizing, not satire. It takes no great feat of imagination to see Seneca deploying his wit to write a pamphlet which tries to be funny as well as sarcastic. And after all, the *Apocolocyntosis* is not exactly a masterpiece; acceptance of its Senecan authorship would not put the philosopher into the forefront of ancient comic writers.

The piece then is a hastily written squib, effective enough no doubt as a piece of propaganda to inaugurate a new régime by discrediting the previous one. The flattery of the still very youthful Nero is kept well within bounds (see 4, p. 212) and the satire against Claudius makes use of familiar charges and weaknesses that may be documented in such later historians as Tacitus, Suetonius, and Dio Cassius. We are given a picture of an absurd, pedantic and capricious tyrant, burdened with a number of physical infirmities and political vices. His head shakes and his speech is indistinct; he is an absent-minded murderer and the slave of his freedmen, and so on. Certain possible satiric thrusts are carefully avoided and this points to an author closely connected with the new ruling clique rather than some independent and anonymous satirist with grudges of his own. Claudius' notorious fondness for women is not touched upon and the version of his death put out by Agrippina, that he died while being entertained by comedians, whereas in fact he was already dead when they arrived, is accepted and made into a joke. The whole question of incest, which might have reasonably prompted some real thrusts because of Claudius' marriage to his niece, is very delicately skirted (8, p. 216).

The signs of haste are equally obvious. In 9, p. 216 Claudius is dismissed from the divine senate so that he will miss the unseemly wrangling among the gods; in 10, p. 218 during the debate on the motion for the deification, Augustus puts a series of direct questions to him. Moreover, once the decision has gone against Claudius and he is taken down to Hades, his ultimate fate is very quickly decided by comparison with the lengthy controversy in heaven. As though the author was tiring of the whole work, the action speeds up and the work ends rather hastily. Claudius, the assiduous judge and puppet of freedmen in life, is handed over to a freedman of Aeacus' to serve as a court clerk.

Given the haste and the unambitious character of the piece I do not find it either offensive or excessively cruel. The charges are standard and the tone, except for some parts of Augustus' speech, where the propaganda becomes shrill and reminiscent of the *Letters to Lucilius*, tries to be light.

In this translation, I have followed for the most part the text of C. F. Russo (Florence, 1948), and I am grateful to Mr Peter Eden for some helpful advice on the disputed areas. The best and most recent biography is to be found in A. Athanassakis, *Senecae Apocolocyntosis Divi Claudii* (Lawrence, Kansas, 1973), pp. 139 ff.

THE APOCOLOCYNTOSIS

OR

THE DEIFICATION OF CLAUDIUS THE CLOD

1. The purpose of the following work is to give future genera-
tions an account of the events in heaven on the thirteenth of
October of this strange year of grace that inaugurated our present
period of prosperity. No offence and no flattery is intended. What
follows is the honest truth. If the reader asks for my sources, in
the first place I will refuse to answer if I am not so inclined. Who
is going to make me? I know that I'm a free man ever since the
death of the fellow who proved the old saying – *be born a king
or a fool!* Should I wish to answer, I'll say the first thing that
comes to my lips. Whoever demanded sworn witnesses from an
historian? But if it is necessary to reveal my source, you should
ask the man who saw Drusilla's ascent into heaven.[1] This person
claims he saw Claudius making the same journey, though 'with
shorter steps'.[2] Willy-nilly, he has to watch everything that goes
on in heaven – he's in charge of the Appian Way, the way by
which, as you know, both the Divine Augustus and Tiberius
Caesar joined the company of the gods. If you ask him, he'll tell
you in private. He'll never say a word to more than one. Ever
since he swore in the senate that he'd seen Drusilla going up to
heaven and, for all that marvellous news, no one believed him,
he has solemnly sworn that he will never reveal what he's seen,
even if it's a murder in the middle of the Forum. I am here
setting down clearly and precisely the unimpeachable story he
gave me and of course I trust he is well and flourishing.

2. Phoebus [3] has now abridged the day's duration,
   Shortening his road, and sleep extends its sway;
   Now Cynthia's triumphs amplify her realm.
   Foul winter plucks the crown from wealthy Fall
   And Bacchus is bade wither on the vine
   While the tardy Vintner [4] plucks the few last grapes.

I think I'll be better understood if I put it this way: it was the month of October, the thirteenth. The hour I can't say for certain – it's easier to get philosophers to agree than clocks. Anyway, it was between twelve and one o'clock. 'That's too crude!' you say; 'no poet is content to describe just dawn and sunset. They all like those descriptions so much that they give noon a hard time too. Will you pass up such a good hour like this?'

> The chariot of Phoebus reached mid-orbit;
> Closer to night, he shakes his tiring reins,
> Sending the curving light down paths oblique.

3. Claudius began to give up the ghost, but he could not find the proper exit. At that point Mercury,[5] as he had always enjoyed his wit, took one of the three Fates aside and said: 'Why are you allowing that poor man to be tortured, you cruel woman? After all his long agony, isn't he ever going to get peace? It's sixty-four years since he began fighting for his breath. Why the malice against him and the country? Let the astrologers be right for once: ever since he became emperor they've been burying him off every month of every year. Of course, it's not surprising they make mistakes and that none of them can predict his last hour – they all thought he hadn't been born. Do what has to be done:

> 'Let him be slain,
> That he who best deserves alone may reign.' [6]

Clotho however said: 'Well, for Hercules' sake! I was going to give him a bit of time until he could grant citizenship to the handful left without it: he'd make up his mind to see every Greek, Gaul, Spaniard and Briton in a toga. But since you like the idea of leaving a few aliens to start the next crop and you insist on it that way, that's the way it shall be.' She opened a small box and brought out three spindles. One was for Augurinus, the second for Baba and the third for Claudius.[7] 'I'll make these three die in one year at short intervals – I won't send him off without company. For a man who used to see so many thousands following him, so many thousands in front of him, and so many thousands around him, it's not right to be left suddenly on his own. He'll be happy with these temporary companions.'

4. This said, she rolled the thread on an ugly spool,
Cut from the imperial line one doddering life.

But Lachesis, hair back, with glittering head,
Pierian crown of laurel on forehead and hair,
Teases the fleeces of white to pure bright yarn,
Guiding with golden touch; new colours now dawn.
The sisters look at their work in awed surmise,
To see cheap wool turn into a mass of gold.
The golden years spin out in a lovely line.
No limits are set. They tease the favoured fleece,
Filling their hands in joy, so sweet is their task.
As if by itself, the work went on; they watch:
Softly the threads turn on to the twirling spool –
Tithonus? his eons – Nestor? his years surpassed.
Phoebus is by to assist and the decades to come
Gladden his heart, so he helps with a song,
Now plucking the strings, now happily passing the wool.
He keeps them to work as he plays and lightens their load,
No praise too much for his lyre, his brotherly songs.
Their hands spin more than they used; and the work he salutes
Surpasses the lot of a man. 'O Fates, spin on!'
Says Apollo, 'Let him see more than a mortal span,
Image of me in looks and beauty as well,
In song and voice no worse. To a weary folk
He brings glad days, to muted law a tongue,
As the Morning Star, setting the stars to flight,
As the shining sun, when his chariot moves first from the line,
So Caesar comes, so Nero appears to Rome,
His bright face glowing with gentle radiance,
His neck all beauty under his flowing hair.'

This was Apollo. And Lachesis, being herself very favourably disposed towards such a handsome mortal, did her work with generous hands and gave Nero a great many years from her stock. As for Claudius they all commanded that

in joy and holy silence the mourners bear him out.[8]

He thereupon gasped his last breath and stopped even appearing alive. However, when he expired he was listening to some comedians, so you can understand that my horror of them is not unfounded. His last words heard came after he'd let off a loud noise from his easiest channel of communication: 'Oh my! I think I've shit myself.' Whether he had, I don't know. He certainly shit on everything else.

5. An account of what happened after that on earth is super-fluous. Readers are perfectly familiar with the events and there is no danger of people forgetting what national celebrations impress on the memory. No one forgets he's happy. Here is what happened in heaven. My informant is responsible for the reliability of the account.

It was announced to Jupiter that there was a visitor of a respectable size and with very white hair. He was somehow threatening, as he kept shaking his head, and he was dragging his right foot. When asked his nationality, he had made some unintelligible answer in confused and indistinct tones. It was impossible to understand his language: he was neither Greek nor Roman, nor of any known race.

Jupiter then instructed Hercules, who had travelled the whole world over and seemed familiar with every nationality, to go and find out where he came from. Hercules was badly shaken by the sight of him at first – he hadn't faced all possible monsters yet. Seeing the strange sort of face and the weird walk and hearing the hoarse and obscure voice that belonged to no land creature but seemed more appropriate to a sea-monster, he thought his thirteenth labour had arrived. On a closer inspection, it appeared to be something like a man. So he came nearer and asked in Greek, as it was easiest for him:

Thy name, thy lineage and paternal land? [9]

Claudius was glad there were scholars there. He had hopes that there would be a place for his Histories. And so, using himself another line from Homer to indicate he was Caesar, he said:

The winds from Ilion to the Cicons' shore,
Beneath cold Ismarus, our vessels bore. [10]

The line after that, however, would have been more correct and equally Homeric:

We sack'd the city and destroy'd the race.

6. He would have put it over on Hercules, who is not at all sharp, if the goddess Fever had not been there. She was the only goddess to leave her temple and come with him: she had left all the other gods in Rome. 'This man is telling you absolute lies,'

she said. 'I'll give you the truth, since I've lived with him all these years. He was born at Lyons.[11] You see in front of you one of Mark Antony's fellow townsmen. I tell you, he was born sixteen miles from Vienne, an out-and-out Gaul. And so, as a Gaul should, he captured Rome.[12] I assure you, this man was born at Lyons, where Licinus governed for years. Now you've tramped over more places than any professional mule driver and you ought to know that there are many miles between the Xanthus [13] and the Rhone.'

Claudius flared up at this point and fumed as loudly as he could. No one understood what he was saying. He was, in fact, giving orders for the goddess Fever to be executed, his shaky hand, which was steady enough only on these occasions, making the familiar gesture with which he had people's heads cut off. He had ordered her to be decapitated, but you'd have thought they were all his freedmen the way no one took notice of him.

7. 'Listen to me,' said Hercules then, 'and stop playing the fool. You've come where mice chew iron. Out with the truth quick, before I knock this nonsense out of you.' To make himself more terrifying, he said in tones of high tragedy:

Say, sirrah, quick, what country hail'st thou from,
Or, smitten by this bough, thou sink'st to earth,
A club that oft hath butchered savage kings.
Why mumble now thy words in tones unclear?
What land, what nation, raised that shaking head?
Speak out. I once did seek the far-flung realms
Of triform Geryon,[14] whose most noble herd
I drove from Western seas to Argos town.
While homeward bound, I saw a mountain crest,
O'erlooking two great rivers, which the sun
Faces direct when first he rises up.
The mighty Rhone with rapid current flows;
Hard by the Saône, in doubt where it should run,
With hushed and quiet ripples laps its banks.
Is this the soil that nursed thee into life?

This was delivered with some vigour and courage. Nonetheless he was not quite himself and was nervous of some sort of *coup de fou*.[15] Claudius, seeing his physique, forgot his nonsense and realized that though he had no one to equal him in Rome, here he did not enjoy the same prestige: whatever your gall, you're cock-of-the-walk only on your own dungheap. And so, as far as he could be understood, he apparently said: 'Hercules, you hero of the gods, I hoped you would stand up for me among the others. If I were asked for someone to vouch for me, I was going to name you, as you know me best. If you recall, I was the one who used to preside in court in front of your temple at Tibur every day in the months of July and August.[16] You know what misery I went through there, listening to lawyers day and night. If you'd had experience of them yourself, as brave as you think you are, you'd have preferred to clean out the Augean sewers:[17] I got a lot more bullshit. But since I'd like...'[18]

8. '... We're not surprised at your charging into the Senate: nothing is barred to you. Just tell us what sort of god you want him to be. He can't be an Epicurean god: they're "untroubled and troubling none".[19] A Stoic god? How can he be "globular, with no head, no foreskin", as Varro[20] says? There *is* something about him of the Stoic god, I now see. He's got neither a heart nor a head.

'For Hercules' sake, if he'd asked this favour from Saturn, he wouldn't have got it, even though he celebrated his month all year round, a proper Saturnalian emperor.[21] So how is he to become a god through Jupiter, after he condemned him for incest, as far as he could. He killed his son-in-law Silanus[22] and why, I ask you? Because his sister, who was the most delightful girl in the world, he chose to call Juno, when everyone called her Venus. He's just said, "Why his own sister, I wonder?" Get back to school, you idiot! In Athens you can go half-way, in Alexandria the whole way.[23]

'Just because in Rome, you say, the mice lick the millstones, is he to set things straight with us? I don't know what he does in his own bedroom – and now "he has his eye on lands in the sky".[24] He wants to become a god. Isn't it enough for him to have a temple in Britain, have savages worship him now[25] and pray that he'll be a Merciful Clod.'

9. Jupiter finally recollected that with members of the public in the Senate it was out of order to speak on the motion or debate. 'Gentlemen of the Senate,' he said, 'I permitted you to put some questions, but you're making the whole thing an absolute sham-

bles. I request you to observe the rules of order of the House. What will he think of us, whoever he is?'

Claudius was dismissed and Father Janus [26] was given the floor first. He was consul elect, beginning the afternoon of the first of July, and was as shrewd an operator as you could wish, always forward-looking and watching his rear at the same time. As he lived in the Forum, he made a long and eloquent speech, which the recorder could not keep up with and which I therefore will not report in case I substitute other words for what he actually said. He spoke at length about the high status of gods. This honour should not be granted to ordinary people. 'Once,' he said, 'it was a great thing to become a god. Now you've made it a farce – not worth a bean. Therefore, to avoid any appearance of speaking against the particular case and not for the principle of the thing, I move that from this day forth no one who "eats the harvest of the soil" or lives off "the grain-bearing tilth" shall become a god. Any person who is declared a god or so spoken of or so depicted in contravention of this senatorial order shall be handed over into the custody of the Infernal Agents and at the next gladiatorial show shall be beaten with rods along with the new recruits.'

Diespiter [27] was next recognized. The son of the Goddess Vica Pota, he was also consul elect and ran a small loan business. He made his living at this and used to sell citizenships on the quiet. Hercules delicately approached him and touched his ear-lobe.[28] Diespiter accordingly spoke on the motion as follows:

'Whereas the Divine Claudius is related by blood to both the Divine Augustus and equally to the Divine Augusta, his aunt, whom he personally had declared a goddess, and whereas he is far superior intellectually to all other mortals, and whereas it is in the interest of the state that there should be someone who can "swallow boiled turnips" with Romulus,[29] I hereby propose that the Divine Claudius be a god from this day forth with the privileges accorded to those of his predecessors with the most unquestionable qualifications and that an account of the matter be inserted into Ovid's *Metamorphoses*.'

Speeches were made on both sides and Claudius seemed to be winning. For Hercules, who saw his own irons were in the fire, rushed here and there on the floor, and kept saying: 'Don't turn me down – I'm involved in this. Next time you want a favour, I'll do the same for you. You scratch my back, I'll scratch yours.'

10. Then the Divine Augustus rose to his feet when his turn to speak came and delivered a highly eloquent oration. 'Gentlemen of the Senate,' he said, 'you are witness that, since I became a god, I have not uttered a word. I always mind my own business. Yet I cannot hide my feeling any longer or conceal the pain, which my sense of honour aggravates. Was it for this that I brought peace to land and sea? Was this why I put an end to civil war, was this why I brought law and order to Rome, beautified the city with public works – in order to ... I can't think of what to say, gentlemen. No words can do justice to my indignation. I must fall back on the words of that great orator, Messala Corvinus, and say, "I am ashamed of my authority".[30] This man, gentlemen, who seems to you incapable of shooing a fly, killed men as easily as a dog lifts his leg. But why am I talking about all those important victims? When a man looks at the troubles in his own house, he has no time to shed tears over national calamities. So I'll pass over them and talk about my domestic problems. Even if my sister doesn't know it, your knee is nearer than your shin.[31] That man you see in front of you, after all those years of hiding under my name,[32] thanked me by killing my two great-granddaughters, one Julia with cold steel, the other Julia by starving her to death, and by killing one of my great-great-grandsons, Lucius Silanus.[33] You will see, Jupiter, whether it was for an unjustified cause. Certainly it was one which reflects on you, if you are to be fair. Tell me, Divine Claudius, for what reason did you condemn any one of the men and women you killed, before you specified the charges, and before you ascertained the facts? Where is this usual? It doesn't happen in heaven.

11. 'Take Jupiter – he has held supreme power all these years. In Vulcan's case alone, did he break his leg

... throwing him by the heel
Sheer o'er the crystal battlements.[34]

He was also angry with his wife and hung her up. Did he ever kill her? You killed Messalina, whose great-uncle I was as well as yours. You don't know about it, you say. God damn you! Not to know about it is worse than killing her.[35]

'He didn't stop dogging Gaius Caesar's footsteps even after he was dead. Gaius had killed his father-in-law: Claudius killed a son-in-law too.[36] Gaius wouldn't allow Crassus' son to be called Magnus: Claudius returned his title and removed his head. In one household he killed Crassus, Magnus, and Scribonia. Three lightweights, but they *were* aristocracy – Crassus in fact was so stupid he could even have been an emperor.[37] And you now want to make this man a god? Look at him – the gods were against him from his birth. All right, let him say the three words one after the other and he can drag me off as a slave. Who's going to worship him as a god? Who'll believe in him? While you create such gods, no one will believe that you yourselves are gods. To get to the point, gentlemen of the Senate, I ask you, if I have been an honest man while with you, if I have raised my voice to no one, make him pay for the harm he has done me. I put this motion to the House.'

And then he read from a note-book: 'Whereas the Divine Claudius has murdered his father-in-law, Appius Silanus, his two sons-in-law, Magnus Pompeius and Lucius Silanus, his daughter's father-in-law, Crassus Frugi, a man as like him as two peas, his daughter's mother-in-law, Scribonia, his wife Messalina and others too numerous to mention, I move that he be severely punished, that he be denied any immunity from trial, and that he be deported as soon as possible, leaving Heaven within thirty days and Olympus within three.'

On the division there was general support for this motion. Without delay, Mercury seized him by the neck and hauled him off to Hell from Heaven,

that bourne from which, they say, no man returns.[38]

12. While they were going down by way of the Via Sacra, Mercury inquired the meaning of the great crowd: was it Claudius' funeral? And it was the most handsome cortège ever with no expense spared to let you know that a god was being buried. There was such a mob, such an orchestration of trumpeters, horn players, and every kind of brass instrumentalist that even Claudius could hear it. Everyone was happy and gay. The Roman

people walked about like free men. Agatho and a few barristers were in tears, but they were clearly sincere. Legal authorities were emerging from the shadows, pale, thin, and scarcely breathing, like men who had just come back to life. One of them, seeing the barristers with their heads together, crying over their bad luck, went up and said: 'I told you it won't always be carnival time.'

When Claudius saw his funeral, he realized he was dead. For they were singing an appropriately rhythmical dirge with a huge massed choir:

> Mourn, mourn
> Ye Roman lads and lasses!
> Sound, sound
> The sad and gloomy brasses!
> In the Forum,
> Sound them for him.
> Brave heart ever,
> Now he passes,
> Braver never,
> Who surpasses
> Him for racing
> Or for warring
> Parthians chasing?
> His light spears
> Hit the Persians,
> His sure bow
> Made swift incursions,
> Lightly foiling
> All attacks,
> Routing Medes
> With painted backs.
> Beyond the seaways
> That we knew
> He made Britons,
> Brigantes too,
> Drop blue targes,
> Be our charges
> In the chains of
> Romulus.
> He brought the Ocean
> Roman *Pax*,

Spread commotion
With our axe.
Weep, weep
For the man's good judgements.
Who could master
Lawsuits faster,
Hearing either
One or neither.
Who will warm
The bench and dock
Through the year
And round the clock?
Minos, retire for him,
Let Claudius instead,
O Cretan lawgiver,
Be judge of the Dead.
Pound, pound
Your breasts
In solemn mourning,
Lawyers for retainers
And all the other gainers!
Weep, weep,
Ye new poetic prattlers
And ye tribes of
Lucky dicebox rattlers!

13. Claudius was delighted to hear his praises sung and wanted to watch longer. The divine herald gripped him and dragged him along through the Campus Martius, his head covered so that no one could recognize him. Somewhere between the Tiber and the Via Tecta he descended into the Infernal Regions. Claudius' freedman Narcissus had already gone on ahead by a short cut to make his master welcome. As Claudius arrived, he met him, gleaming because he'd come straight from a bath.[39]

'What are gods doing with men?' he asked. 'Get a move on!' said Mercury, 'and announce our arrival.' Quicker than it takes to tell, Narcissus flew off. Everything slopes downward and the descent is easy.[40] And so, despite his gout, he arrived in an instant at the gate of Dis, where lay Cerberus, or, as Horace calls him, 'the hundred-headed monster.'[41] He was a bit frightened when he saw that black, shaggy dog, which was certainly not the sort of thing you'd like to meet in the dark – he'd only had a whitish dog for a pet. In a loud voice he cried out: 'Claudius is on his way !'

People came out clapping and singing in Greek – 'He who was lost hath been found, let us rejoice together !' [42] There was Gaius Silius, a consul designate, the praetorian Iuncus, Sextus Traulus, Marcus Helvius, Trogus, Cotta, Vettius Valens, Fabius – all Roman knights whom Narcissus had had executed.[43] In the centre of this singing crowd was the ballet-dancer, Mnester,[44] whom Claudius had cut down to size for his good looks. Around Messalina – for the rumour spread quickly that Claudius had arrived – rushed, first of anybody, the freedman Polybius, Myron, Harpocras, Ampheus, and Pheronactus [45] – all of whom Claudius had despatched ahead to avoid being anywhere where no preparations had been made. Then came the two praetorian prefects, Justus Catonius and Rufrius Pollio, then Claudius' cabinet officers, Saturninus Lusius, Pedo Pompeius, Lupus and Celer Asinius,[46] all men of consular rank, and finally, the daughter of his brother, the daughter of his sister, his sons-in-law, his fathers-in-law, his mothers-in-law,[47] all obviously close kin, and forming into a line they came to meet Claudius.

When he saw them, Claudius cried out: 'The world is full of friends ! How did you get here?' Pedo Pompeius then spoke: 'What do you mean, you cruel bastard? You ask us *how*? Who else sent us here but you, you butcher of every friend you had? Let's get the trial started. I'll show you the bench down here.'

14. He led him before Aeacus' tribunal. He sat on cases that fell under the Cornelian legislation on murder.[48] Pedo requested that Claudius be charged and he laid out the indictment: 'Murdered: 35 Senators, 221 Roman knights, and others to the number of the grains of sand and the specks of dust.' Claudius could not find counsel. Finally, an old crony of his, Publius Petronius,[49] came forward, a fine orator of the Claudian type, and he asked for an adjournment. It was not granted. Pedo Pompeius opened for the prosecution amid acclamation. The defence wanted to reply. The superbly impartial Aeacus denied the request, and with only one side of the case heard, found Claudius guilty and pronounced sentence:

'What he hath wrought, he shall suffer: let justice be done.' [50]

There was a profound silence. Everyone was stupefied, thunderstruck by the strange procedure: this had never happened before. Claudius found it more unjust than unprecedented. As for the type of punishment, there was a long argument about what penalty should be imposed upon him. There were those who said that Sisyphus had been carrying stones for a long time now, that Tantalus would die of thirst unless relieved, and that sometime the brake had to be put on poor Ixion's wheel. It was decided that none of these old lags should be pardoned, in case even Claudius had his hopes raised for something similar.

It was decided that a new punishment should be invented, some useless labour should be thought up, an illusory hope of gratifying some desire. Aeacus then ordered him to throw dice from a broken dice cup. And he began to hunt for the continually falling dice, getting nowhere.

When from the rattling cup he seeks to throw
The dice, they trickle through the hole below
And when he tries the recovered bones to roll —
A gambler who never achieves the desired goal —
Again they fool him: through his finger-tips
Each time each cunning dice as cruelly slips,
As Sisyphus' rocks, before they reach the crest,
Slip from his neck and roll back to their rest.

15. Suddenly Gaius Caesar [51] turned up and claimed him as his slave. He produced witnesses who had seen him being beaten by Gaius with whips, rods and the back of his hand.

The decision was in Gaius Caesar's favour. Gaius gave him to Aeacus. He was put under Menander's orders and made Aeacus' legal secretary.[52]

NOTES ON THE TEXT

1. Julia Drusilla was the sister and, it was said, paramour of the emperor Gaius (Caligula). He granted her divine honours on her death and found a senator, Livius Geminius, who, for 250,000 sesterces, attested to her assumption into Heaven (see Dio 59. 11).

2. An ironic glance at the *Aeneid* (2. 724), where Vergil describes the tiny Ascanius unable to keep up with his father Aeneas. Claudius had weak legs and tended to totter (Suetonius *Claudius* 21. 6).

3. Phoebus and Cynthia represent the sun and the moon in poetry, while Bacchus represents the vine. These lines and those following are tame parodies of epic circumlocution.

4. Probably the Star in the constellation Virgo, which supposedly affects grapes.

5. An ironic touch. Mercury is above all the god of craftiness and subtlety. Athenassalus plausibly argues (*op. cit.* pp. 17 ff.) that Seneca is here playing on a possible double meaning for *anima* (soul/wind) and is caustically alluding to Claudius' notorious propensity to meteorism (or flatulence). Mercury thus becomes a more appropriate god to aid Claudius since in the Homeric Hymn he escaped Apollo by 'a terrible working of the belly, a reckless messenger' (lines 295–6).

6. A quotation from Vergil (*Georgius* 4. 90); the original advises the beekeeper to kill off the worse, if there are two 'kings' in the hive.

7. Augurinus is unknown although it was a surname of the Minucii. Baba is mentioned by Seneca (*Letters* 15. 9) as a proverbial idiot. The three are offered as a sort of ABC of stupidity.

8. A quotation from Euripides' lost *Cresphontes* (Nauck, Fgt. 452). The original context implied that the friends of the deceased should be glad that he had finished with the sorrows of life.

9. A quotation from Homer (*Odyssey* 1. 170), where Telemachus is speaking to the disguised Athene.

10. *Odyssey* 9. 39. Odysseus is describing his adventures to King Alcinous.

11. Claudius was born at Lugdunum, the modern Lyons, on the northern border of Gallia Narbonensis, in 10 B.C. His mother Antonia was accompanying his father Drusus on a campaign against the Germans at the time. Lugdunum became a Roman colony in 43 B.C. under the auspices of the triumvir Mark Antony. The modern Vienne

(*Vienna*), the capital of the Allobroges, was also a Roman colony in Claudius' time and did not enjoy good relations with Lugdunum. The Licinius mentioned below was a Gaul, the slave and later freedman of Julius Caesar; he became procurator of the area under Augustus and his record of rich vulgarity and despotic behaviour was almost proverbial. The implication is that some of his qualities rubbed off on Claudius.

12. The Gauls captured Rome in 390 B.C., but they were regarded as a constant threat until late into Republican times.

13. The Xanthus is a small river near Troy, frequently mentioned by Homer. It would be over a thousand miles away. It might be noted that Claudius' boyhood tutor had been a superintendent of mule drivers according to Suetonius (*Claudius* 2). The goddess Fever cannot understand Claudius' Homeric pleasantries and Claudius' reaction seems very understandable.

14. This was the labour of Hercules that seemed to involve most wandering. After getting the red oxen of the monster Geryones from the fabulous western island of Erytheia, he is supposed to have passed the Alps and Pyrenees, founded the towns of Alesia and Nemausus, and fathered the race of Celts. He might therefore plausibly be expected to come across Mt Fourvière, upon which Lyons is built, and which overlooks the confluence of the Rhone and Saône. The latter river was noted by Julius Ceasar as having an almost imperceptible current.

15. The original is a derisive adaptation of a frequent Greek tragic phrase meaning *the stroke of a god*. My adaptation of *coup de foudre* gives the real meaning.

16. There was a temple of Hercules at Tibur, a Roman resort, and Augustus used to hear trials there (Suetonius *Augustus* 72). July and August were more or less a continuous legal vacation at Rome. Claudius seems to have been taking a busman's holiday. The reading *Tiburi* for *tibi* is, however, Bücheler's conjecture.

17. Hercules cleaned the cattle stables of King Augeas, which had not been cleaned for thirty years, by diverting the rivers Alpheus and Peneus through them.

18. A considerable lacuna follows. It is easy enough to surmise however that Claudius wins over Hercules, who forces his way into the Senate of Olympus, and pleads the cause of Claudius' deification. Jupiter throws the matter open to the House amid uproar and when the text resumes, we find one of the gods addressing Hercules and throwing cold water on Claudius' pretensions.

19. Epicurus had to admit that the gods existed, because we had mental images of them, but he argued that they lived carefree lives in

the clear spaces between the worlds, giving no thought or trouble to men. Claudius had had troubles and caused them.

20. The god or *logos* of the Stoics permeated the world and therefore could be regarded as having the same shape. The quotation from Varro is probably taken from his Menippean satires.

21. Saturn was the father and displaced predecessor of Jupiter. His month was December, a season of licence and carnival. The glance at Claudius' drinking and other habits is perhaps reinforced by the fact that he added an extra day to the traditional four days of the Saturnalia (Dio 60. 25).

22. Lucius Junius Silanus Torquatus was engaged to Claudius' daughter, Octavia. In 48 A.D., at the instigation of Agrippina, who wished her to marry her son, Nero, he was accused of incest with his sister, Junia Calvina, and forced to commit suicide. Claudius even carried out a ceremonious purification. The reference to Juno, Jupiter's sister and wife, points up the implicit reflection on Jupiter himself.

23. One could marry one's half-sister at Athens and of course the Ptolemies of Alexandria frequently married their sisters.

24. From the *Iphigenia* of Ennius.

25. There was a temple and a priesthood established for Claudius at Camelodunum, the modern Colchester. A traditional Greek prayer is parodied here by the substitution of *fool* for *god*.

26. Janus was an important and ancient Roman deity who presided over the beginnings of everything. He was supposed to have power over the entrance to heaven and his month began the year. It is appropriate therefore that he should be one of the two consuls elect who traditionally would open the debate, particularly when the question was whether Claudius should be allowed into heaven. For various historical reasons his statues often had two faces back to back. The reference to the Forum may be explained by the existence of a passage with two entrances called the *Janus Medius*. July was the Roman month for vacation and practically no public business took place in the afternoon in any month. Janus would therefore be consul-designate when the position was totally honorific.

27. The revival of this old Italian god, the meaning of whose name is identical with that of Jupiter's, perhaps hints at Claudius' interest in archaic religion. Vica Pota was also an ancient divinity, the goddess of lucky acquisitions. Unless Seneca, like many ancient writers, is confusing Diespiter with Dis pater or Pluto, god of the underworld and of wealth, who is described as the son of Fortuna, the relationship is invented to explain Diespiter's lucrative occupations. Selling citizenships was a thriving business with Claudius' entourage.

28. The lobe of the ear was regarded by the ancients as the seat of memory.

29. According to Ennius, Romulus, the first King of Rome, was in heaven where he continued to live his old simple life. Turnips would be unwelcome fare for a gourmand such as Claudius. The source of the quotation is unknown.

30. The circumstances in which Messala uttered these words are unknown. Perhaps when he resigned from his post of city prefect in 25 B.C. after five days of office.

31. I read *soror mea* for *sormea*, deleting Graeca with Bücheler. The allusion is perhaps to Octavia's loyalty to her husband, Mark Antony, despite her half-brother's advice to leave him. The original proverb is of course Greek and is the equivalent of our 'charity begins at home'.

32. Most emperors were granted (or took) the title *Augustus*.

33. The daughter of Drusus was killed through the jealousy of Messalina; Julia Livia, daughter of Germanicus, was accused in 41 A.D. of adultery with Seneca, and her death seems also due to the jealousy of Messalina. On Lucius Silanus, see note 22 above. It may be noticed below that Claudius seems now to be present in the senate. If this is not a rhetorical device, it may indicate the haste of the composition of the pamphlet.

34. Homer *Illiad* 1. 591.

35. Narcissus gave the orders for Messalina's death in the name of Claudius. The emperor's absent-mindedness perhaps gave rise to the story that after her execution he asked why she was not at dinner.

36. Gaius had killed Marcus Junius Silanus, father of his wife, Junia Claudilla. Claudius had killed Appius Silanus, actually his step-father, not his father-in-law, and L. Junius Silanus, his intended son-in-law and Cn. Pompeius Magnus, who married Claudius' daughter, Antonia.

37. M. Licinius Crassus Frugi was consul in 27 A.D., Cn. Pompeius being his son and Scribonia his wife. Crassus was engaged to Claudius' daughter, although he never married her. Caligula, according to Suetonius, stripped a number of families of their historical distinctions, including the descendants of the great Pompey. Claudius restored the title *Magnus*. It is fairly obvious that Claudius suspected Crassus of pretensions to the purple, not an impossible idea if we consider the disillusionment with the Julian line and the career of Pompey himself, who might well have been the founder of a line of emperors. The apparent proper names in the MS (*Tristioinas, Assarionem*) do not make sense. I have tentatively adopted Bücheler's *tris homines assarios*.

38. Catallus 3. 12.

39. When Claudius died, Narcissus, Claudius' powerful freedman, was taking a cure at the baths of Sinuessa in Campania. He was put out of the way almost immediately on Nero's accession. The short cut was suicide.

40. A glance at Vergil's *facilis descensus Averno* (*Aeneid* 6. 126).

41. *Odes* 2. 13. 34.

42. A ritual cry from the Egyptian cult of Isis, uttered on the finding of her husband Osiris.

43. Those we can identify seem to have been Messalina's lovers or involved in the scandal of her mock marriage to Gaius Silius in 48 A.D. Narcissus was mainly responsible for their punishment.

44. Mnester was a famous pantomime actor, who had been a great favourite of the emperor Caligula and retained his popularity at Claudius' court, particularly with Messalina, whose lover he was, until he was replaced by Gaius Silius. He was involved in the great scandal also and was executed.

45. Polybius was an important freedman of Claudius' and was his literary secretary. He was forced to commit suicide in 47 through Messalina. About the others little or nothing is known.

46. Catonius was prefect in 43 and was destroyed by the machinations of Messalina. Pollio was prefect in 41 and 44. Saturninus and Lupus were victims of the intrigues of an informer Publius Suillius. Asinius Celer was consul in 38. Pompeius is unknown.

47. These are (in order) Julia, daughter of Germanicus, Julia, daughter of Livia, L. Silanus and Pompeius Magnus, Appius Silanus and Crassus Frugi, Domitia Lepida and Scribonia.

48. The dictator L. Cornelius Sulla had set up a number of permanent courts for different offences. The judicial system of Hades is humorously based on Roman legal procedures. This particular court dealt not only with murder and poisoning but also with those who were given unfair sentences in capital cases.

49. Petronius was consul in 19 A.D., and then proconsul in Asia. Claudius therefore knew him before he became emperor.

50. Aeacus is quoting a traditional Greek tag, first recorded in Hesiod.

51. Caligula, while alive, had been the bane of Claudius' life.

52. As this is probably not the comic-writer, Menander's identity remains unknown. The point however is that Claudius is under the thumb of a freedman as usual and continues with legal work, presumably in the intervals of his punishment.

MORE ABOUT PENGUINS
AND PELICANS

For further information about books available from Penguins please write to Dept EP, Penguin Books Ltd, Harmondsworth, Middlesex UB7 0DA.

In the U.S.A.: For a complete list of books available from Penguins in the United States write to Dept CS, Penguin Books, 625 Madison Avenue, New York, New York 10022.

In Canada: For a complete list of books available from Penguins in Canada write to Penguin Books Canada, 2801 John Street, Markham, Ontario L3R 1B4.

In Australia: For a complete list of books available from Penguins in Australia write to the Marketing Department, Penguin Books Australia Ltd, P.O. Box 257, Ringwood, Victoria 3134.

TERENCE

THE COMEDIES

Translated by Betty Radice

The Roman dramatist Terence (*c.* 186–159 A.D.) is one of the most interesting Latin authors. Although his professed aim was to adapt Greek New Comedy for the Roman stage, he presented sympathetically the stock figures of comedy as human beings interacting on each other, and confronted with the domestic problems that are still ours today.

The six comedies in this volume are his complete output, and range in mood from light romantic comedy through elaborate intrigue to the themes handled with wit and urbanity which delighted Molière. For from the Renaissance onwards these comedies have been a lasting influence on the Western European comedy of manners.

Also published

PLAUTUS

THE POT OF GOLD AND OTHER PLAYS

and

THE ROPE AND OTHER PLAYS

Both translated by E. F. Watling

PENGUIN CLASSICS

'Penguin continue to pour out the jewels of the world's classics in translation ... There are now nearly enough to keep a man happy on a desert island until the boat comes in' – Philip Howard in *The Times*

Some recent and forthcoming titles

THEOPHILE GAUTIER
MADEMOISELLE DE MAUPIN
Translated by Joanna Richardson

SHIKIBU MURASAKI
THE TALE OF GENJI
Translated by Edward G. Seidensticker

THE GREEK ANTHOLOGY
Edited by Peter Jay

THREE SANSKRIT PLAYS
ŚAKUNTALĀ/RĀKSHASA'S RING/MĀLATĪ AND MĀDAVA
Translated by Michael Coulson

THE ORKNEYINGA SAGA
Translated by Herman Pálsson and Paul Edwards